THE GAMBLER'S WIFE;

OR,

MURDER WILL OUT.

BY THE AUTHOR OF

"THE ORDEAL BY TOUCH;" "THE IRON MASK;" "THE ASSASSINS OF THE CAVERN;" &c.

Oh! tell me not to ease my heart with tears—
Tears cannot reach a grief so deep as mine!
Let others weep; and with their tears wash out
Their lesser sorrows: mine are all dried up!—*Old Play.*

LONDON:

PUBLISHED BY EDWARD LLOYD, 12, SALISBURY-SQUARE,
FLEET-STREET.

THE GAMBLER'S WIFE;

OR, MURDER WILL OUT.

BY THE AUTHOR OF "THE ORDEAL BY TOUCH," "THE IRON MASK," &c.

CHAPTER I.

THE BRAZEN MASK.—THE SPANISH DAGGER.—THE GUEST'S MURDER.—THE RETURN
TO THE GAMING-TABLE.

SILENCE, sad and solitary—no one to cheer her—no one to utter to her one kind word—no friendly voice to greet her ears—no kind face with the soft, beaming expression of tenderness to meet her gaze; but all dreary, blank, and desolate, sits the Gambler's Wife. Her head rests on her hands; her infant slumbers; the clock has already struck the hour of two.

The room in which she sits is one of large dimensions. There were indications, too, about it, that it had once been of elegant and rich aspect, as regards its furnishing and decorations; but all is faded. The portable articles of comfort or of luxury have been one by one taken from it, and nothing remains but those embellishments which cannot well be converted into money.

One table, a child's cot, and two miserable chairs, compose the moveable furniture now of that apartment, which has seen within its precincts the gay, the rich, and the beautiful; that apartment which has rung with the laugh of light-hearted revelry, in which strains of sweet, spirit-stirring, joyous music, have floated in the air; and in which a beautiful wife slept the calm sleep of innocence and joy. Alas! how changed now is every-thing! Where, now, are those little indications of a happy household, which were wont to present themselves to the eye of every one who set foot across the threshold of that house? Who now ever hears the happy, careless laugh from an unburthened spirit, in the now deserted apartments?

But let us look at her whom we have named the Gambler's Wife. Alas for her, poor thing, that we should be compelled to give her such a title!

She is young, and she is beautiful. Nay, the very bloom of girlhood still lingers on her cheek; her figure is light and graceful; her hair dark, and falling in massive folds upon her shoulders; while the small hands upon which rests her fevered brow, are white as ivory. She rocks gently to and fro. Perhaps she still fancies she is endeavouring to soothe her child to sleep, although it lies for a time serene and quiet in its cot, a stranger to its mother's miseries. But hark—she speaks!

"Oh, heaven! and has it come to this? Is this, in truth, the climax to my day dreams of happiness? Oh, God! oh, God! when will all this end? But one year since, and I was happy—one short year! The sweet flowers that adorn the fair summer time, have not blown again, ere I was happy. What am I now? Where, now, is all the long-continued joy which I told myself was surely mine? My child, too—that dear little one, who yet has but for two short months opened its sweet eyes to the light of day. Must that gift of God perish? Oh, no—no—no! he will come back to us—he must come back to us. Some angel of good will yet whisper in his ear better counsels, and I shall look upon his face again. Hush—hush! Is—that his step? Yes—yes—it is—oh, it is. He comes—husband—Harry—dear Harry—'tis he. Hush!—no—God, no! The footstep passes on, and I am desolate again!"

She once more relapsed into the attitude of woe which an expectation of the arrival of her husband had roused her from, and her dejection seemed more intense than before; for she now gave utterance to low moans of anguish, and what she said was for a time scarcely articulate. At length, tears—bitter, scalding tears, came to her relief, and then, when that burst of feeling was over, she spoke again.

"He wooed me, and he won me. I knew not what love was until he came and whispered the soft, soul-enchanting word in my ears. Yes, he won me; he taught me to love him; he taught me to centre in him my whole hopes of earthly happiness; and what has been my reward? A blighted heart—a wasted frame; agony beyond all com-parison. Oh, what will be the end of this? What is that? His knock? Yes, it must be. Hush! hush! Do not move, my child. It must—it must be he. Your father comes at last. Welcome, welcome! I hear his foot upon the stair. There is music in the sound. 'Tis he! God of Heaven! no, it is not he!"

A footstep did ascend the staircase; for it was in a house let off in different suites of chambers that they lived, that gambler and his wife; and now she gave herself up to despair, for the clock had struck three, and there seemed to be no prospect of any return of her husband. He had parted from her with taunts—taunts from him to her, because she would have warned him from a course which was destroying him.

The child still slept. That was a mercy! Yes, the beautiful child lay still in its couch, breathing gently, and little dreaming of the sadness at its poor lone mother's heart. She rose and paced the room; she wrung her hands in agony; she dashed away the tear-drops that ever and anon clustered in her eyes, and then, as she was about to speak, there came another footstep on the stairs.

She flew to the door and listened. The footstep came nearer—nearer still; but she would not this time tell herself that it was her husband's. She dreaded to awaken, as she had done before, a hope which would have but to be quenched again. That would be too horrible, and so she did not speak.

Nearer, nearer still came the footstep; and now it pauses, and there is a low tap upon the door. To open it with frantic haste was the work of a moment, and she exclaimed,—

"Henry, Henry, is this you? You have thought better of it, and come back to me. You have repented you of the idle words you spoke, Henry. You have come to me— Ah! it is not he!

A strange man, of sinister-looking aspect, and whose countenance was adorned with a horrible squint, stood on the threshold of the door; and although, in consequence of his obliquity of vision, he seemed to be regarding some object on the staircase, he was in reality glaring at Jane Hoffenden, for that was her name, with all his might, while his lips were curled into a most hideous leer.

"So, my pretty one," he said, "you are still alone."

Jane at once made an effort to close the door; but the stranger's foot was across the threshold, and she could not do so, although she tried her utmost strength.

"Ha! ha!" he said, "it won't do. I have come to see you and to speak to you. It won't do. I will say what I have come to say."

"Begone. My cries shall find me assistance. Begone, I say, begone. Help!"

"Psha! Do you think, now, I care for your cries? Look at me, and ask yourself if I am the likely man do so. Besides, I bring you news of your husband."

"Of my husband!" exclaimed Jane, shrinking back, so that the stranger had a free passage into the room; "of my husband! Oh, what of him—speak your message quickly—speak. No—no harm has come to him? Oh, relieve my fears."

"All in good time," said the unprepossessing individual, as he turned and closed the door after him; "all in good time. I have seen him within this half hour, madam, and as I thought you would feel lonely, I thought I would come and bestow a little of my good company upon you."

"Insolent!"

"Nay, nay, wait a bit; you don't know who you are speaking about, yet. You don't seem to be very luxuriously situated here. Ah, Harry Hoffenden was drinking champagne when I left him. Ha! ha! the poor dupe; he was winning a little; and thought it would last. Well, I can find a chair for myself, although there ain't much choice, madam. One a piece for us, I see. Come, now, be seated, and I will soon explain my errand, and there will be no bones broken if we don't agree about it."

"This intrusion," said Jane, trembling, for she was fearful of the man, and he kept between her and the door, so that there was very little chance of escape; "this intrusion is most unjustifiable. Leave me, I implore you; leave me, oh, leave me! There is misery enough here without your adding to it. I know not who or what you are, but I implore you to leave me!"

"What! leave you, after taking all the trouble I have to find you out? Oh, no, I couldn't think of it; and as to knowing who and what I am, you shall soon do that. Listen to me, Jane Hoffenden. I knew you by sight before you were married, and I loved you. You start, because you never heard of it; but I will tell you why you never heard of it. You were surrounded by gay young sparks, who were breathing all sorts of flatteries in your ears. I knew you would marry one of them, most likely the worst; and what chance then had I, although I did love you with a love that they, in their common, cold, every-day natures, were incapable of feeling."

"I do not want to hear this—I ought not to hear it."

"But you must. Destiny has now settled that the time has come when I can plead my suit. You must hear me, Jane, and you shall. We met once——"

"Ah, I do remember, now; your face met my eyes for a moment, and—and——."

"And you were terrified, I remember well. A young party of friends were out together; you strayed a little; I was watching you, and suddenly appeared before you. I put on what I intended for a look of affection; you fled in affright, and I heard you tell your friends that a strange man—one of the ugliest you had ever seen, had been making faces at you."

"I did—I did."

"Well, from that moment I vowed that you should be mine. It is your destiny; I knew and felt that it was then. It is your fate; you shall be mine, Jane, you shall be mine; for, as I then loved you, I love you still: and I should fancy, now, that you have shaken off some of the romance of your disposition, and know better how to appreciate a man of my many attractions."

The hideous countenance that he put on was beyond all description, and Jane knew not what to do to get rid of so unwelcome an intruder. She hoped, and yet she dreaded, her husband's return from his gambling orgies, for she knew his violent implacable temper, and that murder might ensue.

"Leave me," she cried; "once more, I ask you to leave me. And, if you have any pretensions to the character of a gentleman, you will not let me ask in vain. I am another's; and, let the conduct of that other be what it may, it affords no sort of justification to you for this visit. I know you not—I do not wish to know you, and I will not know you."

"Hard words. But let me tell you how I came to think of you. You have a cousin named Andrew Ewart. It was he, boy as he was, who first painted you to my imagination. in all your charms."

"Andrew?"

"Yes. He loved you. But he was too much of a boy to tell you so. He went abroad, and died. Ha! ha!"

"Alas! another tie is broken. And Andrew loved me?"

"He did; but what's the use of a dead man's love? I am am here and living, ready to love you well and truly as I always have loved you. I tell you it is your destiny to be mine, and you cannot avoid it. It must, it will be so; it's of no use for anybody to fight against their fate."

"Such an argument," said Jane, with more of scorn and loathing in her manner than she had yet exhibited, "has no power; I blame myself much for holding so long a converse with you, and I shall command you to begone."

"You command!"

"Yes; as I have a right to do here, beneath my husband's roof, in his absence. Dread his vengeance for this insult upon me, and carry it no further."

"Indeed! and you thus speak of the man who has virtually deserted you—who is at this moment at the gambling table; while you and your child are left here, for all he cares, to starve? This is the man whom you defend, and whom you talk of as your protector. Ha! ha! fine words; but your own heart tells you the fallacy of them. You know that you are but making an attempt to elevate a man, who cannot be elevated, into something that he has no pretension to. Your husband is not your protector."

Jane was compelled to hold by the side of the child's cot for support. There was a dreadful truth in the words that were thus uttered by the stranger; a truth which she could not but, to herself, admit, however humiliating it was for her to do so.

But she would not seem so to barter away her husband's honour; but was upon the point of putting an end to the painful interview by calling for assistance, when the intruder suddenly stepped towards her, and throwing his arms around her, exclaimed,—

"You are mine. No power on earth shall, or can prevent you from being mine; I have long loved you, Jane!"

"To be foiled at last, villain as you are!" exclaimed a voice, and at the same moment the door was dashed open, and a young man rushed into the apartment, and clutched the stranger by the throat, with a vehemence that threatened his immediate strangulation.

"To be but foiled at last, villain!" he repeated; "and now you shall have the reward of all your base treachery towards me."

"My cousin Andrew!" exclaimed Jane. "Oh, thank God for this deliverance."

The ugly intruder who thus was suddenly pounced upon by one whom he believed to be dead, seemed to be absolutely paralysed by the suddenness of the event, which was perhaps, the one of all others which was farthest away from his thoughts; and for a few moments he shook like a reed in his antagonist's grasp. Speak, probably, he could not, in consequence of the gripe upon his throat, which the other kept; but he soon recovered himself sufficiently to make some resistance, and disengaging one of his hands, he plunged it into his breast, and drew out a long, sharp, double-edged, foreign-looking dagger which glistened in the faint rays of the candle-light.

Jane saw the action, and, nerved by despair and dread, that Andrew Ewart would meet his death from his generous attempt to save her, she flung herself between them, and clung so heavily to the villain's arm, that he could not strike the blow he intended.

By a sudden snatch at its hilt, then, Adrew disarmed him of the dagger, and flung it to the ground; and then the whole effort of his antagonist seemed to be directed towards an escape.

Whirling and struggling in each other's grasp, they reached the head of the staircase; but as Andrew Ewert had never let go his original grasp wholly, he had an advantage, and by a sudden effort he succeeded in flinging the villain backward down the staircase, which he descended with a loud cry of terror.

Andrew, himself, tottered on the brink for a moment, and it was only by suddenly flinging himself backward on the landing, that he saved himself from falling.

"Thank God! thank God!" exclaimed Jane, and she sank on her knees by the side of the child's cot, and held her clasped hands up to Heaven in thankfulness and prayer.

The tumult had awakened the infant, who, by its cries, added to the confusion of the scene; and faint, pale, and exhausted by the efforts he had been compelled to make for his own preservation, Andrew Ewert rose and tottered into the room again.

His wish was to have pursued the ruffian, whom he knew well; but he found himself quite incapable of doing so, and he was compelled to be satisfied with the amount of punishment he had inflicted upon him by casting him down the staircase.

CHAPTER II.

THE EXPLANATION.—THE GAMBLER'S RETURN.

For several minutes now, in the apartment which had been the scene of so much confusion and uproar, there was a silence as of the very grave itself.

The child had ceased its cries, and composed itself to sleep again. The young mother was praying still, but uttering no sounds; for hers was that prayer which comes gushing from the heart too quickly to be clothed in words, and Andrew Ewert was drawing breath after his rapid and fearful encounter with one who most unquestionably would have taken his life if he could have done so.

And if he had been in a condition to speak, he was not the one to interrupt Jane in her present occupation, and he sank upon the chair so recently vacated by the ugly stranger, feasting his eyes with the sight of that being whom he really loved so tenderly, and whom he had not now beheld for the space of two years.

At length Jane had sufficiently recovered herself to speak: and, turning to Andrew Ewert, she held out both her hands to him, exclaiming—

"Oh! Andrew, what do I not owe to you for thus saving me from a villain!"

"You owe me nothing, Jane. I—I ought not, perhaps, now to call you Jane."

"Yes, Andrew. Call me by the old, familiar name you were wont to address me by when we were boy and girl together. Oh, what a world of sadness have I gone through, Andrew, since last we met!"

"And I, Jane—and I—I heard that you were married, and God knows I hoped that you would be happy! I became the victim of that man whom I was this night happy enough to rescue you from.   He persuaded me that he would get me a place on board a merchant-vessel; but, instead of that, I found myself sold to a piratical vessel.   It is needless to tell you all I have suffered, and how I escaped back again from the coast of Morocco to England; but, as good fortune would have it, I met the rascal to-night, and followed him."

"Oh, what a happy chance!"

"But, Jane, is it indeed true what I have now heard,—that you are united to one who prefers the gaming-table to the charms of home with thee?   Can it be possible? Alas—alas! you need not answer me in words.   That averted face, dear Jane, and that sigh spoke too plainly the truth of such a proposition!"

"It—it is true, Andrew," she said, and she burst into tears.   It is too—too true!"

He was deeply affected, and, at the moment, a wild thought crossed his brain that she would be much happier to fly with him, and forsake the man who showed how little calculated he was to appreciate the bright jewel he had won.   But as this thought grew into something like a tangible shape, he glanced towards the cot in which the child was sleeping, and that sight at once brought him to himself, and dissipated the vision.

"Jane—Jane!" he cried; "do not weep.   Your tears each fall like drops of molten lead upon my heart.   Do not despair, but still have a hope that happier days may come."

"Never—never—never!"

"Nay, say not so.   Your husband may see the mad folly of the course he is pursuing and amend his mode of life.   Have you any idea what impulse it was that first drove him, to so desperate a resource as the gaming table?"

"I cannot tell.   All is mystery to me.   I know nothing but that for six months we were too—too happy, and then a change took place, and he became what he is. Whether it be that he has evil counsellors, or that, as I sometimes suspect, that there is a something upon his mind which requires mad excitement, such as the gaming-table can alone bring to him, to stifle the thoughts of,—I cannot tell.   But the effect is terrific! Ruin, irretrievable ruin stares us in the face.   Nothing can save us now.   Nothing—nothing!"

"Yes, Jane; I can save you, and I will.   I must see, and converse with your husband; and by, perhaps, convincing him that I have the means of extricating him from any pecuniary difficulties, I may induce him to alter his course of life completely."

"And—and—is it possible there can be so much generosity?"

"Do not call it by such a name; but if I should succeed in doing anything that may be of service to you, say that it is done from a grateful recollection of many a happy hour spent in your society, dear Jane.   That is the feeling that will prompt me to do my best."

"Oh, Andrew! if, indeed, you should be successful, what shall I not owe you! The devotion of a life would be too little to repay you.   I love him still; and if he but be reclaimed from the evil way into which he has fallen, we might yet be happy."

"And you shall, dear Jane.   By an accident of fortune, which at some future time I will relate to you; I am rich, Jane, and can convince your husband of the policy of quitting the gaming-table; and when once the spell is broken which his constant visits to it have thrown around him, without doubt he will acquire better habits."

"These are hopeful words!"

"Oh, Jane! I saw, even now, something like the shadow of one your old smiles flit across your face.   You will, you must be happy; while I—but forgive me—oh, forgive me for this slight allusion to myself!   I—I meant it not, Jane—I meant it not."

The look of hopefulness vanished from the face of Jane, as she now suddenly recollected what the insolent stranger had said about the state of Andrew's affections, and she could well understand the sort of struggle that was going on in his breast, and the great amount of virtue and self-denial he practised in talking of taking steps to make her happy with one who had plucked the fair flower he would himself have wished to wear for ever in his heart of hearts.

"Andrew," she said, gently—"Andrew."

"Speak on, Jane. Your voice reminds me of old times, when we were children, and so very, very happy."

"Yes, Andrew; but the past must be forgotten, and we must only remember that we esteem each other, and that, with the pure and holy love of brother and sister, we will and may, in the sight of Heaven, regard each other."

"You are right—you are right."

"By no word, look, or action, shall a reproach be founded; and we shall be able to call down God's blessing upon us, Andrew—shall we not?"

"Yes—yes," he gasped. "You are my better spirit, Jane, and one word from you will suffice to chase from my heart all dark and unholy thoughts. As dear kindred, we will feel for each other the affections of kindred, and, so far as it is possible for me to do so, I will strive to turn your husband from his path of misery."

Jane stooped over the child to conceal her tears, and kissed its soft cheek, while Andrew stole a hasty glance around the room, and, with a sigh, witnessed the desolation of its aspect. He saw what once had been, and what was now; and then he wished to ask a question which he instinctively shrank from putting to his cousin; and that was, if the gamester had left her in want or not?

It was a strange hour in the morning, too—nearly four—and he knew not whether to wait until Henry Hoffenden should come home, or go away and trust to meeting him at some more seasonable hour. The latter question was, however, solved by Jane, who looked up and said—

"I know not when he may return; but this is about his time. There is a couch in yonder apartment, where you can rest, Andrew. I will watch, and when he comes I will tell him who is here, which will prevent any misconstruction on his part—that is to say —if—if——"

"If what, Jane?"

"If he be sober enough to listen. But should you hear him in a state which prohibits the possibility of his hearing reason, Andrew, let me pray you to leave, and return some few hours hence. You will find another door from your room opening upon the staircase, and you can go at once, and he need not know of your most innocent visit; but if he shall come home heated with wine, there is no knowing what mad-brained jealousy might take possession of his faculties upon finding you here."

"Alas! my poor, poor Jane," said Andrew, "the more I hear of the man to whom you have yoked yourself to life, the more I dread that he will be proof against all persuasion to a better course."

"We will hope," said Jane, faintly; but it was very faintly indeed.

Andrew Ewert did not press this theme more; but he approached the cot in which lay the slumbering infant, and, as he looked in its face, he said, in a tone of voice as much as if he were speaking to himself as addressing her—

"And this, Jane, is your child?"

"Yes, Andrew; I ought not certainly to give way so much as I do to despairing thoughts, ought I, while I have this little one to comfort me? Oh! how happy we might be, if Harry would but forget that dreadful gaming-house, which has come between him and a better nature. You do not know him, Andrew; and in your mind you may condemn him, as I can indeed hardly wonder at your doing; but he is not all so bad as he appears. There are good thoughts and good feelings in his nature, which like rare flowers in a neglected garden, still hold possession of the earth, although nearly hidden from human observation by clustering weeds. You will yet, I hope, Andrew, have reason to feel that my choice has not been altogether a heedless one."

"I can, at all events," said Andrew, "feel that he has a treasure, even if he knows not its value."

Jane sighed, and a tear glistened in her eye as Andrew stooped and kissed the child. She knew that that kiss was a pure and holy one, and that it came from lips that had never been profaned by falsehood or deceit.

"I will leave you as you desire," said Andrew. "I am myself much fatigued, Jane; but I will not, if I can help it, sleep; and should your husband return and be in any state that can enable me to speak to him, I shall, I hope, be able to do so effectually; or do you think I had better seek him?"

"Alas! I know not where to direct you to find him."

"Then there is no resource. It is a strange thing, Jane, but, when I was abroad, a man, who had a great repute as a conjuror and fortune-teller, prophesied that something very important and very dangerous would happen to me on the second day of September."

" Indeed !"

"Yes; and it has happened. The danger was, no doubt, from the dagger of that ruffian, concerning whom I will tell you some strange particulars at another time ; and the important event will, I hope, be the reformation of your husband."

So saying, he left the room in which Jane and her infant were, and went into an adjoining room, where there was a couch against the wall, and on which he flung himself, for he was extremely tired.

He had picked up from the floor the dagger which had been by him wrested from the hands of the assassin, and he placed it by his side, and then fell into a long train of anxious thought concerning the fate of Jane, and the probability of his being able to exert sufficient influence over the mind of her husband to induce him to leave the gaming-table, and embrace the happiness which was within his reach.

"It is strange—very strange." he said, "that the greatest difficulties are always encountered in persuading people to their own good, and that it is so much easier to persuade them to evil."

This was a melancholy truth which young Andrew Ewert had hit upon, and it was one which made him feel a little doubtful of the success of the attempt he intended to make upon the better nature of Henry Hoffenden. Indeed, if he had not had money to back his arguments with, he would have altogether despaired of producing the least good effect ; but, assisted by that most powerful of all arguments, he did think that there was a chance of doing something yet for the happiness of Jane.

As these thoughts passed through his mind his senses became gradually involved in slumber ; and although he several times started awake, he would, upon finding that there was no noise and no sound of voices, subside again into repose, until at last he was really in a deep sleep, from which no slight thing would awaken him ; for the young and the innocent sleep soundly, and Andrew Ewert came up to both of those conditions, for in age he was not yet nineteen, and a more single-minded, innocent heart than his never beat in a human bosom.

And so we will leave him for the present, while we look after the proceedings of the villain over who, mere' boy [as Andrew was, he had obtained so signal a triumph.

CHAPTER III.

THE GAMING-HOUSE.—THE SUGGESTION OF MURDER.

THE force with which the villain fell down the staircase was so great, that, for some few minutes, he lay in the passage completely stunned and motionless, and had the time been any other than what it was, namely, between three and four o'clock in the morning, he would no doubt have excited some compassionate attention from passengers; but, as it was, he lay quite unobserved by any one until he recovered.

We have already said the house was one of those very large ones which are to be found in some parts of London, and which, owing to their size preventing them from readily getting a tenant, are made into separate suites of chambers, and let out to different tenants accordingly.

The door had been removed altogether, and separate outer doors put upon the different floors, so that, as in the inns of court, any one could walk up the staircase without, however, getting admission to any of the chambers any the more readily than as if each had been in reality in a separate house, defended by its separate street door.

Thus, then, when the man with the obliquity of vision fell down the staircase, he lay in the open passage until he recovered a little, and gathered himself up.

His first care was to ascertain what amount of injury he had sustained, and he was gratified to find that they were confined to bruises, for no bones were broken, or joints dis-

THE GAMBLING HOUSE IN THE NEIGHBOURHOOD OF LEICESTER SQUARE.

[At one of the principal tables sat a young man, who, but for the storm of passion that was called into existence upon his face, would have been handsome. . . . He had before him money,—a confused pile of notes and gold. . . . He suddenly scrambled it all together, and exclaimed in a low voice,— " All—all upon the next throw !"]

located, which was rather a wonder, considering the height from which he had fallen, and that the steps were of stone.

When he found that he was comparatively uninjured, his thoughts reverted to the person who had got so completely, in consequence of the suddenness of the attack he had made upon him, the mastery over him, and, shaking his clenched hand up the staircase, he said, in suppressed. but bitter tones—

"I will have a revenge for this that shall be as complete and bitter as ever the revenge of any human being was. You shall both—you, Jane Hoffenden, and you, Andrew Ewert, suffer for this night's proceedings to an extent you little dream of. You shall find, and that before long, too, what Roderick Murdo's capable of doing."

Appearing, then, quite satisfied in his own mind that he had the power to put his threats into execution, he walked away at a rapid pace towards the west-end of the town, and crossing Leicester-square, he rushed up one of those dull streets which lead out of the northern side of that locality—streets which at no time have been able within the memory of the present generation to boast of anything in the shape of virtue or good-ness as regards their inhabitants.

The morning light was gently stealing over the great metropolis, as he paused at the door of a house in this street, and he was about to enter, when suddenly a female form came rapidly towards him, and clung to his arm entreatingly, as she exclaimed—

"Stay, father, oh! stay. Stay, I implore you. I have followed you the whole night, because I know you are intent upon some scheme—a day of repentance for which will surely come at last."

"D——n! what do you do here?" cried the fellow.

"Oh, hush! hush!" said the young girl, for young she was. "Hush! father; do not use to me those dreadful words, I implore you. Remember, that I am your child—your own Mary."

"Then what the devil do you do in the streets at such a time as this, I should like to know?"

"To follow you—to attend upon you as your good genius, and to endeavour to with-draw you from pursuing some unholy course which I am certain you meditate. Oh! do be persuaded by me to return home now, at once. I heard you before you left this evening, say to yourself, that you would have revenge."

"How dare you listen to what I say, girl! Go home, and by——"

"Oh, hush, father, hush. Do not utter those dreadful oaths. You know not what an awful sound they have to me, who are unused to them."

"Take that, then, for meddling," said the brutal fellow, and he struck the young girl a savage blow on the side of the face, that made her reel again, and compelled her to sink upon a door-step, on which she sat wringing her hands, and exclaiming—

"Oh, God! oh, God! has it come to this?"

"Yes," he cried, "it has come to this, and it will come to this as often as you come prying into my affairs, and dogging me about from place to place. Go home, and make yourself comfortable; for, if you make war against me, you will soon find, that, like everybody else who does so, you will in time get the worst of the bargain."

The young girl did not speak, but she rose, and walked slowly away. The villain watched her as she went, and then muttered to himself—

"I shall have some trouble with her yet, and I almost regret—no—no, I don't regret that either. I have had my revenge in that quarter, and kept my word."

He ascended the two steps that led to the door of the house at which he stopped, and tapped in a familiar manner at it; a small square piece, that, when it was closed, looked like one of the panels of the street-door, was opened instantly, and a voice said—

"Who knocks?"

"One of the old well kept and right sort," was the reply.

"All right; come in."

The door was opened only just wide enough to admit one person, and the man whose name was Murdo entered the gaming-house hall. This was as plain and unornamented as it could possibly be, and crossing it rapidly, he ascended a flight of stairs, at the top of which was another, from an opening in which an accurate survey could be taken of any one who ascended the staircase; so that even if the outer door was passed, and there should be anything in the appearance of the visitor which was not liked, he would got no further than the top of the staircase.

In this instance, however, the scrutiny was satisfactory, and the upper door was opened by a man stationed at it, who greeted the new arrival by the name of Captain Murdo.

"Are the rooms full?" he said, "and is Hoffenden here?"

"Yes, to both questions," said the man; "and I heard some one who came out say, that Hoffenden seemed halfmad to-night."

"Indeed! With drink or play?"

"Oh! that I cannot tell you. Perhaps a little of both, you know, captain; but, for a young hand, he is an out-and-outer, they say. I don't see much of inside myself; but I hear a good deal, you know, from one and another, as they go out."

"Of course—of course. Everybody knows that you can be trusted."

"Thank you, captain—thank you, you screw-eyed old vagabond," added the door-keeper to himself, when Murdo had passed on. "I never get anything more solid than a compliment from you."

A little further on from this door was another, which yielded either way to the touch; and beyond that again, was a very heavy massive curtain indeed, reaching from the ceiling to the floor, and which quite had the effect of excluding all ordinary sounds from the interior of the gaming-saloon, into which Captain Murdo now at once made his way.

It was a gorgeously-fitted up place, although not equal to some of the more favourite haunts of the aristocracy, in the close neighbourhood of St. James's Palace; but, still for a second-rate hell, which it was, there was much to charm the eye in it, and to dazzle the senses.

The room itself was a large one, and was tolerably well filled with persons, who were almost all engaged either in betting or playing; and the confused mass of sounds that came upon the ears of any one entering from the quiet of the streets at such an hour, was most prodigious, and for some moments quite confounding.

The various cries incidental to the different games that were being played; the exultation of the winners, and the loud and deep curses of the losers, altogether made up a scene which quite justified the ordinary name of hell being applied to such a house.

At one of the principal tables sat a young man, who, but for the storm of passion that was called into existence upon his face, would have been eminently handsome. But now that he was flushed with wine, and that a run of ill-luck had driven him almost frantic, he looked more like a demon than a living man engaged in any proper avocation.

It was quite evident that he scarcely knew what he did; sometimes he would laugh long and loud, as if he were almost mad with mirth; but yet it was a laugh that made some even of the guests of that house shudder to hear it, so strange, forced, and hollow was it.

Then, too, it was a laugh that would stop so suddenly, that it seemed as if done on purpose to create surprise. And then, at times, with the most horrible oaths and imprecations, he would continue the game.

He had money before him—a confused pile of notes and gold. God knows where he had got it from, but now he suddenly scrambled it all together, and cried in a loud voice—,

"All—all upon the next throw!"

"How much is there, sir?" said the man who was presiding at the table.

"Don't ask me," shouted the other, who was Harry Hoffenden; "how should I know how much I have? You can count it when the chance is over. Quick! quick! damnation! Quick. I say. More wine! Is there not a glass of wine in the place?"

The man who played against him for the bank, did so with the greatest coolness, and the result was, that in half a minute more, the little rake of the presiding genius of that demoniac place had swept away all that Hoffenden had a moment before possessed.

"Make your games, gentlemen, make your games."

"Yes," said Hoffenden, as he rose, "make your games, gentlemen; I have made mine. I wonder if it's a fine night on—on the river now. I—I wonder——"

He reeled rather than walked to one of the windows, and there he was closely followed by Captain Murdo.

For a moment or two he was left to his own bitter reflection, and, from the attitude of Murdo, we might believe that he quite exulted in and enjoyed the misery which the young man was evidently suffering, and that that misery was most acute, was soon evidenced by the amount of suffering that he observed he endured, for suddenly, with a deep groan, he flung himself upon the window seat, nnd seemed to be completely prostrate.

Then Captain Murdo touched him lightly on the shoulder, and that touch seemed at once to arouse him from that state of lethargy into which he had fallen, for he exclaimed, in loud and angry tones—

" Who dares lay hand on me ?"

" Pho ! pho ! Mr. Hoffenden, it is a friend. I have something to say to you in perfect friendship, and in perfect confidence, if you will listen ; and I can likewise tell you how to better your condition.'

Hoffenden looked up at the hideous face which was turned towards him, and he almost seemed to doubt if that was the man who had spoken to him, for, owing to the peculiarity in Murdo's eye, he seemed to be looking from him, instead of to him.

" Did you speak ?" he said.

" I did, my friend ; and when I have told you what it is necessary for you know, you will find that I am fully entitled to the name of friend. Will you hear me here, or will you come out ?"

"The air here is pestiferous and hot—I will come out. I am proof against all calamity ; and, therefore, care not what you say. Come on—come on."

Hoffenden rapidly left the gaming-house, followed by fhe fiend, Murdo, who was intent upon luring him to destruction, by making him an instrument by which to gratify his own revengeful passions. They were quickly in the street, for, on leaving his gaming-house, there were none of the precautions incidental upon entering it, for they were not required, and the doorkeepers at once opened the doors for any one to emerge at pleasure; and it was no new thing for them to see a person rush out with frantic gestures, and in such a state of madness from loses as would have made it certainly a dangerous thing to have interrupted them, so that a kind of official celerity in opening the doors for the exit of gamesters was obtained by the two doorkeepers, from their practice in that branch of their duty.

" Now, sir," said Hoffenden, as he took off his hat to allow the cool morning air to blew upon his brow—"now, sir, what have you to say to a man who has not a farthing in the world, nor a friend ?"

" You wrong him who addresses you, when you say that."

" Indeed—do I ?"

" Yes, you do ; but to business. You are a married man, and now and then a pang, short, but severe, crosses your mind at the thought that you are sadly neglecting your wife and child."

Hoffenden made a gesture of impatience, and the captain added—

" I will spare you from having that pang for the future. Your wife has a cousin, named Andrew Ewert, who calls upon her and consoles her, while you are at the gaming-table."

" Devil!—fiend !"

" Call me what you like; I never care what an angry man says to me ; but it certainly does seem to me as if I deserved thanks, instead of abuse, for taking special pains to put a man in a position to save his honour, as I have for you."

" No, no, it cannot be. Jane false ! Oh, no, no."

He leaned against the railings of a house, and turned of an ashy paleness ; and then suddenly, as the warm blood rushed to his cheeks, and he dashed his hat upon his head, he clutched his companion by the arm with startling energy, saying—

" Prove to me what you say, or I will, if it be unfounded to that extent to make me call it a lie, tear the foul tongue from the throat that has given breath to the words."

" Putting on one side altogether," said Murdo, coolly, " the probability of my objecting to your taking such liberties with my tongue, and the fact of my being by far the stronger man of the two, I can only repeat my statement, and say that I am willing to go with you while you make the inquiry."

"You—you do not mean to tell me he is with her now?" gasped Hoffenden.

"How can I, when I am here, and you live in the Adelphi? But I mean to tell you that he was with her to-night."

"You—you swear that?"

"If you please, I swear it; not that I consider my swearing it adds anything to its truthfulness, for I hold that what a man of temper will coolly say, he will as coolly swear to."

"True, true—that is true. Come on; I thank you already, for your manner is such as to impress me with a strong idea of your truthfulness. Come on, I say. Home, home—oh, what a word is that now to hear!—God, what a word. Oh, Jane, Jane, can it be—can it be?"

"You seem rather disturbed?"

"Rather disturbed! Rather! but you cannot feel as I feel; oh, no—no. Oh, God, no. I am as a man awakened from some dream of fancied security. If it should be true—oh, if it should be true!"

"What will you do—will you have revenge?—Devilish revenge—such revenge as shall make people, when they tell the tale of your wrongs, end it by saying, 'Such was the manner in which Henry Hoffenden was treated; but was he not amply avenged?'"

"Yes—yes."

"You would have blood? There are some stains that nothing will wash out, or cover up, but blood."

"There; and this is one of them—I will have blood."

"You will kill them both—you will not let either of them live—nay, you must not hesitate; for, on my soul, it is what I would myself do—kill them both. And yet—yet, when we come to think how frail woman is, and how you have neglected Jane——"

"Neglected who? You called her Jane as if you knew her intimately."

"Who, I? Oh, no, you called her Jane, you know, and I adopted the word, for which I apologise. Of course I ought to have said Mrs. Hoffenden; but I spoke hurriedly, and I must confess that the wrong which has been done to you stirs me more than you would suppose by my outward bearing."

"It is no matter, sir."

"Nay, but it is of matter, if, by a mere stray word, I offend you. If you would take my advice when you reach home, you should, without giving time for any specious tale to be prepared, at once put the question to your wife as to whether or not the cousin had been there; and then I would hear no more than the answer, and be that even in the negative, you will be able to judge by her manner if she speaks true or false."

"I shall, I shall."

"Most assuredly you will; and if she say that he has not, you—you——"

"Will still be able to come to a correct conclusion."

"Then I personally am willing to abide the issue; and now I will tell you how I came to know as much. I was, strange to say, thinking of you as I neared your home, or rather the house in which you have your home, and as I walked slowly past the open doorway, some one came out; yes, some one rushed by me suddenly in coming out, and a glance let me know who it was, for I have seen the youth before."

"It was Andrew Ewert? and she, when last she spoke of him, affected with friendly solicitude to bewail his probable fate; for nothing she said, having been heard of him for a time, she feared that he was gone from this world."

"Indeed! Mark you the hypocrisy of that. She knew—she must have known that he was alive and well, as I shall show you; for when he had got a few paces from the door, fancying me, no doubt, a stranger, and inattentive to his speech, he said, in hurried accents—

"'I must warn her not to let the jealous fool, her husband, think that I have set my foot in London again so soon. I will return. Besides, is it not worth returning to get one kiss from those ruby lips——'"

"D——n!"

"' One more embrace from those encircling arms, and ——' "

" Hell and furies! Peace! peace! I will have revenge! ay, such revenge as even you shall admit to be bitter and complete! Yes, I will have revenge—revenge. Say no more! I want no prompting! My honour is like a polished mirror, the least breath will dim its lustre! Such a stain must be wiped away, and, as you say, with blood! Ay, with blood must it be wiped away, if necessary! I need no prompting, I need no urging on to do a deed which shall fill the mouths of men with expressions of wonder and awe!"

Thus conversing, and that villanous Captain Murdo urging on all the furiously awakened passions of the gamester, to do some frightful deed which should give him his own revenge, they reached the doors of the chambers in the Adelphi, where he, Hoffenden, resided.

And in that strangely awakened whirlwind of passion he never thought of how, even if Jane had really fallen, instead of being the creature of purity and goodness she really was, he, by his neglect, had himself to thank for such an effect. He never seemed to think that he was the person who was to blame for all that it was possible might have occurred in his once happy home.

But thus is man ever unjust to woman. Thus it is that he seems to think his manhood and his strength gives him a licence to commit iniquities which his gentler and weaker partner must be covered with shame and reproach if she make but the smallest advance to; and thus was it that Henry Hoffenden, although he was the injurer, considering himself a very ill-used man, as he stood on the staircase leading to his chambers in the Adelphi, full of dark and evil thought.

Before, however, he entered the chamber—for he could do so at his pleasure, as he had a key with him—he turned to Captain Murdo, and said, in a voice of agitation,—

" Will you wait here for me? God knows, I am now desolate of heart, and may have need of much good counsel yet."

" My dear fellow, I shall do all that you can possibly ask me to do. Rely upon me in any little emergency of this nature, I beg, for I shall always be most happy to be of service. But you remember my caution, I hope."

" Your caution! what was that? I thought you urged me on to my revenge, instead of cautioning me."

" I did say that it was incompatible with your honour not to be avenged ; but I cautioned you to abstain from attempting aught against your wife. Do not stain your manhood by lifting up your arm against her. You ought, and I hope you will be fully satisfied by punishing the seducer; let the seduced seek for what consolation she can from her own thoughts."

Hoffenden trembled as he replied, after an anxious moment or two's pause—

" I should not have expected this of you. No—no—not of you, of all men. Did you speak to me of blood even now ?"

" I did. But you should remember that, although you, by neglecting your wife, and spending your time at a gaming-table, may have left her peculiarly liable to temptation, and although you may find at the bottom of your heart, consequently, some excuse for her, there is none for the man who, taking advantage of such circumstances, has contrived your dishonour."

" Yes, yes ; that is very true. I—I have neglected her. But—but—well, well, I will not seek to excuse it, or to fritter it away. I have neglected her, I know I have; but I did not think of this."

" No ; we seldom think deeply of the loss of any treasure, until the thief has stolen it from us."

" It is so. Then, and not till then, are we able to estimate the value of that which we have cast from us. Oh, Jane—Jane!"

" What were you saying? Whither do your thoughts point now ?"

" To Jane—to Jane! Oh, if I could but have foreseen——"

" Yes ; that is the fool's argument when something has happened. If he could have foreseen! Why, Hoffenden, if we could foresee what is going to happen next, we should be divinities all of us. Shake off this woman's mood that is come over you. Do you not see that already the daylight has come, and that you will have little time in which to act? Enter your own room at once, and be what you seem to be—a man. Vindicate your honour!"

"There is a side door here that leads to the inner chamber next to the bed-room of my wife. I have a key that will open its latch. What if I make my way there first, and—listen? I may hear something."

"Be it so. I will keep watch here, in case any one should attempt to escape; not that at such an hour as this, with the full light of day glaring upon him, and your return expected, the author of your dishonour is likely to be here."

"I do not think my return is even expected," said Hoffenden, sadly. "I have been away for days together, so that is no argument against his being here."

"Enter at once. Any other one who trusts your courage less than I, would say that you shrunk from the task that is before you."

"Shrink! No, no; there is no shrinking here. My heart feels like a lump of marble in my bosom; but it does not shrink."

As he spoke he produced the key of the latch of the chamber door that opened it on the outer side, and though his had trembled so that he could scarcely accomplish the simple operation of turning the lock, he in another moment passed into the chamber.

Captain Murdo folded his arms upon his breast, and his hideous eyes seemed to be looking all manner of ways at once, while he seemed to be laughing, for a strange sort of convulsion shook his frame, although no sound came from his lips at all indicative of mirth.

"Yes," he muttered—"oh, yes; there will be blood flowing before the world is twenty-four hours older, in this spot—human gore; and the half-stifled shriek of the dying will fill the air with pleasant music to my ears—very pleasant music. There will be blood—yes, blood spilt—red, sparkling gore, springing from the green earth to heaven. Ha, ha, ha! and I shall see it—and I shall see it!"

CHAPTER IV.

THE MURDER IN THE SPARE ROOM OF THE OLD CHAMBERS.

AND what must have been the feelings of the gambler's wife during the weary time when he, who was the great enemy of all goodness and virtue, was endeavouring to effect the destruction of the only one, who for a long time past had bestowed a word of kindness upon her?

With what agony of mind, and with what a frenzied imaginaion she waited still the return of him, whom she still loved, despite all the cruel conduct he was guilty of; him whom she would still have praised, still have defended against all aspersions. But such is woman; she clings to her idol still, under any and every circumstance; where once she has bestowed her heart's best affections, there she clings even to the ruin of what once was happiness.

And so it was that Jane clung to the man, whose evil and desultory passions made him prefer a gaming-table, with all its wild and feverish terrors, to the truly blessed calm of existence, with her who ever welcomed him with smiles, and who should have been the very sunshine of his existence. Strange perversion of human nature ever to cast away the happiness it has within its grasp, in the pursuit of some new meteor of the fancy, that glitters but to betray.

Who ought to have been happier than he, Henry Hoffenden? He had won the affection of one, who, in person and in mind, would have lent a lustre to the proudest diadem queen ever wore; and then—then, when he had achieved such a triumph—then, when he had won the golden prize, he cast it from him as if it were worthless.

But woe, woe be to him who thus casts aside a loving trusting heart. That day of vengeiance is sure to come to Hoffenden. His heart is soft as that of the hyæna searchng for its prey. He listens at the door. He wants to overhear the counsels of that heart he has so nearly made desolate. And now he is in the room. Now he has fairly passed the doorway, but he staggers back. God of heaven! what an expression is upon his face. Who would know him now? The only sound that comes from his lips is a strange hissing one, scarcely human. He has grasped the arm of the arch fiend who has brought him so far, and dragged him in a couple of paces, and then he points to the couch on which lies the unconscious sleeper, and looks in the face of Murdo.

"Did I not tell you so?" whispered Murdo. "Ha! ha! Did I not tell you so? Am I a false prophet now? Did I not tell you?"

Henry Hoffenden lifted up his arm, and seemed about to say something sudden, loud, and violent; but the other stopped him, and laid his hand upon him, whispering—

"Hush! hush! Who placed yon knife so temptingly at hand? Do you see it—I say do you see it?"

"I do—I do see it. Ha! ha! Oh, yes, I see it, and I feel it too. It is here—here in my hand, and it shall soon be in another's heart."

"Remember!"

"Remember what—my dishonour—my wrong? What else am I to remember?"

"That with this one sacrifice your vengeance should be satisfied. Contrive nothing against your wife. But if—hush! hush! Do you not hear her voice? Hush! she speaks to the child."

"Oh, God!" they heard her utter; "oh, God! not yet returned. When, oh, when shall I look upon his face again?"

"Mourning her lover, of course," whispered Murdo, in the ear of Hoffenden.

"And what," added Jane, "what now has life in store for me? Nothing—nothing. What will become of me now? Oh, how I hope, and yet how I dread to look upon him."

"Conscience, you hear," whispered Murdo, "makes itself a little heard.

"And what will be thy fate, my little one? My darling, what will be thy fate? Alas! alas! that thou wert ever born; and yet—no, no. Oh, God! forgive me."

"Humph! you hear that?"

"Hush! hush! hush! I hear, but know not how to translate. Oh, what can I think?"

"Do not think. The hour for thought has passed away, and that for action has arrived. Look about you."

"Hush! she is praying."

"And well she may. Who has more need of prayer than the guilty wife?—who more need to pray that the poor fool, who she thinks knows not his own dishonour, may always remain in, to her, such a blissful state of ignorance. Oh, yes, of course, she prays."

"Demon! fiend! Why do you tug so at my heart? Ha! what cold touch is that?"

"You laid your hand upon the knife-blade. The coldness reproached your tardy purpose. But I see you are one of those who are content to talk, and not to act. Farewell."

"Do not leave me—do not leave me now, I pray you, but stay and see that I am not one of those who shrink to strike in the name of injured honour. No, no, no; I am not one of those."

"Are you not?"

As he spoke, he pointed deridingly to the sleeping form of Andrew Ewert, and Hoffenden understood the implied reproach of inconsistency. He made a step towards his victim, and raised the dagger in his hand.

"To his heart," whispered Murdo; "to the heart of the man who has desecrated your home, and made you the ridicule of the world. To his heart, I say to his heart, Hoffenden, or do not do the deed."

"It is done," said Hoffenden; and like a flash of forked lightning the glittering steel descended upon its victim, burying itself up to the hilt in the unhappy young man's bosom. Oh, what a dreadful scene was that! With awful and ready tact, Murdo stopped the scream which would have issued from the lips of the poor murdered man, by placing his hand upon his mouth, and in another moment he was incapable of uttering any sound but a dull, rattling noise in his throat, which had an awful signification.

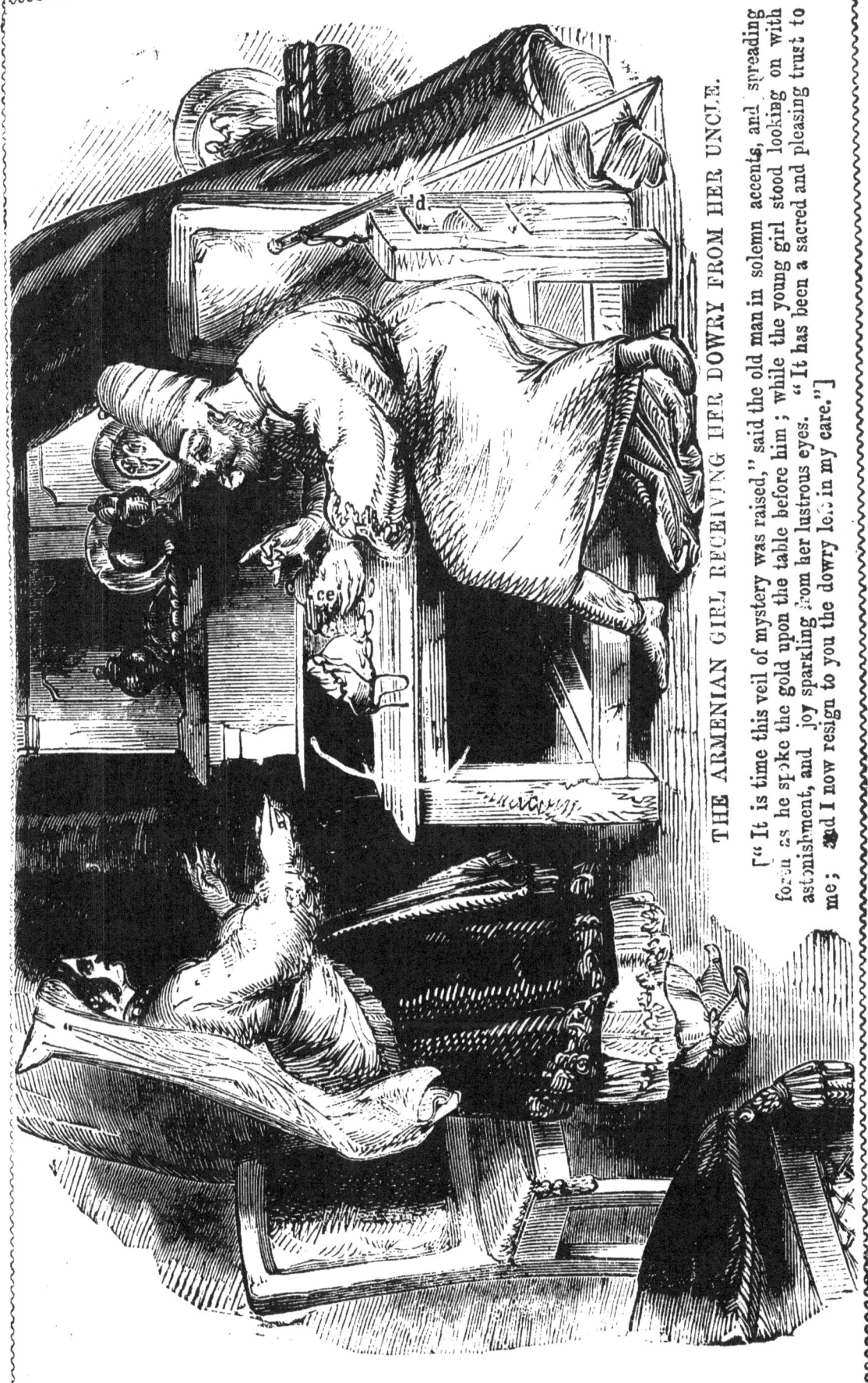

THE ARMENIAN GIRL RECEIVING HER DOWRY FROM HER UNCLE.

["It is time this veil of mystery was raised," said the old man in solemn accents, and spreading forth as he spoke the gold upon the table before him; while the young girl stood looking on with astonishment, and joy sparkling from her lustrous eyes. "It has been a sacred and pleasing trust to me; and I now resign to you the dowry left in my care."]

Hoffenden, when he struck the fatal blow, fell backwards, and remained propped up strangely against the wall of the apartment, with his feet doubled up under him, and his hands outstretched, as if he expected that the murdered man might yet have strength to rise and grapple with him.

It was a horrible scene! Some frothy-looking blood bubbled up from the wound and spread around the spot through which the poniard had passed; and, although from internal bleeding the lungs refused to aid in the production of any articulate sound, the struggles of the victim were frightful. Roderick Murdo sprung upon the couch, and seized Andew by the hair, on each side of his head, and held him down; but the limbs of the dying man were drawn up with horrible energy, and the arms were tossed about in wild disorder. Then suddenly releasing one of his hands from the hold he had of the poor victim's head, Murdo plucked out the poniard from the body, and then, with an awful, frightful gush the warm blood bubbled forth like as if from a fountain.

It fell upon the clothes, and upon the face of Hoffenden, who felt what a relief it would have been even to him to shriek, far suffocating sensation came over him as he saw the gasping efforts of the murdered man to get breath; and, at the time, he felt as if the poniard was deep in his own heart.

"But, now, surely he is dying.—Yes, he is more still, and a change has taken place upon the features.—Yes, he is dying. The limbs hang flaccid and motionless; and the warm heart's blood wells forth with a bubbling sound. God of Heaven, what new impulse is that! He half rises and turns upon Murdo, who has relaxed his hold, and has but barely time to grapple him by the throat, and fling himself across him, hoping, by his whole weight to keep him down. It is a fearful struggle, a horrible struggle—not a struggle for life or death, but a struggle to die. The last awakened energies of life all concentrated in one convulsion; and the struggle of the dying man was appalling; he tossed Murdo off him as though he had been a feather's weight, and in his turn grappled him.

"Help! help!" gasped Murdo, "help!—He will kill me."

But Hoffenden could not help him. He was too paralised himself with what was occurring to move, and so the frightful fight went on until Andrew Ewert suddenly became motionless, and rolled over upon his back a corpse.

Yes; the deed was done, and the consequences had yet to come.

Oh, what an aspect did that poor victim of lawless passion and of false testimony present—dabbled in gore, and the eyes—those eyes which had never beamed malevolently upon aught human, shining with a lustre that was not of this world. They seemed bent upon him, too—Hoffenden, the murderer—the man who had struck the death blow; and upon the now sad face there was an unutterable expression of reproach, for the previously convulsed features had composed themselves to a state of repose, and the feeling a contemplation of them would have awakened in the mind of a stranger, would have been one of unmitigated grief, rather than the desperate convulsive vehemence that, but a few minutes before, had so much distorted them.

All was over; but how strange it was that no alarm had reached the next apartment. How strange it was that Jane was so still while the deed of blood was doing. Could it be possible that she, in such close proximity, too, as she was, heard nothing of that frightful struggle. That was the strangest thing of all.

"Are we watched?" said Murdo.

"God knows—God knows!" ejaculated Hoffenden. "Where is the knife?"

"What do you want with it?"

"To plunge it into my own heart. I cannot live now to be the slave of a recollection which would drive me mad. The act might have been a justifiable one, but it is none the less horrible."

"Psha! What is your wife about?—that is the question."

"I—I cannot tell. All is still. Is she watching us?"

"If so, we are lost; and the only resource is——"

"What? Oh, what?"

"Another death. The lives of a thousand women should not stand in the way of my personal safety. If she knows too much, she——"

"Hush! I hear a footstep on the stairs. 'Tis her's—'tis her's! There, look through the keyhole, and you will see; she has been out on some errand."

"To fetch the police?"

"Oh, no—no; she could not act composure so well. Besides, she is alone. Listen, listen—oh, listen, and speak not a word."

Murdo looked through the keyhole of the door, and he saw that it was Jane Hoffenden who was returning, and in her hand she had a small jug of milk. The fact was that she had waited until it was light enough to go to a neighbouring dairy with the only piece of copper coinage she had, to get its value in milk for the child; and she had been absent just long enough for the frightful deed of blood to be committed in the adjoining chamber which we have detailed to the reader.

They now heard her speak to the child.

"Darling," she said, "I have not been long from you, and I have brought you milk. Alas! your father comes not; but this will drive off for a time the pangs of hunger, which I can bear myself, but cannot see you bear."

Thus conversing to that little one, without whom she would indeed have been desolate, she sat down, little suspecting the occurrence that had taken place so close at hand, and which, if she had known it, would have convulsed her soul with horror, and produced probably some act of desperation, such as in her calmer moments of distress she could have no notion of.

"All is right," said Murdo in a whisper. "Who will say now that providence did not work with us by removing the only witness we had to dread, at the very moment when her absence was most desirable?"

"Hush—hush! What is to be done? How is the deed now to be concealed? What if she come in here and see the dreadful sight? Will she not denounce us at once? How are we to dispose of this victim? How are we to hide a deed which, in its consequences, if discovered, must be fatal to us?"

"I have thought of all that. You must now go into the next room by the other door, opening on to the landing-place. You must temporise with her. You must tell her that you have seen Andrew, and made an appointment with him for to-morrow; and you will have the satisfaction of knowing that it is here, for you must come to dispose of the body. Then you must say that fear of an arrest for debt forces you instantly to remove, and take her away at once."

"To where? I have no funds."

"I will supply you with sufficient funds to answer that purpose. I will not desert you now that I have brought you thus far in safety through this perilous enterprise. You will tell her to go with the child and wait for you at the corner of the street; then you will carefully lock up the chambers, and to-night, at an hour after sunset, meet me here; and during that time I will think of some mode of getting rid of the body."

"It—it must be so. I rely wholly upon you."

"You may—you may. Go and do it at once. Is there any fastening to this door of communication?"

"Yes, a bolt on this side. Do you not see it?"

"I do; it is fast. Be quick, or some suspicion may arise. You can please her, you know, now, by telling her you will reform a little, and not frequent the gaming-table so much, but make yourself comfortable at home."

"Comfortable!" said Hoffenden, with a shudder.

"Yes; and why not? It is but a human life, after all, that you have taken—a ticklish possession at the best of times, as we all know; and, besides, your provocation was surely sufficient. Go—go at once, and do as I require you, I have a cooler head than you, and am more likely to advise you for your safety."

Hoffenden now was as a mere child in the hands of the villain Murdo, who could just dictate to him any course of conduct he pleased; for he seemed to be really both physically and mentally prostrated by the deed he had, with so little reflection, and so little evidence to back out the presumption upon which he had set about it, committed. Truly might he say, as he did, that he had something to recollect, which would cling to him for the remainder of his existence, brief or long.

If, however, he had been in a condition to reason upon the matter, he could not probably have come to any better arrangement than that which was proposed to him by Murdo, and he accordingly obeyed his injunctions by leaving that room in which was such damning evidence of murder, and proceeding to the other door leading to the chambers.

CHAPTER V.

THE MEETING AND THE PROMISE.—A TRUSTING HEART'S DEVOTION.

JANE HOFFENDEN was bending over her child to kiss its brow, as it composed itself to sleep again after the tiny meal it had had, when she heard the rattle of a key in the lock of the room door, and with a feeling now of certainty that it must be her husband, she stood with clasped hands and a face of deep anxiety concerning the state he was likely to be in, expecting his appearance; for, alas! on the few occasions, in the course of a week, that she did see him, he was often flushed with wine, and unable to listen to the voice of affection or reason.

And even now, when he made his appearance before her, there was a strange sort of unsteadiness in his gait and movements that made her at the moments suspect that her fears of inebriety were but too true, and that she was about to have a repetition of some sad scenes that had before passed between them.

But a glance at his face alarmed her. It was a death-like paleness, except upon one spot, and there was a smear of blood. She had never seen him present so dreadful an aspect, and the slight stagger in his gait now she was more inclined to put down to the score of illness that inebration.

She flew to his side, and clung to his arm, as she said,—

"Oh, Harry! you are not well. You are very, very ill, Harry, and you are right to come to me. Sit down—sit down, and tell me—oh, God! how pale——"

"Hush, Jane—hush! I am—well enough—that is—I—I have had a slight fall. Am I pale?"

"You are, Harry; and on your cheek is a spot of blood."

"Blood—blood! whose blood? Take it off—take it off, or it will cling to me like a pestilence. I feel it now! Take it—oh, for God's sake, take from my face that spot of blood! It rests upon me like the avenging hand of God!"

With a furious gesture, he wiped that particle of gore from off his face, and then, shuddering, he sank into a chair which Jane brought to him; and the alarm that she felt at his strange manner chased every particle of colour from her cheeks, so that she was to the full as pale as he was, and for some moments she scarcely knew what form of question to put her fears into. At length, as he continued silent, and only looked tremblingly about him, she spoke.

"Harry—Harry, speak to me. What has happened to disturb you thus? Oh, tell me what has happened, Harry! You are not at all yourself. Something dreadful——"

"No—no—nothing! That is to say—I forgot; we must leave here at once. I am pursued for a debt—a mere debt, and must get out of the way of an importunate creditor; and—and, Jane——"

"Yes, Harry."

"I have taken a better thought, and shall be more with you, Jane, than I have been —a much better thought."

Jane burst into tears. She had not heard such words from him for many a day, and they completely overcame her to hear them now so suddenly come from his lips, when she least expected them. She sobbed like a child.

"Hush! hush!" he said, "Jane." I—I will be a different man now, if you will go at once—at once, Jane."

"Anything, Harry—oh, anything! You know you have but to hint at your slightest wish and it becomes my law. Oh, Harry, Harry, shall we really and indeed be happy yet? Oh, say that we shall, and let it be with one of your old familiar smiles that you say it, dear, dear Harry."

"Very happy."

He uttered the words, but they were uttered in such an abandonment of despair, that they wore a mockery upon their own ordinary meaning.

"But you have something, Harry, on your mind, I know you have; some danger threatens you, or you are hurt more than you will own; but there is one here who will advise with you; one who will, with all sincerity of heart and soul, be of assistance to you. My cousin, Andrew Ewert."

"Stay," cried Henry Hoffenden, as Jane was about to proceed towards the door of the next apartment. "Stay; I—I have seen him."

"Seen him, Harry! Oh, God! that spot of blood. Some quarrel!"

"No!" he shrieked. "No—no. There was no quarrel; we have made an appointment for to-morrow, and he is gone. We have had no quarrel, and we shall have no quarrel. All will be peace between us."

"All should be, Harry, for he means you well; a more disinterested, noble heart never beat, except your own, dear Harry, in those happy times when first we knew each other, and when first we loved—those happy, happy times, which surely shall come back again. See, Harry, our little one is sleeping; but even in the calmness of repose I can trace the father's features in the infant's face. Is the child not like you, Harry? Look upon its face again. Nay, why do you turn aside?"

"Jane—Jane! your cousin, Andrew Ewret, ought to have loved you."

"He did—he does."

"Ah!"

"But with such a soul, and such a principle of honour, as makes his love a pride and a satisfaction. He loves me well enough to wish me to be abundantly happy with you. Did he not tell you so? Oh, you know little of him if you think that one unworthy thought could find a home in his heart. If you had heard him speak, how you would take him to your heart as a brother, and you would love him. Shall I tell you, Harry, that my great hope is for you to be so charmed by his good companionship, that you will seek with him for such pure sinless pleasures, as shall be sweet to reflect upon the delight without one pang."

"Peace! oh, peace! Do you believe in Heaven?"

"Do I believe in Heaven? Oh, awful question. Can you doubt——"

"Will you swear by its name, then, and by every hope you have in this world and the next; by your child's eternal welfare; by all that you hold sacred, that—that you are innocent, and that the love of Andrew Ewert is such a love as you have described to me? Will you swear?"

"I will swear—I do, as God is the judge of all."

"Then—then," said Harry Hoffenden, rising—"then I—I——"

He could say no more, but, completely overpowered by conflicting emotions, he fell to the ground heavily, as if he had, at that instant, surrendered up his spirit to be judged by that Heaven, whose ordinances he had in so fearful a manner outraged. The alarm of Jane was excessive; she uttered a shriek, and flew to the door for aid; but before she could lay her hand upon the lock it was opened, and Murdo stood upon the threshold.

The sight of this man, who had so recently insulted her, was sufficient to make Jane recoil from the door, aye, quicker than she had approached it; besides, there was an expression upon his face which was such that it was enough to make any one shudder to look at it.

Slowly, amid the dead stillness that reigned in that apartment, he entered it completely, and closed the door after him, still keeping his eyes fixed with the glare of a basilisk upon poor Jane. But when he came a little closer to her, she found strength to speak, and she recoiled further from him, saying,—

"Help—help—husband—help!"

"'Tis I shall help him," said Murdo. "Cease this clamour; it is not required. 'Tis I shall help him; and let me advise you, to prevent discord, not——. Hush, he moves."

"Where am I—where am I?" said Hoffenden. "Is it all a dream? Oh! thank God, I am saved. It is not real—I am in my own house. Oh! Jane, Jane! I have had an awful dream. I thought——"

"Silence! said Murdo, in a loud voice; and, stooping over the prostrate form of Harry Hoffenden, he with one hand lifted him to his feet by an exertion of prodigious strength, such as few men indeed could have been at all equal to.

"Silence. Look at me!"

"God! it is real."

"Harry, Harry, what is the meaning of all this?" cried Jane, frantically. "Oh! tell me what has happened, and how is it that you look about you with such horror-stricken eyes? I appeal to you to command the absence of this man from your house."

"Ha, ha! Good!" laughed Murdo. "Mr. Hoffenden, am I not your friend?"

"Yes," grasped Henry.

"And am I not welcome ?   Speak, am I not welcome?"

" Welcome to kill me !"

" Psha ! you are disordered, and know not what you say. Remember what you have still to do. If you like to do it alone, I will leave you—if not, I will remain. Say which of these two propositions you prefer ?"

" Oh, do not leave me. I shall go mad if I am left."

Jane sat down and wrung her hands despairingly. She could too plainly see that she had no power over the mind of her husband, in the presence of that dreadful man ; and that it was quite clear, for some reason or another, he had a controul over him, which Hoffenden dare not even make the attempt to shake off. What it could be that bound them together, she could not think ; but it was agony to know that there was a bond of union of that sort, and to think that there was the man who had so grievously insulted her enjoying the positive protection of her husband, in repeating such conduct if he chose.

All the feelings of a virtuous and high-minded creature, such as she was, revolted against such a state of things, and she spoke with a sudden energy that alarmed Hoffenden, and surprised Murdo.

"Harry," she said, " it can be but recently that you have taken that man to be your friend, and I tell you that he is a base and a most unworthy person to hold such a place In your heart. Do not ask me now to tell you more, but be content to dismiss him from any home of yours."

" Really," said Murdo, " you must allow me, my good friend Hoffenden, to explain this little matter to you. I called here before we went you know where, hoping to find you at home, to tell you of you know what; and Mrs. Hoffenden, I suppose, mistook the ordinary every day civility of a man who has travelled much, for gallantry of a warmer character than was correct. That is all, and I pledge my honour I meant nothing."

" 'Tis false," said Jane.

" I—I—know not what to do. Will you drive me mad between you?" said Harry.

" Between us ?" said Jane. " Good God, husband ! Can you speak of me thus, in conjunction with that man ?"

" That man, madam, is your husband's friend," said Murdo, " and one without whom, your husband will tell you, he does not wish to do."

" I—I think," said Hoffenden, his lips quivering as he spoke, and his whole frame betraying the greatest emotion, " I think that we ought to believe Mr. Murdo, when he tells us that upon his honour he meant no harm. I—think so, Jane, and for my sake——"

" No more, no more, Harry. This subject shall never again be originated by me. Let Mr. Murdo enjoy the triumph he has obtained, and the position he has gained ; but let him feel that he holds it upon sufferance, and that his future behaviour must be squared upon the most exact model."

" You are too hard upon me, madam," answered Murdo. " You are much too hard."

Jane did not condescend to make him any reply, and he whispered into the ear of Hoffenden—

" My great offence was, that I saw Andrew Ewert here.   That was my great offence against your wife. Do you not see that clearly enough ?"

" But you did not tell me you had been here at all."

" I intended."

" And she has taken a solemn oath of her innocence."

" Of course."

This reply was simple enough in itself—indeed it was as short as possible ; but it had a world of meaning in the tone in which it was uttered, and the manner which accompanied it ; and once more suspicion, that monster so easy to raise and so difficult to lay, arose in the mind of Hoffenden with regard to the purity of her who, alas, was of too noble and exalted a character to be understood by him whom destiny had mated her.

Far different, indeed, ought to have been the fortune of poor wretched Jane Hoffenden; and had she been the wife of one who could have appreciated the prize in the lottery of matrimony he had drawn, she would have been not only herself the happiest of the happy, but have formed a world of felicity for another.

The humiliation now of having to endure the presence of the man whom she had before feared to complain of to her husband, for fear of exciting his too great wrath, was immense ; and no wonder such a person as Jane felt it acutely. She now made up her mind, when she should be alone with her husband, to make a stronger stand than she could in Murdo's presence, against any intimacy with him ; for when he had the liberty o putting in a word, the conversation was too painful and too degrading, for her to continue it.

The idea that came across her at once was, that some money transaction accounted for the supremacy that he (Murdo) had temporarily obtained over her husband's mind ; and again she sighed to think that that must be in truth all owing to that detestable vice— gaming.

"Be quick," whispered Murdo to Hoffenden. "Time presses, and I would have you seek another home."

"Yes, yes—I——"

A low tap at the door now aroused the guilty man, and he sprang to his feet with terror depicted upon his face.

"Who—who knocks?" he said.

The knock was repeated as before, and Murdo walked to the door, saying, "Allow me to answer for you."

He flung it wide open, but no one was to be seen. Not a soul was visible on the staircase ; and as there was no place in which any one could hide, and as it was almost impossible that they could get into any of the other chambers so quickly , the knock remained a mystery, which there seemed to be no means of clearing up.

"Who—who is it ?" gasped Hoffenden. "Who wants me ?"

"No one. Some accidental sound has been mistaken for the knocker. There is no one here, and the staircases are quiet. Will you go at once? It is your better course. Have you explained to Mrs. Hoffenden the necessity for your immediate departure ?"

"Yes—yes. Come, Jane, come. The child—the child. I am glad to leave here."

"And I am willing," whispered Jane to him, " to go to the world's uttermost wastes with you, Harry. I have but to get something from the next apartment, and then——"

"No!" almost screamed Hoffenden; and then making an effort to appear calm, he added, "Never mind it now, Jane—you shall come again ; never mind it now, Jane. I —I will bring you again, myself. Come away, if you would indeed do my bidding, Jane. Come away at once, I pray you. Oh, come, come."

Thus implored, although much wondering at the reason of it, she complied with the request to come away at once; and merely wrapping the child up in some of its clothing, she hurried from the room, closely followed by Hoffenden, after he had been, by the directions of Murdo, most specially careful in fastening the chambers, so that no one should intrude into them during his absence, and discover how dreadful an object lay in one of them.

It was broad daylight now by the time they reached the street, and many passengers were bustling along, some intent on business, and some on pleasure ; but all envied by that unhappy wretch, who felt that he had done that deed of blood which there was no recalling.

CHAPTER VI.

A NEW SCENE.—THE THIEVES' HOUSE IN THE MINT AT SOUTHWARK.

At the time of which we write, that peculiar district of London, known as the Mint, at Southwark, was only just beginning to be deprived of some of its exclusiveness, which for so long a time had made it a sanctuary for all sorts of evil-doers, and a complete hotbed of vice in every possible shape for the supply of what may be called the metropolitan market.

There was a time, some twenty years anterior to the period when the circumstances took place which we are now laying before the reader, when the police as little thought of breaking up the thieves' quarters at the Mint at Southwark, as the thieves would dream of asking for a seat on the bench at the Old Bailey. Indeed, it would not have been safe for the officers to have attempted a seizure in such a sanctuary as the Mint ; and as the effort of the police in those days was not to put down crime, but to catch criminals, those seminaries of iniquity went on flourishingly.

But, as we have remarked, at about the period of our tale—viz., 1800, some efforts were being made to root out those dens of infamy, which had the effect of causing greater circumspection in their conduction.

There was one house in particular where, up to the latest period, such an academy of vice was kept, that it alone was more than sufficient to engage the whole of London, and send out pickpockets, housebreakers, and footpads enough to furnish plenty of work for police-officers and police magistrates for years to come.

It was a large, rambling, old-fashioned building, and in its exterior presented nothing remarkable. For many years there had been a placard in the window of "lodgings to let," and it had hung there so long, that it had got brown and dusty to an extent which almost precluded the possibility of reading it. But nobody thought anything of that, because it was so large a house that there might be plenty of rooms always to let in it.

The police, however, and certain of the magistracy, knew perfectly well that it was a thieves' training-house ; and it had such a reputation for secret places and dangerous characters, that, unless some daring offender was wanted, it was left alone, and even on those occasions it was only watched, so that the gent might be caught coming out or going in some day.

On the occasion when we wish to introduce our readers to this mansion of the arts, a close, small rain was falling in the streets of London, which tended very much to drive everybody within doors whose avocations did not compel them to bide the pelting of the pitiless storm, and a large assemblage of persons were in the large room, as it was called, of the house, which was ostensibly kept by a man named Oakes, who was hung in 1823 for murder.

This Job Oakes, as was his name, certainly reigned at the head of a despotic government, for no one attempted in that house to interfere with his management. It was, "Stay and do as Job Oakes pleases, or go and be ——— ;" and that elegant sentence was actually on the chimney-piece in one of the rooms, as well as the capital letters, W.T.L.W., which all new comers were expected to translate, or mulcted accordingly for the knowledge in divers quarts of some intoxicating liquid.

But the brotherhood, as they were sometimes called—that is to say, those who really might be considered to belong to Job Oakes's establishment, were not many, and it was only those who got into the more secret parts of the house ; a few large rooms of which, on the ground-floor, were only devoted to the use of all thieves alike who chose to make it a house of call.

The great majority of what are called the put-up robberies of London were concocted at this house, and in those Job had generally a share.

In defiance of all public-houses, and trouble about licences, and so on, Job furnished his visitors with what liquors they wanted, as well as tobacco, so that the place became irresistibly attractive to the light-fingered fraternity.

On this particular night, then, in consequence of the rain, the art of picking pockets could not be called into very active requisition, because the class of people whose pockets were best worth picking did not come out when the elements were in an unfavourable state, and consequently that branch of professional industry was not pursued with effect ; and the professors of it indulged themselves with pots and pipes, and talked over past achievements, and the probabilities attendant upon campaigns to come.

There was no sort of doorkeeper and no kind of ceremony to be used in entering the house ; only a stranger would be certain to be reeognised in a moment, and unless then he could give "respectable" reference, he got into trouble.

It did not by any means often happen that a person unknown to the fraternity made his appearance ; but, if he did, he meet with a reception not calculated to induce him to repeat his visit.

To attempt to enter into anything like a descriptive chapter of the saying and doings of the throng of persons who were in the common rooms of the house, would be to take up too much of that space within which we propose keeping the limits of our story, and therefore we proceed at once to a small private apartment belonging to Job Oakes himself, but he was not alone in it at that time.

Besides "the Job," as he was most familiarly called, there was a man of sharp, intelligent features, respectably dressed, and with a half open mouth, as if always ready for a smile upon the smallest possible provocation that could be presented to him, and he was listening, or pretending to listen, to what Job was saying to him ; while two lads were close at hand, listening with the most marked attention to what passed.

These lads were very different in appearance. One was a large boy of his age, and of

THE CHAMBER OF CRIME.

[Murdo advanced, and seizing Hoffenden with his disengaged hand, he dragged him to the door, while with the other he held the light. . . . Hoffenden bent his gaze on the couch—it was empty. Not a vestige of the murdered corpse was there.]

coarse, shrewd-looking features, with deep-set, cunning-looking black eyes, that shone out of his head like polished beads.

The other was a fair, unassuming-looking boy, rather timid-looking in appearance, and with a handsome, sensitive face, across which half-a-dozen varying expressions would flit in a moment.

"Mr. Bolster," said Job to the man who affected to listen to him with such difference, although, in reality, it was a mere piece of acting on both sides for the special benefit and behoof of the two boys—"Mr. Bolster, I told you a month ago that I revered you, d—n you, but I couldn't, blow you, take any more kidlings. Now you know I had lots o' money along o' the last two, and here you brings me two for nothing, Mr. B. Is that ere the ticket, blow you?"

"You are quite correct," said Mr. Bolster, "you are quite correct, Job Oakes, Esq.,— for that is your proper title, and, if you had all your rights, I believe, sir, you would be Lord Oakes."

"That ere is not the kivestion, Mr. B."

"No, that's uncommonly true, it is not; but you know, sir, that good nature is a rock I am so continually splitting upon, that it's a wonder I ain't by this time shivered all to bits. And, feeling an interest in these two lads, I brought them here with the hope that you would be so good, sir, as to take them in to educate."

"I ought not to do it, Mr. B., I ought not to do it; but, if you recommend them, why I don't mind stretching a pint."

"Sir, how can I express my grateful feelings—would you like me to stand on my head?"

Job frowned, as much as to say, "You are going too far now;" and then, turning to the boys, he said—

"Can you do anything to warrant Mr. Bolster's recommendation?"

"A little," said the dark one, and he laid on the table a large silver spoon.

"Oh, indeed," said Job; "well, well, we can get on by degrees, you know."

As he spoke, he took up the spoon and put it into his pocket, and then he continued— "What can you do, my pretty little kid with the blue eyes?"

Before the boy could answer, Mr. Bolster interfered, and said, in a voice of assumed respect—

"With all deference to you, sir, I was thinking that to get among the ladies he would be just the sort of person. A pretty boy, you see, sir—a very pretty boy, one may say. Don't you think, sir, he could take a purse or two, without much trouble?"

"He might," said Job, stroking his chin, "he might. Follow me, my lads; and you too, Mr. Bolster; of course I shall be glad of your company."

Job Oakes led the way into an apartment of tolerable size, the sight of which seemed much to surprise the boys, for it seemed to be full of all sorts of odd-looking mechanical apparatus, the various uses of which appeared as if they would positively defy conjecture. There were stuffed figures, too, in different parts of the room, both male and female, some of which hung by their necks, while others, again, were propped up from the ground.

"You see," said Job Oakes, "this is one of our school-rooms!"

As he uttered these words, a deep groan was heard, and Job paused and glanced towards the chimney, from whence the sound seemed to come.

"Hilloa!" he said; "is Adams not dead yet?"

"May I take the liberty, sir," said Mr. Bolster, "to inquire who you mean, and what it is that induces Mr. Adams—who, if I recollect rightly, was a nice-looking young lad, who came to you—to utter such a groan?"

"Well, Mr. Bolster, if you must know," said Job, "young Adams went on very well for a little while, but at last he ran away, and told some people he knew all about being here. It has cost me twenty pounds to catch him; but if he had been laid at the bottom of the sea, I'd have had him up, for I never forgive a breach of confidence, and I always catch a boy again, if he goes away and peaches, if it costs me a thousand pounds."

"Ah, I know that; but what's he groaning for, sir?"

"I have wedged him up the chimney, and intend to light a fire and roast him."

"Good God! sir, that will, I suppose, be an end of him."

"Yes, blow you, it will. The end next the fire will be done first, and then he'll gradually drop like fat into the grate, till he is all gone, sir. That's the only way to manage it, sir."

"It's dreadful to think of, Mr. Oakes; but if boys will go away after once coming here, and peach, what can they expect but to be caught again, and stuffed into places and burnt alive ?   I think, sir, it's the mildest thing you can do with them."

That all this was intended to strike terror into the two lads, there is no doubt, and that Mr. Job was getting up a nice little plot, by the assistance of an old stager, is evident enough.

The boys did look at each other rather aghast, at this exposition of what was the probable fate of deserters ; and well they might, for the groans began to be quite energetic, so much so, indeed, that Job declared himself out of all patience, and, taking a light, he set the fire in a blaze.

" Oh, murder !'' said a voice in the chimney ; " oh, murder !   I'm being done brown. Oh ! oh ! oh !''

Dab came something down on the fresh-lighted fire.

" Oh !'' said Job ;   " that's one of his shoes.   His foot will catch all the sooner, that's all, and a good riddance he will be.''

The cries in the chimney now became quite appalling—so much so, indeed, that Mr. Bolster said—

" If I might humbly advise, sir, I would give Mr. Adams a poke, and put him out of his misery at once.   These young gentlemen have nerves, you know, sir, and it's rather unfortunate this little affair has happened just now, because I am sure you may depend on both of them, sir."

" Oh, no doubt of that," said Job, as he took from a corner something that looked like a roasting spit, and commenced at once ramming it up the chimney with great vehemence, until the cries and groans gradually subsided, and it was left to be inferred that Mr. Adams was dead, and had, in this signal manner, paid the penalty of his great indiscretion and treachery.

What real effect this little interlude had upon the two candidates for admission into the art and mystery of taking possession of other people's property, it is impossible as yet to say.   They looked as terrified as Job could desire, and with that he was compelled to be satisfied for the present.

" Now, young fellow," he said to the stoutest of the two, " you see that purse hanging at the end of that stick from the ceiling?   What you are wanted to do, is to take it down, for it's only hooked on, with two fingers of your left hand—this way, you understand.   You must make a sort of jog trot run at it, just as if you were going along the street, you know, and take it as you pass.   You comprehend all that, blow you ?"

" Yes, blow you," said the boy.

" What ! you infernal rascal !   How dare you speak to me in that way?   I'll pretty soon let you know who I am, if you come any of your insolence, you young vagabond. —I had better tell you at once that that won't do."

" I begs your pardon," said the boy ; " I didn't go for to do it, sir, I can swear."

" Well, for this once, we will let it pass ; and now, my young shaver, you will be so good as to try your hand on what I told you."

" Oh, I think I can do that easy enough, sir.   It don't look difficult.   Two fingers only, and as one trots by it.''

" Yes, exactly.   Now, Mr. Bolster, I hope you will turn out to be correct, sir, and that this is really a clever lad, sir.   I hope he will turn out to your satisfaction, sir. You see, sir, he seems to set about the trial with a good spirit."

" Never fear," said the dark-looking lad to his fair companion.   " Never fear, Charley ; I'll manage it."

The lad then, by direction of Job, went to the further end of the room, and, assuming a sharp, careless sort of trot, he made the attempt to snatch the purse with his two fingers as he passed it ; but to accomplish that feat was, apparently, more difficult than he had imagined, and the failure brought with it some consequences.   He hit the piece of wood with his fingers instead of the purse, and it immediately swung over on its centre, and the other end of it dealt him a whack on the head that made him reel again.

" It's not quite so easy as it looks," said Job, taking a pinch of snuff.   " How do you feel now ?''

There's a lump on my head as big as a turnip—a little turnip, I mean.   Oh, d—n it !''

" Ah ! you don't seem to like it.   Now you, my fine fellow, come and try your luck. Here is a stuffed figure, you see, of a lady.   Now, here is a pair of scissors ; I want to see how you would manage to cut her pocket open, for that's the sort of thing that you will suit. The women won't suspect you with your innocent looks."

What would have resulted if this one had failed, he had no opportunity of knowing; for he used the scissors very cleverly, and succeeded, to the great admiration of Job, in extracting sixpence, current coin of the realm, from the pocket of the stuffed figure without any accident whatever.

"Bravo—bravo!" said Mr. Bolster. "Upon my life, that's good. Bravo! I believe, Mr. Job; you will be inclined to admit that to be very good for a beginner?"

"Very fair—very fair," said Job—"very fair, indeed. The lad will get on; but the other is an awkward lout. However, boys, you can have what the house affords, but you must not be idle. Now tell me your names."

"My name," said the dark-haired boy, "is Job."

"What?"

"No; it's Job Smith, not Job What, master; and this here little chap's name is Charley Green. That's what they call him when he's at home. I takes care of him, and he takes care of me, and that's all about it."

"Do you know," said Job, "I rather think you are too clever to live long?"

"Likely; but I know how long I shall live, so that satisfies me, don't it, Charley?"

"Yes," said the other boy, timidly.

"How long, then, may that be?" asked Job Oakes, with some amount of curiosity.

"As many nights as days, short of one either way, as the case may be. I thought every fool knew that."

Mr. Job looked rather blank for a moment at being thus, as it were, sold in his own house; but he soon rallied, and, shaking his head at his namesake, he said—

"You are a deal too sharp to live long, that's a fact, and so you'll find unless you pull in your horns a bit. I never knew a very clever lad like you have more than a short time of it. So, take warning; and now, my boys, I have other fish to fry, and you may go about your business; and, if anybody asks you any questions here, Mr. Job Smith, tell them you are No. 82; and you, Mr. Charley Green, will be No. 83, if you please."

"We think, do you know, sir," said Job Smith—"we think we know a gentleman that used to come here."

"Do you?—then, you had better, by a great deal, keep the knowledge to yourself. It's quite sufficient for you that you know me, and quite honour enough, my lad. Take them away, Mr. Bolster—take them away."

Mr. Bolster beckoned to the boys to follow him, and he conducted them from the private into the public part of the house, where the strange assemblage of guests were to be seen. He was very eager to induce them to partake of some strong liquors that there abounded, and which he liberally offered to pay for; but the boys refused, saying that they preferred leaving, and the dark one remarked—

"Who knows but we may have some luck in the way of business to-night that will quite set us up. But you may depend upon seeing us to-morrow, whether we have or not."

So saying, they left, and when they got into the street, and were out of sight of the house, he who had called himself Job Smith hung back a little, and said to his companion—

"I hope you are satisfied with me, Miss Maria? I did the best I could, you know?"

"Yes," said the other, in the now unmistakable voice of a girl; "oh, yes, Robert, and I shall report as much to my uncle; and although it is true we have made no discovery as yet, we may do so, you know, when we go again."

"Yes, Miss Maria, we may; as you say; but it won't do, of course, to begin too early."

"Oh, no, no. When we go again, don't forget to take something to stop them from having any suspicion."

"Oh, no, Miss Maria. But I do wonder your uncle likes to send you on such an errand, miss. It's sharp work, and rather dangerous, if we should be found out, don't you think? What a rap on the head that piece of wood did give me, to be sure—I feel it now."

"If," said the girl, turning a pair of flashing eyes upon him; "if anything of the sort had happened to me, I would soon have let them know what it was to offend me. The first portable article should have made an acquaintance with his head."

The tone and manner of the girl were so different from those she had assumed in the thieves' house, that if Job could even see her, he would, indeed, have been surprised; for she was completely transformed from what she had been, to a little spirited, fiery creature, who seemed just adapted for perilous adventure of all sorts. Her step was firm and buoyant, and her whole figure, although decidedly *petite*, seemed to dilate as she walked with the consciousness of power; and the sort of deference which the other paid to her was sufficient to show that this was habitual to her, and that it was by no means a new thing.

They walked on, the girl preceding the boy, till they crossed one of the bridges, and then, in a street at the back of the Strand, they stopped at a large house, which, however wore but a dingy appearance, and there they paused; and the girl produced a key, with which she opened the street-door, at which she entered, leaving it swinging behind her for Robert, as she called him to come in at.

He did so, and carefully closed the door behind him.

Who or what this girl was, we shall in due time discover; but sufficient for the present to say, that the large, dingy-looking house into which she went, was in the occupation of a man named Aminadab Foxley, who was one of the most celebrated and expert thief-takers in London, and whose very name was dreaded by evil-doers; for he knew no fear, living as if he had a charmed life, which state of mind seemed to have brought with it, as it not unfrequently does, its own protection, for nobody ever heard of its being hurt, strange to say, or of any harm coming to him although he undertook adventures connected with thief-catching that other officers would shrink from.

But even Foxley did not venture into the house in the Mint, which we have spoken of. He was too well known personally for that—much too well known; and had he put his head into any of the rooms of that building, he certainly would have stood a good chance of having it knocked off.

There must have been some strong motive to induce Miss Maria as she was called, to adopt such a disguise as she had, and to venture within the precincts of that desperate establishment of Mr. Job Oakes.

CHAPTER VIII.

THE MEETING BETWEEN MURDO AND HOFFENDEN TO REMOVE THE BODY.

IT is not a difficult thing to get a lodging in London, if those who seek it can show that they possess that key to the hearts of all landladies—money; and, as Murdo placed it in the power of Hoffenden to do that, he soon suited himself, not far from his old abode, with a tolerably comfortable home.

For the first time, too, for a long period, he actually gave his wife some money without an accompanying reproach upon the necessity of women eating and drinking like the rest of humanity; so that she began indeed to think that better times were dawning upon her, and that the interview she fancied had taken place between her husband and her cousin Andrew had effected this change.

"And so, indeed, it had; but little did she suspect how it had done so.

Hoffenden took Jane aside to one of the windows of their new abode, and said to her,

"Jane, you may be assured that Captain Murdo is my friend, and has shown himself to be so, or I should not treat him with the confidence I do. You may depend upon that Jane; and therefore I hope you will not misconstrue any little fault in his behaviour to mean something more important."

This was a most humiliating speech for such a man as Hoffenden to make; but it was a ten times more humiliating one for such a person as Jane to hear made; and she looked in her husband's face with a mingled expression of affection and disquietude, as she said,

"Oh, Harry, you do not know him. Make any sacrifice to give him back any money that you may owe him. Do anything but continue an intimacy with him, which will be sure to end in something terrible."

"You know not what you say."

"I know too well. I tell you, Harry, I was only saved from that man's violence by my cousin Andrew Ewert, whom I long to see again."

"Yes, you long to see him again. Strange—strange; very strange!"

"What is strange, Harry? You seem to be wandering in your mind, and to know not what you say. Oh, tell me all. What is it that has placed you at all within the grasp of this man, Murdo, as you call him?"

Harry Hoffenden shuddered, and seemed about to say something, which he suppressed, and said instead,—

"Jane, I must have a distinct promise from you that you will not attempt, on any pretext whatever, or for any object whatever, to go near our old chambers. I am hunted by the myrmidons of the law for debt; I—I know not who might follow you, so that your going there might consign me to a prison."

"Say no more, Harry; say no more. I will not go. Do you think that for one moment I would expose you to such a danger? But you must promise me that I shall not be subjected to the visits of Murdo, for those I could not endure. You must promise me that much, Harry."

"Yes, yes. I will speak to him upon that head. Be at peace—be at peace."

Jane sighed deeply, for she could not but perceive how strong and dangerous a hold Murdo had obtained of her husband; and the more she thought of it, the more she convinced herself that pecuniary obligations must be the cause of all that; and this thought was the more annoying, when she came likewise to consider how very little occasion there really had been for such a state of things, and how happy they might have been, had not the allurements of the gaming-table seduced Harry away from better courses.

She tried now to draw his attention towards his child; but she saw that his mind went not with the words he spoke, and she desisted, leaving him to take what course he pleased.

He left the place, for there was now about him a nervous restlessness which prevented him from remaining long in one spot; and, oh, how he longed for the night to come, when some effort might be made to chase from his mind the dread of a discovery of the ghastly spectacle which was to be found within the precincts of his late habitation; and yet, when the dim and dusky shadows of evening did begin to show themselves, the most horrible apprehensions took possession of him, and his dread of looking upon the corpse fe the man he had murdered almost drove him to madness.

Again was Jane left alone, to thoughts of the saddest description. In addition to her husband's passion for gambling, which had already caused her so much misery, was his acquaintance with the wretch Murdo, and the fearful consequences that were likely to result therefrom.

To endeavour to drive away these thoughts for a brief time, she took up a book containing a selection of small tales, and tried to fix her attention upon one of them. It was a simple story, and some of its passages reminded Jane of the sunshine of her former days. It ran as follows:—

The sun was setting, and beneath the waving branches of a tall, tree reclined two youthful creatures, watching its departing grandeur. They seemed to be absorbed in the splendid light before them, and they sat as if entranced, with hand locked in hand. They wore the picturesque garb of Armenia, and the figures of both set off their dresses to the greatest advantage.

"Zuliema," said the youth, at length, as he turned his dark, flashing eyes upon the maiden by his side, "my own dear one, is it not sad that two hearts, bound together as ours are by the deepest affection, should be destined to meet with so much opposition to our wishes?"

"Alas? Achmet, our fate is not singular. The legends of our fair country tell of many similar. But can I wonder that your father should object to our union, when my hand is empty—when she whom you would make your bride is dowerless?"

"Then let us fly, Zuliema. My sword shall earn us a living in a foreign, but friendly land."

"I cannot consent, Achmet. My life exists but in your prosperity—your glory; and though my love for you is beyond all else in the world, I will not consent that you should sacrifice it for me."

The young lover still urged the dark-eyed maiden to fly with him—he painted to her in the most glowing colours the happiness they should find in each other's company—the bliss that would be theirs for the remainder of their lives; but the maiden, faithful to her love, and the future prospects of her lover, refused to consent, though her heart might break in the struggle.

Slowly and mournfully they left that spot, around which the dark shades of night were now quickly spreading; and, as they disappeared, a rustling among the branches of the tree under which the lovers had been seated, was heard, and then an old man descended to the ground.

He raised his hand and eyes to Heaven, as if in thanksgiving, and then he also left the spot.

* * * * * * *

In a room rudely, and yet richly furnished, sits an old man. His dress is that of a noble among the Armenians; and a deep frown rests upon his features. A quantity of gold coin lies on the table on which he is leaning. Before him stands a girl, whose countenance betokens the firmest resolution. The latter is Zuliema; the former, the old man who descended the tree.

"Well, girl," said the old man sternly, "has not imprisonment yet subdued thy spirit? Do you, a nameless—dowerless girl, still refuse to consent to my proposition? Marry this Nemon—destroy at once the foolish hopes my son entertains of ever unitng himself to thee, and not only shall land and flocks be thine, but gold, countless gold. Persist in thy obstinacy—dash to the ground the ambitious hopes I had formed for him, and you know the alternative—death."

"Then let it come," said the maiden, sadly, "since Achmet is lost to me for ever. I have known but little joy, save in his love, since I was a child. Deserted by my parents—left to the kindness of a herdsman, my childhood was passed in poverty and neglect, till his coming brought a ray of sunshine across my desert path. That dream has been dissipated, and with it let me also pass away."

The maiden's head sunk upon her breast, and she appeared to be lost in sorrow; while she was thus occupied, the frown vanished from the face of the old man. and was replaced by the serenity of happiness. He pronounced her name in a gentle voice, and the young girl started to her feet, as if stricken by lightning.

"It is time the veil of mystery was raised," said the old man, in solemn aspects, and spreading forth, as he spoke, the gold upon the table before him; while the young girl stood looking on with astonishment, and joy sparkling from her lustrous eyes. "It has been a sacred and pleasing trust to me; and I now resign to you the dowry left in my care."

The revulsion of feeling was so great that Zuliema could not speak, and she expressed her astonishment by a gesture, while the old man proceeded,—

"My brother, when you were very young, suspected your mother of infidelity, and her life paid the forfeit. You were confided to the herdsman, who was sworn to bring you up as his own, and he kept his oath. Years passed on, and your father received evidence of your mother's innocence; but he was then on his death-bed. He gave you to my care with the dowry of a princess. I then learned that you loved my son, and I determined to test your love. I have tested it—and found it beyond price; and now for its reward."

He clapped his hand twice; a door at the further end of the apartment flew open, and the next moment Achmet and Zuliema were locked in each other's arms.

* * * * * * *

When Jane had concluded this tale, she threw the hood aside, for she found it impossible further to fix her attention, and she relapsed once more into her saddened train of thought.

* * * * * *

So much had happened since the murder, to render the innocence of Andrew Ewert painfully apparent to him, that Hoffenden felt all the agony of having committed a murder that was objectless, and the consequences of which would haunt him while he lived; without even the sorry feeling in addition, that he had done a deed of wild justice, in taking the life of Jane's cousin, who might be as innocent of wrong towards him even in thought, as it was possible for any human being to be.

But he, at a moment when he was half maddened by his losses at the gaming-table, and when he was heated with wine, had been made believe the dreadful tale; and he dare, not now, sitnated as he was, quarrel with the man who had so horribly deceived him. No; he was completely in Murdo's power, and, like the fascinated bird who cannot move from the deadly glare of the rattle-snake, he felt that all his faculties of resistance to Murdo's dominion over him were gone.

The moment of uneasiness and apprehension that came over him as the hour arrived at which he was to accompany his arch-tempter to the chambers where lay the dead body, was fearful in the extreme; and from the preceding day, to the evening of that one on which it became necessary to undertake so loathsome a task, ten years of age seemed at the very least to be added to his appearance.

Even the society of Murdo, however, was grateful to him. Anything but loneliness suited him now ; for the companionship of his own thoughts, certainly, was the worst he considered that he could be subjected to ; and yet we may guess what sort of feeling he must have had towards Murdo, when we review all the circumstances in which they were involved together.

It was about half an hour after the sun had set, that they stood together on the Adelphi Terrace, waiting for a greater amount of darkness to ensue, in order that they might commence their nefarious proceeding. Hoffenden was clinging to the railings to prevent his excessive trembling from being noticed by his companion ; while Murdo, with his arm crossed upon his breast, was looking upon the water, as it rippled gently in the decaying light of the departing twilight.

" Have you," said Hoffenden, " matured a plan by which, with any degree of safety, the—the—the——"

" Dead body," interposed Murdo. " Why do you hesitate ? You mean dead body ; and why not say it therefore, at once ?"

" Well—well ; have you matured a plan by which it may be removed ?"

" I have. I purchased this morning a large trunk. It must be placed in that, and taken to your own home."

" Oh—no—no !"

" But I say yes. We must place the body in that trunk, and lock it up carefully. Then, I propose getting some animal, a dog, probably, and bringing it into the room, and slaughtering it on the couch where he breathed his last."

" Good God ! what superstition is that ?"

" None. I do that solely for purpose of accounting for the blood that we should otherwise find it quite impossible to get rid of."

" Oh, I see. I understand, now ; a most excellent plan, it seems."

" It is the only one I can think of ; and we can afterwards, at our leisure, devise some means for the complete and safe disposal of the body. Have you anything better to propose ?"

" Nothing—nothing. It is most ingenious ; and the only thing about it that I shrink from, is the having the body brought to where I live now. If that could be avoided, I should be glad, indeed."

" Where else will it be safe ?"

" Well, well, I see all the arguments of the case ; and I cannot help agreeing with you ; so it must be done, despite the dreadful idea of a companionship with such an object, even for a short time."

" Yes, it must be done."

" So you think it now too soon to set about our errand ?"

" Well, scarcely so. We can go to the chambers now at once, I should say. I have ordered the trunk to be brought there about this time, so we may as well be there to receive it. Come on, come on."

He took the lead, and the shivering Hoffenden followed him. Alas ! where was now all the impatience of spirit which really did once characterise that young man ? Where now the candour and the openness of behaviour which had won the heart of Jane, and made her think that in uniting her fortunes with him she was taking a step which would be likely to ensure her future happiness ? All gone ; the consciousness of guilt, like a fell blight, had fallen upon him, and he was no longer what he once had been. He had changed at once and completely from what he was, to a crawling, timid man, subject to all descriptions of tyranny from one who before he would have defied.

And now they stood by the staircase that led up to the room of murder, and, as they did so, Murdo pointed down the street, saying, as he did so,—

" Behold ! there comes the coffin of Ewert."

" Coffin !" exclaimed Hoffenden, as he looked in the direction, and saw a porter slowly approaching with a great chest on his head ; " coffin ! oh, yes ; I—I had forgotten the chest—but do not call it a coffin."

"There is only a slight alteration in shape. Hilloa, my man, you are bringing that to Mr. Hoffenden's chamber, I presume ?"

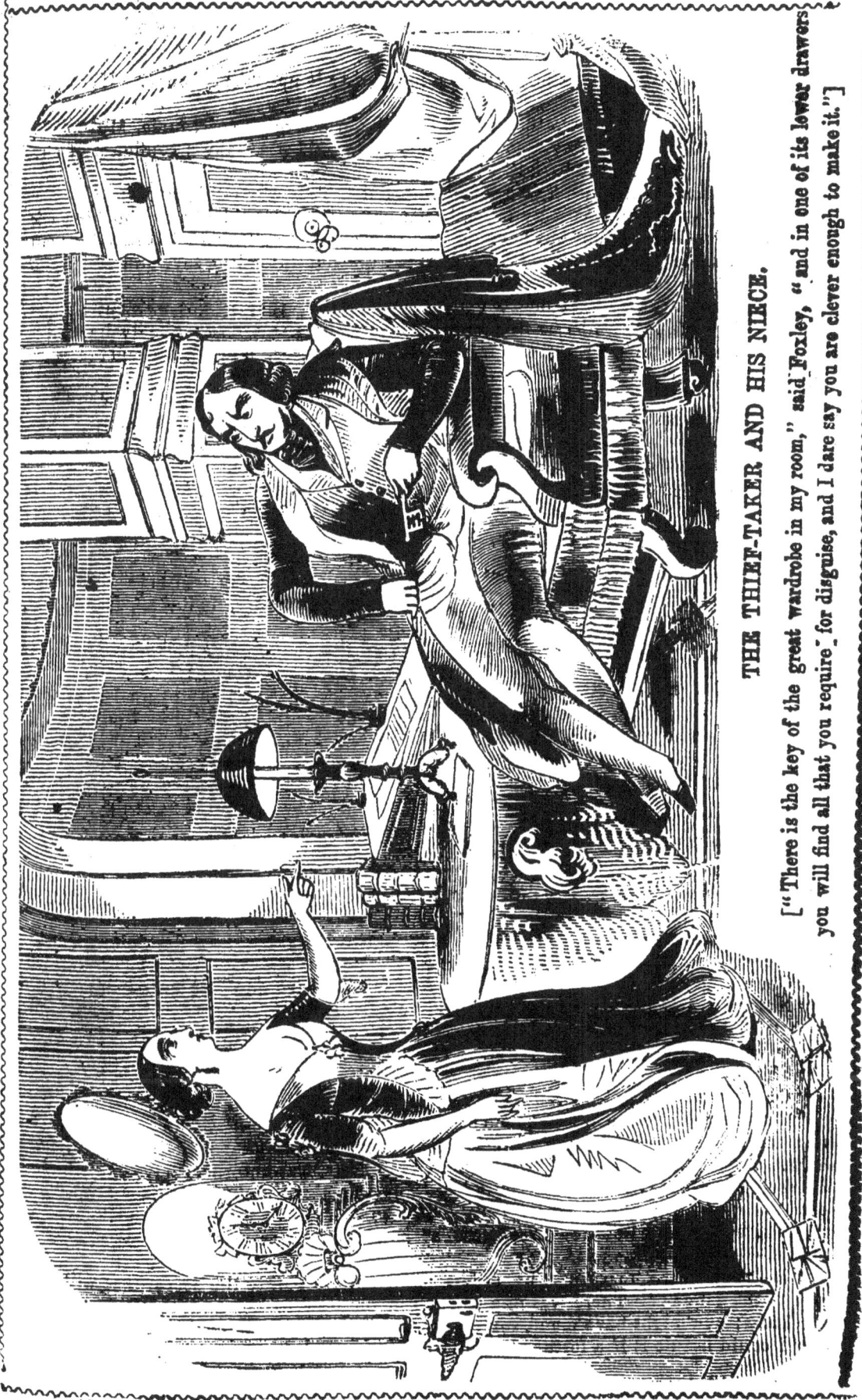

THE THIEF-TAKER AND HIS NIECE.

["There is the key of the great wardrobe in my room," said Foxley, "and in one of its lower drawers you will find all that you require" for disguise, and I dare say you are clever enough to make it."]

"I am, sir," said the man.

"Then here is that gentleman, and you may bring it up-stairs at once. Have you your keys, Hoffenden?"

"I have; come on, this way, this way. Into the front room, of course, Murdo?"

"Certainly—certainly. Why, good gracious, you would not make a confidant of the porter by taking him into the back!"

"No—no. Hush! oh, hush! No, of course not. This way—this way."

The porter's attention was very much taken up with the load he had upon his back and head, or else he could not but have noticed the extreme agitation of Hoffenden; an agitation that made him say a hundred things he did not intend to say, and which, do what he would, he could not conquer.

Murdo looked at him with such a glance of contempt, that it was evident he saw completely the state into which he had brought his victim, and how entirely he might triumph over a man whose imagination was so full of horror, and whose nerves were so little under his own command.

When they reached the landing from which the doors of Hoffenden's chambers opened, the wretched and guilty man shook to that degree that Murdo was compelled to take the keys from him and open the chambers himself; for Heaven only knows how long Hoffenden would have been in doing so in his agitated state.

"Can you not put on at least some outward show of composure?" he whispered to him; "your destruction, sooner or later, is certain, unless you can conquer this exhibition of feeling."

"I—I am quite calm."

"Calm? Psha! One would think you had committed all the crimes in the calendar. This way with the trunk, my friend, which, you are aware, doubtless, is paid for. There is half-a-crown for yourself."

This extent of liberality was quite unexpected by the man, and he looked twice at the half-crown before he could make himself believe it to be a real one; but when he was satisfied beyond all dispute upon that head, he showered down such a profusion of Irish blessings and thanks upon Murdo's head, that it was difficult to get rid of him at all.

"There, there, go," said Murdo, "that will do; I am quite satisfied that you are extremely grateful; but, as it was a heavy box, I thought you entitled to a proper reward for bringing it. There, go away, now, for we have no time further to spare."

Thus urged, the man departed to liquidate the half-crown at the nearest public-house he came to; and Murdo and Hoffenden were alone in the chamber.

"Do you think it will hold him?" said Murdo, as he pointed with a grin of satisfaction to the box. "Do you think it will hold him?"

"Oh, yes, yes, it will. I am quite calm now—I will be very calm—do you not see how calm I am?"

"Remarkably so; indeed, considering that you tremble in every limb; but, come, I have brought with me an assistant in our enterprise."

"Oh, no, no; you have not trusted any one! We are ruined—lost—betrayed!"

"Not quite. What I trust is a brandy flask. Drink, and gather from the warm spirit an artificial courage, since you have not a real one. The grateful fumes, too, of the liquor will wage war against the noxious vapours that ascend from yonder room. I can scent him now."

"Oh, horror! horror! I can picture to my mind how he will look."

"That is well; you will not be surprised when you see him. Come on, I say, come on; each minute now is full of danger. Come on, and do that which is to be done at once. I was told this morning that Foxley, the officer, was known to have something in hand of importance, and he lives close by. The thought struck me, that it might concern us by-and-by; but as all seems calm and quiet here, we are as yet safe."

"Foxley? Yes; he—he—lives close at hand. If he were to suspect us, we are ruined—quite lost!"

"But how is he to suspect us, unless you yourself betray the secret that will bring you to the gallows? There was one thing you omitted to do, and that was to search the body; you might have found something of value about him, you know."

"I could not do it if a fortune lingered in his pockets for the taking."

"The more fool you. I am amazed that a man who had the courage to strike the blow you struck, had not the courage after to look upon his victim."

"It was not courage that struck the blow, it was madness. Oh, Murdo—Murdo, I do believe that Jane is innocent!"

"Yes. Ha! ha! you have a most substantial reason. Because she told you so, you believe her innocent. Oh, fool, fool! did you for one moment suppose that she would confess her guilt? But let me advise you, Hoffenden,—behave to her as before, or rather better, for you have taken vengeance enough. Let her wait and wait in vain the coming of her lover, and, in her daily doubts and anxieties, you will have ample revenge."

"I could reconcile myself to what has happened if I could think her guilty; but I cannot."

"Be it so—be it so. Of all the confiding fools on earth, a confiding husband is the worst. Oh, oh, oh! Hoffenden, I am surprised at you. But, come, time presses; drag the box in after you. Oh, this door is bolted on the inner side, and we must go round to that which opens on the staircase. Go and open this one for me, and I will drag in the chest."

"No, no, I cannot—I tell you, I dare not enter that chamber alone. I feel as if I had a certainty that the dead man would rise and spring upon me. It is useless urging me—I cannot, dare not, do it—if my life depended upon it, I cannot do it."

Murdo saw that Hoffenden spoke no more than the truth when he said this much; although, in his malignant nature, he would gladly have inflicted upon him the suffering of going first into that apartment, he was, in a manner of speaking, compelled to do so at once.

"Give me the key," he said, angrily; "your own fears are your greatest enemies, and if you come to death for this deed, I feel assured you will have yourself to thank for your own betrayal. Give me the key."

Hoffenden handed him the key which opened the outer door of the next room, and Murdo, taking the only light they had, at once proceeded to use it.

The few moments of suspense that Hoffenden suffered were dreadful ones, although he was a little the better for the draught of ardent spirits which Murdo had given him, and which, at any other time, would nearly have been sufficient to produce intoxication; but it is a no less strange than true phenomenon of the human mind, that any great anxiety deprives intoxicating liquids of much of their power over the frame.

He heard Murdo rattle the key in the lock; and heard the door opened. "Now—now!" he gasped, "he looks upon the dead, and soon he will summon me to do so. Hush! he comes—he comes! Oh, dreadful sight that I shall now have to encounter! Oh, horrible consequence, to be compelled to look upon the form we have struck with death. Yes, I hear the bolt. Now—now!"

Murdo flung open the door of communication between the two rooms, and with the light elevated in his hand, so that it cast a full glare upon his face, he presented himself to the eyes of Hoffenden, with an expression of so much alarm, that the latter felt at once that there was some cause for fear, and uttered a cry of despair; for to see Murdo shaken, was indeed to think that something fearful had happened.

"What is it? Good God!—what is it?" he cried.

Murdo advanced clear from the doorway, and pointed into the room, saying—

"Look—look!"

"No—no—I dare not—I dare not! It is a sight of greater horror than ever you imagined. I dare not look, Murdo; you know I dare not. Do not press me to do so."

Murdo advanced, and seizing Hoffenden with his disengaged hand, he dragged him to the doorway, while, with the other, he held the light; and, as he pulled his victim, as poor Hoffenden might truly be called, he cried—

"You shall see all that is to be seen. Raise your voice, if you please, and alarm every one within this house. I care not; but you shall come. The consequences of making an alarm be upon your own head."

Hoffenden had just sense sufficient left to feel the danger of attracting attention by making a disturbance, so he gave up the contest, and allowed himself to be dragged on, while the perspiration stood in heavy drops upon his brow, and he shook in every limb.

Now he is on the threshold of the room. Another step, and he must stand within the precincts of that dreadful apartment, in which he, Hoffenden, knew so fearful a spectacle awaited him.

"Look!" cried Murdo, "look, I say, and tell me what you see."

It was with the resolution of desperation, that at length Hoffenden did draw himself up, and bent his gaze upon the couch. It was empty—not a vestige of the murdered corpse was there!

CHAPTER VIII.

THE INQUIRY.—THE SUDDEN STROKE OF FORTUNE TO HOFFENDEN.

To depict the astonishment of Hoffenden, when he saw that there was but a vacant couch in the apartment, in lieu of a dead body, is beyond the power of all language. He rubbed his eyes, as if he doubted the fact of his being awake or not; and then he looked at Murdo for an explanation of a mystery, which he considered must be known to him; for who else could have removed the body? But there was an appearance of alarm and consternation even upon the face of Murdo, which went far to contradict such an assertion.

"Oh, speak to me," cried Hoffenden; "tell me that you have done this—tell me that, to spare me, you have, ere this time, removed the body. Is it not so, Murdo?"

"I know not," said Murdo, "what words to use to convince you that I am as much surprised as you can be; but that I am, I can tell you, without deception."

There was a something about the tone in which Murdo spoke, that was sufficient to produce conviction in any one's mind, and Hoffenden staggered back into the front apartment again, and sunk upon a chair with a groan of anguish; for he made up his mind that all was now lost, and that his apprehension would soon follow as a thing of course, at the instance of whoever had removed the dead body from the chambers, and who must be supposed cognisant of the deed that had been committed.

It would seem, too, that such an idea was not very far from the mind of Murdo, for he stood in a listening attitude, as if he expected each moment to hear some sound that would proclaim danger.

Hoffenden began to wring his hands when he saw these evidences of alarm in Murdo's manner, and to bewail his wretched lot; but the other stopped him, by exclaiming vehemently—

"Peace, peace, I say. It is a time for action, not for silly wailing and weeping. Peace! there is danger, and it must be met like men, not like weeping women. We are in a trap."

"A trap—a trap! What mean you by that, Murdo? You, you think we shall be apprehended, I suppose? Oh! save me."

"Have you arms?"

"No, no, no."

"Then take this pistol; I have a pair of others if it shall become necessary to use them. My opinion is, that we shall not be suffered to leave this place without an attempt being made to capture us. By some most damnable accident, the dead body has been found during the day, and removed, of course. We are caught, I say, in a trap of our own making."

"To make resistance were madness. We are lost—we are lost."

"It may, or it may not avail; but we cannot make our situation worse than it is. That is impossible, and I am not disposed to submit patiently and calmly. Hark! I hear footsteps coming up the stairs. Now, by Heaven, Hoffenden, if you do not assist me in making something of a defence, my last effort shall be directed against you. But tell me, you must know the chambers well, is there no means of escape?"

"None, none whatever. The chimney——"

"D—n the chimney! You may attempt it if you like, but I will not."

"I was going to say that the chimney was too narrow; and, besides that, there were bars across it, which forbids the least chance of an escape by such means. Already I feel as if the gripe of the executioner was upon me. I am lost, lost, lost!"

Rap, rap, came a knock at the door of the chambers, and then all was still.

"Who knocks?" cried Murdo; "who knocks?"

"A friend," said a voice, "who wishes to save you some inconvience, namely, of walking, for I have a coach below."

"Good God," said Hoffenden, in a whisper; "you do not mean to open the door?"

"Yes, I do, though. What's the use of keeping it shut? Blow out the light, Hoffenden, and we will trust to good luck. Do not fire unless you have hold of your man with one hand, and can touch him with the barrel of your pistol. Now not a word, not a word, but keep yourself as lively as a young antelope, for you may want all'your wits about you if these are Foxley's men."

There was a curious rattling sound in the lock of the door, which, to Murdo's practised ear, betokened the fact that the officers were attempting to pick the lock ; but officers are not so expert as thieves at such work, and it was some moments before the door yielded ; but the instant it did so, Murdo sprang forward, and levelling a pistol at the head of a man who presented himself, he shot him dead upon the spot.

"Come on," he cried to Hoffenden, "come on," and he dashed down the staircase, followed instinctively by the latter, with the most frightful amount of speed. Indeed, he scarcely touched the stairs, but clinging in some strange way to the balustrade, he half fell, half slid down, till he reached the bottom, when he was immediately grasped by a powerful man, who said—

"You are my prisoner," and who at the same time aimed a heavy blow at his head with a short brass staff, loaded with a lump of that metal, with lead in the centre of it, at its further extremity.

Then, as if by [magic, the man let go his hold, and fell upon his face on the stone passage of the hall, and Hoffenden, hearing the voice of Murdo, saying—

"This way—this way!" sprang over him, and darted off in the direction of the sound, which was to the left, and down Adam-street.

In the dim evening light, the unhappy and half-maddened Hoffenden could just see the shadowy looking figure of Murdo as he darted onwards, and turned down one of the narrow streets leading to the river : and, with a blind reliance upon him, Hoffenden pursued him, hoping to come up to him, fancying, too, each moment, that he heard the sound of pursuers' feet coming rapidly after him.

The latter idea was, however, a delusion, for such was not the case, inasmuch as there seemed to have been but two men bent upon their capture, and one was unquestionably killed, while the other was too much injured by his sudden fall to be able or willing to carry on a pursuit after men who seemed so well able to defend themselves from any attack.

When Hoffenden did overtake Murdo, he found him at the head of a small flight of stairs which led down to one of the little landing-places on the river side, where boats could be hired, and he was talking to a man who was putting on his jacket, as if getting ready to do his duty in a wherry.

"Quick—quick !" said Murdo, as he saw Hoffenden approach. "My friend, here— although you would scarcely think so to look at him—is one of the most impatient men in the world, and a regular fire-eater. Quick—quick, I say !"

"Ready now, sir," said the man. "This way, gentlemen, if you please (gents were not invented then). This way. Now, Bill. Pull her in oars or sculls, gentlemen ?"

"A pair of sculls will do. You seem a stout fellow."

"I rather think, sir, I can pull as well as most on the river. Now if you please."

Hoffenden made no remark, but jumped into the boat after Murdo, who sat down with an appearance of great coolness, as he said to the waterman—

"Southwark. The Bull-steps."

"Yes, master—I know, sir. They keeps as good a drop of beer at the Bull as any waterman would wish to drink. Ah! it makes one dry to think of it, it does."

"When you get there you shall taste it."

"Thank you, master. I know'd when you comed down, master, I had a trump in my boat."

The wherry shot through the stream at a quick rate, and the bridge at Southwark soon came dimly in sight. Then Murdo leant down to where Hoffenden was sitting, and whispered—

"I'm going to introduce you to some friends to-night."

"Friends—what friends?"

"You will soon find what they are, and who they are. But, for the present, be contented with the knowledge that they will do you no harm, and may do you some good. Did you ever hear of Job Oakes?"

"Never."

"Oh! you are out of the world; but, however, situated as you are, you ought to know where to go to on an emergency, if you should be hard pushed. Job Oakes keeps a house in the Mint at Southwark, and let you have done what you may, you will be safe there you may depend; and such is the nature of the place, that a minute search would scarcely find you."

"Indeed!"

"Yes; it is well worth your while to know of such a place; and, besides, when we get there, I can tell you what I have arranged for you as regards the future. You must live, you know."

"Yes—yes; and that is a subject that agonises me to think of. What is to become of me and Jane, and the child? We are, in very truth, destitute!"

"Psha! There's lots of wealth in London."

"Yes; but those who have it keep it."

"Yes, if they can. But hush! this is not a conversation to carry on here."

"Heaven knows I have need of counsel from some one; and if you will give it to me now I shall be grateful."

"All are not lost who are in danger. Come on, and I will soon show you this place of safety; for I rather think you will need it, considering all things, although I am myself a little puzzled to know what has exactly led to the scene we had to go through at your chambers. This is the house I spoke to you of, as being kept by a man named Job Oakes."

As he spoke, Murdo stopped before the same mansion which we have already introduced to the reader in connexion with the two lads who played so strange a part in the private rooms belonging to Mr. Oakes, and who, for some reason or another, were intent upon prying into the internal economy of his establishment.

CHAPTER IX.

THE THIEF-TAKER AT HOME.—MARIA DECLARES HER SENTIMENTS TO HER UNCLE.

SINCE we have made rather repeated mention of Mr. Foxley, the thief-taker, it will be just as well for us to introduce that eminent character to the reader in his own house, which was in one of those cross streets that run from one to another of the larger ones which go from the Strand to the river at such regular intervals.

The time is evening, but not late; and Foxley is sitting in a large room, by a table covered with papers, which he now and then appeals to as he makes entries in a book which is before him.

He was a man not of large build; but his frame seemed to be so well knit together, and he was so ugly, that it appeared to be almost impossible he could come to any injury. He wore a wig of a lightish colour, something like the back of a very indifferently-coated tabby cat; and lying on the table before him were two large holster-pistols, the stocks of which were turned towards his hands, so as to be ready for immediate service if requisite.

Altogether, such an iron-looking, repulsive scoundrel was seldom to be met with.

Suddenly he rung a hand bell, which was answered by a man.

"Have Peterson and Jarvis come back yet?" he asked.

"No," was the brief reply. "But young Skinder is here, and says he wants to see you."

"Ah, indeed!—he here! Oh, tell him I'll see him in a few minutes. You may bring him in in about five minutes by the hall clock. You understand?"

"I ain't a fool. Of course, I understand. What do you go on saying that for, I should like to know? Understand, indeed! as if I was a *hass*."

"Oh, you amiable brute!" muttered Foxley, when he was gone; "if you were not honest now, how soon I would put a stopper upon you; but you are faithful to me, and you know I know it. So, young Skinder has actually come, has he? Ho! ho! ho!"

The glee of Mr. Foxley at the idea of young Skinder coming, seemed remarkably like that sort of merriment which some tiger might be supposed to feel at the gratifying fact of some small animal, whose carcase he considered to be of a delicious flavour, having strayed into his den. Who young Skinder was we shall soon gather from the edifying nd highly characteristic few words that passed between him and Foxley.

As an individual, young Skinder was not the sort of person whom you or I, reader, would have chosen for an intimate acquaintance. He was a most diabolically cunning-looking rogue as ever stepped. There was a twinkling expression about the little grey eyes of young Skinder, which looked anything but open and candid, and his red, close crop of hair certainly did not come up to the popular standard of beauty.

Just before this individual made his gracious appearance in the presence of Foxley, the latter had gone into an adjoining apartment, which was quite close, and made some arrangements, which sounded very much like moving a number of hoards about; but what it was remained a mystery to all but Foxley himself.

Then he seated himself at his table again, and the five minutes he had stipulated for having nearly expired, he heard some footsteps coming, and in another moment young Skinder made his advent.

We should be decidedly wrong if we were to say that this gentleman came quite unsuspectingly into the presence of Foxley. On the contrary, he kept at a respectful distance from that *public character*, and seemed quite ready to make a spring upon anything or anybody who should interfere with him. The candle was rather in the way of his making a minute examination of the face of Foxley, and he moved in order to get clear of its dazzling influence, as he said—

"You see I am here, Mr. F., at last."

"Yes, at last," said Mr. F., "you are here. I'm afraid you have been up to no good since I last saw you, Skinder. You know my rules well enough."

"Yes, I know I ought to have shown myself before."

"Rather."

"But I have been getting up a good lot in Hereford, and I hoped to have done some good for you Mr. F."

"Oh, you are quite sure, Skinder, that you did not set up a little in business on your own account? You are quite sure of that, I hope, and that you had no hand in clearing out my store at St. Alhan's?"

"Me, sir!" Can you suspect me of anything so base? I didn't know that your store had been cleared out. I swear I had nothing to do with it."

"Well, I am not a suspicious man."

"Why, how was it, Mr. Foxley? You don't mean to tell me, sir, that any of the family have been bad enough to play you a trick, I hope? That would be dreadful. After that, I should say there was no honour among thieves."

"So should I. But, you know, Skinder, that at St. Alban's I had as pretty a little storehouse of things, that had been got by tramping and smashing through the neighbouring counties, as any man would wish to see. As circumstances turned up, I from time to time made a good thing of returning such things to their owners, as you well know; and the party who had swagged them in the first instance always had his share.'

"Yes, Mr. F., you always behaved like a trump, you did."

"Well, I'm glad to hear you admit that. But, what would you actually say, now, to the fact of that store, worth, as it was, two thousand pounds, at least, being pounced upon by the police one day, and everything taken away? What do you say to that, Mr. Skinder, eh?"

"It makes my hair stand on end, sir."

"Does it. Well, I can tell you it made mine stand on end when I first heard it, and some one must have betrayed the place. If I did wrong in suspecting you, Skinder, I am sorry; but the fact is, I don't know who to accuse; the thing has been so cleverly done."

There was a slight twinkle in the corner of Skinder's eyes as Foxley gave this unqualified praise to the manner in which he had been treated, which showed that Skinder belonged to human nature generally, and that he felt praise from Foxley was praise indeed.

"Well, sir," he said, "I tell you what I don't mind doing. I'll give a whole week to trying to find out who did it. If it's any of the family, I think, by some means or another, I shall be able to detect him. You know, sir, it might have been an accident altogether."

"Oh, yes—oh, yes; you are very kind in your offer, Skinder, but time to a family man is of too much value, so we will let the matter rest; only, if I do come across the fellow who did it, his time of life after that shall not exceed one hour."

Skinder winced a little, for the keen eyes of Foxley were fixed upon him, and he knew well he was suspected; but he did not know that Foxley had positive information that he was the man who had played him so treacherous a trick.

"Sir." he said, "if the man who did it was my own brother, I'd take him by the throat and bring him to you."

"Thank you—thank you. Hush! somebody's coming."

"If you please, sir," said a man, popping his head into the room, "here's Mr. Lake, the sheriff."

"The sheriff," said Skinder—Sheriff Lake? Oh, he knows me. Don't you remember how Sheriff Lake knows me, Mr. F? I can't be seen by him, or else he'll want to have something to say to me."

"Oh, yes, I recollect. By Jove, Skinder, yes. Let me see. Hide in that cupboard, No, no. That room; there's nobody there, and I don't mind you overhearing what the sheriff has to say to me, Skinder. It's only something, I dare say, about general business."

"Thank you—thank you; I won't listen. Only put me out of the way."

Skinder scrambled up his hat, which he had laid upon a chair, and darted into the oom, which was profoundly dark; and the moment he had done so, Foxley rose and closed the door of communication.

There was a loud shriek from that apartment, and then all was as still as the grave.

"It's done," said Foxley, "it's done, and done well, too. The fool—the idiot—to fancy I was going to be braved by such a shallow head as his! Well, well, Mr. Skinder, you have met your deserts; you will not act as a warning to others, because they will not know your fate; but I know it, and am gratified to have had my revenge. You are now a mangled corpse in the common sewer, and may possibly be picked up down the Thames, on the Isle of Dogs, to-morrow."

He then waited several minutes, as if even he dreaded that some cry or some appearance of his victim might yet reach his senses, if he went too prematurely into the room. Then he took the light, and cautiously opened the door, and entered it.

In the centre of that apartment was an opening of about five feet square, so that it was next to impossible that any one could be there in the dark above a minute without plunging down.

The light was far from being sufficient to penetrate into those profound depths; and as Foxley stood over the yawning gulph, he put his hand to his ear and listened; but the only sound that met his ear was a low murmuring one, which he expected, and which sounded like the dash of distant waters.

"He is safe enough," he muttered. "The fool! who thought he could play with me. He is safe enough. If there be another world, young Skinder, you and I may meet in it, but never again in this—no, never again in this!"

He stooped and looked anxiously at one of the edges of the opening. There was a dash of blood upon it, and he at once conjectured how that had happened. The wretched man had fallen forward, of course, when he missed his footing in the room, and that was when he had struck his face a heavy blow, and that he had left a dash of blood to mark the spot.

THE INSULT, BY MURDO, TO THE GAMBLER'S WIFE.

"Ah," said Foxley, "he fell, no doubt, heavy; but he has fallen surely, and all is well."

Mr. Foxley then set about restoring the room to its original aspect, and this he did by closing the yawning and terrific looking aperture, by turning over it the two halves of a trap-door, which, when thus c'osed, was sufficient to cover up the centre opening; so that although a suspicious observer might, possibly, have noticed that there was something unusual in the floor, nine out of ten would not think of looking.

Besides, in order to make matters still more secure, Foxley took a square piece of carpet, and laid it very evenly over the trap-door, and, as it extended considerably beyond it, there could be no suspicion, unless some slight inequality of the boarding, or a certain slight sinking at the spot where the edges of the folding trap-doors met, engendered it.

And those little indications of the existence of such a means of getting rid of trouble-some people Mr. Foxley could not get rid of, so he ran his chance of them.

When he had completed all these little arrangements, he returned to the next room rather pleased with himself; for he had, since finding out, which he had done a whole week before, the delinquency of Mr. Skinder, nourished towards that individual a deadly hatred, and he had hardly dared to hope that he would have visited him.

Nor would Skinder have done so, but that Foxley kept his own counsel so well, that he never let any one know that he had a suspicion of him.

With respect to the sham announcement of the sheriff, Foxley had a number of signals, which enabled those who attended upon him, to know who he wanted announced.

Thus, when he was tired of any visitor, he would touch a little nob close to him in the wall, which looked like the head of a round button, but which rung a bell, and forth-with some fictitious visitor was announced, which gave him a good excuse for getting rid of the one he had with him.

But he did not get of all of all of them by means of the opening he had from the next apartment, down to the common sewer. Oh, no. Foxley had a number of visitors whom he was glad, from time to time, to see again, and whom he wished just to see long enough to get from them all they had to say, but no longer.

In fact, this man, who had, by the force of a strong natural sagacity, reduced thieving and thief-taking to a positive and well-worked system, acted quite like a minister of state; and that room in which he sat might be considered his private cabinet, in which he gave orders, and granted audiences.

He had reasoned upon the connexion between the trade of thieving, and the trade of apprehending thieves; and, of course, he came to the conclusion, that both were possible, but that the latter was quite dependent upon the former, but not, in its complete integrity, quite so good a thing as regarded pecuniary results.

From such a state of reasoning, Mr. Foxley had gradually come to the opinion, that he might, with great effect, combine the two in one.

Accordingly, he got up a regular organized system, by which he kept gangs of thieves in his pay, and dealt in all sorts of articles; negotiating with people, who had been robbed, for the return of their property, and most rigorously bringing the justice any one who did not work for him.

By this nefarious conduct, he certainly made large sums of money, and he likewise received a kind of tribute money, or "black mail," from such persons as Mr. Job Oakes, who, on payment of a certain sum, were permitted to carry on their trade as well as their skill permitted them to do.

This Job Oakes, however, had lately thought proper rather to throw off his allegiance upon Foxley, and to consider himself strong enough to be independent; and conse-quently, Foxley was anxious to break up his establishment.

He had already made a communication to the authorities regarding Job's house in the Mint, and he was told that, as soon as the perpetrators of any serious crime could be traced to be connected with Job's place, he, Foxley, should be armed with full powers of action.

He was, therefore, calmly waiting such an event, when some of the circumstances off our story gave him great facilities in carrying out his plans of vengeance against the rebellious Job.

When he sat down in his own room again, he was silent for some minutes, and then he muttered,—

"Yes; Murdo, as he now calls himself, shall suffer. I will catch him tripping some day, for I am convinced that he holds a sort of communication with Job Oakes that I like not. If, now, I could but get some one to go to Oakes's who was unknown, all would be well. There's that scoundrel Bolster, who so narrowly escaped hanging last sessions, I am told that he caters for Job in getting youngsters to become pickpockets.—Ha! who's there?"

He heard some one turn the handle of the door, and in another moment a young girl stood before him. She was young and handsome. Her age could not be much more than sixteen, and that was rather apparent from her manners and countenance than from her general appearance, which was *petite* and girlish, almost to childishness, in the extreme.

"Well, Maria," said Foxley, with a slight touch of reserve in his manners; "what may you want?"

"Uncle," said she, "I have come to ask you the usual question."

"What may that be?"

"You know well. Have you found any news of Michael Clifton?"

"Why, really, Maria, I have not. You know as well as I that he went away from here of his own accord, and that I know nothing of him whatever. I have set people on the hunt for him, and I am led to believe that he has been in some way picked up by a man named Job Oakes, who keep a house to teach young gentlemen the art of picking pockets, in Southwark; but Job denies it, and I cannot find out that it actually is so."

"He must be rescued from such a life."

"Very good."

"It is strange, uncle, that I have heard you boast, that you could do anything you set your mind upon; and yet you are completely foiled in this matter of discovering where Clifton is. You know he is a great friend of mine, and you know that I would not see him perish if possible. He is of a wild and reckless turn of mind, that may be easily played upon. He is adventurous, too; but he is generous, and requires to be led into a good course to follow it."

"Well, really, Maria, you don't do me common justice. You know that you were destitute, and that I took you in; and you told me that this Michael Clifton, the orphan son of your nurse, had been so kind to you that you would not desert him."

"Yes; I told you that I would accept of no asylum unless he shared it."

"Good; and I consented, and took you both, which was some years since; and everything went on very well, till Michael suddenly took it into his head to disappear."

"You cannot then, or will not find him?"

"Nay, I have tried; and, as I tell you, I think he is at Job Oakes's in the Mint, at Southwark."

"Then I will seek him there."

"You Maria—you?"

"Yes; I will adopt some disguise which shall gain me admittance, and take Robert with me. I must rescue Michael, if it be possible so to do, and I will."

Foxley leant his head upon his hand for a few moments in silence, and he was evidently engaged in deep thought, for the words of Maria had awakened in his mind a train of reflection, which he thought might terminate in something that would be favourable to his own views. At length he spoke in a confidential tone, saying—

"Maria, what you have just said has set me thinking."

"Well."

"Listen to me. You talk of going with Robert in some disguise to Job Oakes's. Now, the fact is, that I am very anxious indeed to know something of the economy of Job Oakes's house, but I cannot depend upon what is told me by any one; and if you thought that you could manage to keep up a disguise, you might, I think, without much danger, go there, and find out all you want to know yourself, as well as do me a great service. Are you willing, Maria, to undertake it? Do you think you should have nerve enough?"

"Nerve enough!" she said, while her eyes flashed again. "Who dares to doubt it? What do you want to know?"

"As accurate a plan of the premises as you can let me have, and as good a description of all you see there as possible; besides, I want to know if a man, whose real name is Murdo, goes there. You cannot mistake him; he squints awfully."

"I am willing," she said.

"You are? And will you set about it at once?"

"To-night, if you will provide me with the means, and tell me how it must be accomplished. I must have a boy's suit, and for the manner I shall put on, you may leave that all to me. Whoever sees me, shall take me for a timid, shrinking boy, such as I have often seen, and such as I can act to the life."

" You are a clever girl, and I always said you were, Maria. In this house not one half of the secrets of which you know, I have every sort of disguise. I will show you a large wardrobe, in which you cannot fail to find what you require. And now let me explain to you how you shall get admittance, without trouble to Job Oakes's house."

The girl listened to him with attention, and he proceeded to say—

" There is a public-house in Cannon-street in the city, called ' The Chandlers' Arms. It is a rather questionable place ; but if you go there, you will find yourself in strange company, and ten to one but you will be spoken to by a small man, with light hair, and of an insinuating address, named Bolster. He will ask you if you are on the lagging lay."

" I understand."

" Ah, you have not finished your education here for nothing, Maria ; and I do think I could back you out for family patter against any one in London."

" Go on," said the girl impatiently, " go on."

" Well, you need only tell him sufficient to make him think that he has picked up a couple of prizes for Job Oakes, and he will make you an offer of introduction to his house. He gets a price for every young pickpocket he takes there, and goes about like a recruiting sergeant doing his best."

" I understand ; it shall be done, and nothing shall fail for want of tact on our parts, for I know I can trust Robert well."

" Good ; I believe Robert will go through fire and water, poor devil, for you, Maria; but it won't do to go empty-handed to Job Oakes. You must take something with you— a silver spoon, or some trifle, to show that you have been industrious, and which will serve to pay your footing. Now do not embark in this scheme, if you have any doubts in your mind about whether you should like to go on with it or not."

" I see you don't know me yet."

" Well, excuse me for making the remark, and go and make your own preparations There is a key of the great wardrobe in my room, and in one of its lower drawers you will find all that you require for disguise ; and if any alteration be required, I dare say you are clever enough to make it."

" Yes," said Maria, as she took the key, " I will manage all that ; and if I find Michael, and rescue him from a course of life I am quite resolved he shall not lead, I shall be well repaid for any risk I run myself."

So saying, she left the room, and Foxley, when she was gone, muttered to himself—

" What a strange girl ! If she but knew who it was that first reduced her to the poverty that made her a dependent upon my bounty, she would not be very well pleased, I'm thinking. A strange girl—a spirit, too, she has, which I should not be sorry to see quelled ; for if she grows up as she is now, she will perhaps give me some trouble."

He arose and paced the room with uneasy strides, as if some recollections had come across him of a troublesome character ; and then he sat down to his books again with a toss of the head, muttering—

" Well, well, that's all past and gone, and what's done cannot be undone, if one wished ever so much to do so. Hang care and regret ! They are enough to kill a cat."

———

CHAPTER X.

THE ADVERTISEMENT.—HOFFENDEN'S FORTUNE.—THE BRIBE TO FOXLEY BY MURDO.

Amid all the various mutations of fickle fortune, none are so desperately provoking as those which, after a man has done something which prevents him enjoying the favour of of the blind goddess, shower upon him her golden stores.

And how often is it found in real life that such is the period when the wealth, which in an earlier period would have been so pleasant to receive, is showered upon a man ? Either age has incapacitated him from the enjoyment of fortune, or, driven to despair—as in the case of the celebrated Eugene Aram—at the want of that fortune which he panted for, he has just done some deed, the frightful consequences of which cling to him, and poison every possible enjoyment.

It is not thus when a man spends the prime of his life in the acquisition of fortune, although we shall frequently hear persons, who have taken but a superficial view of human nature, pity such men, and talk of them with a degree of contempt, for wasting a whole lifetime in the acquisition of that which they can never enjoy.

This, however, is a gross mistake; for, in all human undertakings, there is an immense amount more of pleasure in the pursuit than in the possession.

A successful pursuit of any object which we fancy will be happiness when attained, is the pleasaniest condition of which the human mind is at capable; and hence those persons who do spend a life time in the accumulation of a fortune which they intend to enjoy by spending it at some time or another—which time never comes—really do enjoy it a hundred times—ay, a thousand times over.

They spend it in imagination. They know what they can do; and it is a principle of human nature not to care much for the actual doing of that which we can do at any time we please.

We have been led to these remarks by a circumstance which occurred just in the midst of all those affairs of which we have endeavoured to give the reader a succinct and clear description. That circumstance consisted in an advertisement which appeared in a morning paper, and was to the following effect :—

"If any one can give information of the present place of abode of Mr. Henry Hoffenden, he will be liberally rewarded; or if that gentleman should chance to see this advertisement, and will call upon Messrs. Stevens and Gill, solicitors, No. 3, South-square, Gray's-inn, he will hear of something considerably to his advantage."

This advertisement had, it appeared, been inserted in the morning papers several times before it caught the eye of any one who felt interested in it, and then it was Murdo who saw it; and we will fancy him, in company with Hoffenden, at the house where he had been advised to take refuge for a time.

They are in a private room of the establishment; for the case of Hoffenden is considered decidedly a dangerous one, and one that consequently requires great caution in its mode of treatment; for any sudden attack upon the public room might be quite successful, whereas the private apartments of the establishment were tolerably safe.

"Hoffenden," said Murdo, "have you any expectations?"

"Expectations of what? What do you mean?"

"I mean, have you any money expectations? Have you any relatives who are likely to die, abroad perhaps, and leave you any sums of money? I do not ask for idle curiosity, but really from a particular motive."

"The question is easily answered," said Hoffenden, with some bitterness. "I have not one."

"It's very odd, then."

"What's very odd?"

"Read this advertisement, and judge for yourself. It may be a trick, after all, and, if such, you cannot be too careful in taking any notice of it. What do you think of it?"

Hoffenden read the advertisement with marked attention, and when he came to het names of the solicitors, he said—

"I do not think it a trick."

"You do not?"

"Certainly I do not; because these solicitors know my family, and would not lend themselves to anything of the sort. It is, I am inclined to believe, a *bona fida* affair altogether. You may depend that, just at this very awkward juncture, something has happened that might otherwise have been of service to me. And here am I, hiding, and unable to help myself, or even to stir abroad, in consequence of wha ıha s hapı ened. Curses on my own precipitancy—curses on it, I say!"

"Oh, don't despair; all are not lost that are in danger, and something ʻɲaɟ bʒ done yet. Don't you know that money is all powerful in this country, and that eveʼyɩrime here has its price? Don't make yourself uneasy if this affair should turn out to be a profitable one; for you will find, if it does, that you can buy your way to freedom."

"Indeed!"

"Yes; as a matter of course, I should say; I know the man you have to deal with. Foxley, the officer, is not the sort of fellow to refuse to make a good bargain. Why is he an officer at all? Why does he trouble himself with the apprehension of thieves, but because it is a money-making business; and if it be more profitable, in any instance, not to apprehend the criminal, why, he will not. It's a matter of the simplest and most ordinary calculation with him, of course."

"Think you so?"

"I know it. But do you remain here in safety, while I go and make the necessary inquiry for you of these lawyers, and we will soon see if enough money is come-at-able to move the flinty heart of Foxley. Why, after all, he would only get forty pounds by hanging you, and eighty another way would be doubly pleasant, you see."

"I will leave the matter in your hands to manage how you like, Murdo; only get me my liberty out of this infernal place. Oh, what a fool I was to meddle with murder!"

"Not at all. You got rid of a man who was in love with your wife; a fellow who was conspiring against your peace; and, although her virtue may have stood the test, we have no need to thank anybody who makes the attempt. I tell you again and again, that although I believe your wife sufficiently innocent, that you may very well afford to forgive her for the past, you have no need to feel any regret about the death of Andrew Ewert."

With this Murdo left Hoffenden, and proceeded to Gray's-inn.

There can be no moral doubt, whatever, but that this ruffian had thoroughly made up his mind to abide by his victim until he had achieved his destruction. The admiration which he had conceived for Jane Hoffenden, probably, was at first not more than a man, such as he, would be likely to feel for a really beautiful woman; but the contempt with which she had treated his addresses, and the decided loathing which she had manifested towards him, had inflamed his passion, at the same time that it implanted an amount of revengeful feeling in his heart, which he longed to pay off at the first opportunity.

As regarded poor Andrew Ewert, his bad feelings were glutted to the utmost, and against him he had achieved a vengeance which he had hardly hoped, but which now, whenever he thought of it, gave him the most unbounded gratification.

"And he was gradually getting Hoffenden into such toils, that he would find it difficult, if not, indeed, quite impossible, to escape from them in a short time.

How far he will succeed in his insidious designs against the peace of mind of Jane Hoffenden, remains yet to be seen; but one thing is quite clear, and that is, that he intended to play upon her fears for her husband's safety, by letting her know that he was in possession of a secret that would compromise his life.

That he thought would, at all events, keep her silent, almost under any insults, and he had a great opinion of the effect to be produced by perseverance.

"Worn out," he thought, "by solicitation, she will become broken spirited, and yield to me at last, surely, and when she finds that to complain of me to Hoffenden, and so produce a collision between us, places his life at my mercy, she will be broken-spirited and unable to call to her aid all those indignant virtues which now possess her heart. Oh, I shall triumph yet, although I am not exactly the handsomest man in the world to win a lady's heart. But what care I?—I love wine, money, and beauty; and so long as I can enjoy all three, I care not if I were as ugly as Vulcan. Indeed that little accident makes my triumph so much the greater."

So far he was right; and, in a good line of ambition, to get over any disadvantages is a justifiable subject for congratulation; but the case is widely different when, as in the present circumstances, nothing but the greatest amount of villany is contemplated.

Murdo had no idea of walking, and accordingly he hired a hackney carriage, which soon took him from the Mint to Gray's-inn, where he had no difficulty in finding the lawyers' offices.

Upon inquiring for one of the principals of the firm, he was ushered into a private room, where sat a little elderly gentleman, with a pair of blue spectacles perched on his nose, and who took a blue look at Murdo, as he made a half inclination of his body towards him.

"I have called, sir," he said, "in consequence of an advertisement which has appeared making an inquiry for one Henry Hoffenden."

"Oh, do you know where he is?"

"Yes; but, as Mr. Hoffenden, who is my most particular friend, happens, at this present juncture, to be in a little difficulty, he has sent me to learn the particulars of what it is that is to his advantage."

"Oh, he is generally in some little difficulty, I believe," said the lawyer; "at least that is the character that we have heard of him, and that he likewise was not very particular in his choice of associates, which seems to be confirmed."

The attorney, as he uttered these words, looked hard at Murdo, who could not but feel that this very left-handed compliment applied to him most particularly.

"Humph!" he said. "You may think so, sir, if you please; but you will oblige me by stating what it is that is to the advantage of Mr. Hoffenden, my most particular friend."

"It is no secret," said the attorney. "Money often gets into bad hands. Mr. Hoffenden had a brother named Horace, who went to India a friendless lad. He fell down dead in the streets of Bombay eight months ago, after being left a widower by an Indian lady, whom he married."

"Yes, sir. Well?"

"He died intestate; and the consequence is, as he has no child, that his brother, Henry Hoffenden, is heir-at-law to all he has died in possession of, which principally consists of his wife's fortune, which she left wholly to him, and completely unencumbered."

"Well, sir, but the amount—the amount? That's the most interesting part of the business. It's the amount, sir, that I want to know."

"I don't doubt that. I should say, in round numbers, about £180,000."

"What! what—£180,000? You—you don't mean that, old fellow? D—n it, we will lead a glorious life now."

"I don't doubt but you will. You look as if you would; and, as we don't like the connexion, I decline transacting any more business than we can help with Mr. Hoffenden. You will oblige us by taking to him our compliments, and saying that we shall be glad when he will come and take the affair off our hands entirely. Our Indian agents sent the business to us, and we are anxious to get rid of it as quickly as possible."

"You shall be favoured to that extent, you may depend, sir," said Murdo, rising and buttoning his coat up to the chin; "and I can only say that, for a lawyer, you are the d—dest old fool I ever came near."

With this piece of insolence, Murdo at once left the place, before the attorney could make any reply to him, and he hastened with great speed to Hoffenden, to whom he broke the intelligence.

The breath of Hoffenden was almost suspended as he heard the intelligence, and, for a moment or two, he seemed ready to faint away, and really alarmed Murdo, who was terribly afraid lest the goose he now expected to lay him such golden eggs should die, and deprive him of the share he fully intended to have of the fortune.

"Why, Hoffenden," he cried. "Hilloa! what's the matter? You look as pale as a ghost. What's the matter, I say? Cheer up. Come now, rouse yourself. I suppose I ought not to have told you in such a hurry what a piece of luck had come across you."

"I am better now," said Hoffenden; "I am much better now. It was the sudden surprise—that's all. I am much better now. You—did not say £180,000, did you?"

"Yes, but I did though. That's what they told me, and I congratulate you, my dear fellow. You will now be able to enjoy life as it ought to be enjoyed by a young man like yourself, you know."

"Good God! and I in such a situation!"

"'Tis a glorious situation!"

"You surely forget—you surely forget, Murdo, how I am situated."

"No, I don't. I don't forget at all. You are putting yourself out of the way about that fellow Ewert, but I'll bring you through that, you may depend upon it; why, it ain't worth a moment's thought, you may take your oath. Make yourself easy about it."

"You—you really think so? Oh, what a career opens before my eyes now, if I dared contemplate it. I certainly did not at all expect money from such a quarter. I and Horace were never friends."

"Never mind that. He has turned out a very good friend, for all that, Hoffenden. Never mind where the money comes from, so that it does come from somewhere. Why, you will be able to do what you please; and as for the little secret which might at any time mar your happiness, and place you at the bar of the Old Bailey, it will be safe in my hands, you know."

"Yes; that dreadful secret!"

"Why call it a dreadful secret? Have you not the power of making it a safe one? What could I gain by telling it? What might I not lose by doing so, in fact? Pho—pho! you know how to make me keep a secret."

"I understand you—I understand you. You shall have no cause to complain of a want of generosity in me. You shall be well paid."

"Oh, don't put it in that shape—don't call it pay. We will manage to see something of life, my boy, between us. Somehow I can hardly fancy it real, upon my word. But, Hoffenden, you must get an immediate advance from the lawyers, and that will enable you, you know, to carry on the war; besides, terms can be made with Foxley, whom I had better see as soon as possible in the matter."

"Will there be no danger in seeing him?"

"None at all. He is the most comfortable man in the world to do business with, I can assure you. There's no difficulty. It's merely a matter of money. If you can agree with him, well and good; if not, there's no harm done, and the affair rests where it did."

CHAPTER XI.

JANE HOFFENDEN IN HER NEW HOME.—THE DREAM.

LET us now, for a brief space, turn our attention to her who is most of all to be pitied in all these transactions which are taking place—the sweet, beautiful, and suffering wife of Harry Hoffenden.

Alas! it is grievous to think that one so fitted as she is to adorn and lend a lustre to any station of life, should be so grievously and so sadly situated as she now is. Wedded to a man who was only enamoured of her beauty, and who totally lacked the power to appreciate her for those mental excellences which were most truly hers, she was most truly to be pitied by all who can feel for suffering virtue, or wish that the best of God's creatures should likewise be the happiest.

But how seldom is such the case! On the contrary, it seems as if, in this world, it was one of the greatest of curses to have sensibilities far beyond those which belong to ordinary natures; and as if to such, along with the power to feel the extatic joys which are strange to others, is likewise given the unhappy capacity to feel more acutely the many evils which human life is so full of.

This surely was most particularly the case with poor Jane Hoffenden. She felt that she no longer held her husband's heart in those silken ties of happy bondage which once it had been his delight to own the existence of; but which, alas! now he had so completely shaken off as to leave not the shadow of their once glorious presence behind.

Where were all those hopes of continued joy with which she had commenced her married life? Alas! all scattered to the winds; and although she was to the full rational enough to know that there was sure to be a change of some sort, still she did not expect that that change would take the form of utter alienation, as it had done.

"He might have loved me less," she would say, "but he need not have discarded me altogether from his heart. The one I could have borne with, and uttered no murmur; but the other crushes my heart."

It is hard to say whether the charms of the gaming-table took first a hold of the imagination of Harry Hoffenden, and hurried him away from home, or he got *ennuied* at the

JANE'S DEFENCE OF HER HONOUR.

quiet life and the domestic endearments of his own fireside, and flew to the first excitement that presented itself as a change.

There are men who never can settle down into the calm of domestic felicity, but who seem to have been born with such a natural love of change, and such a restlessness of disposition, that they never can remain long satisfied with the lot which fortune has given them, and of this unhappy class was Harry Hoffenden.

We say unhappy class, because what can be more unhappy than that perpetual worry of the mind after something which is not, in preference to that which is? The love of change is as unquenchable a feeling as it is a wretched one, unless fortune is such with the erratic individula that he can indulge himself.

But that state of things is rare, and it is commonly indulged at the expense of everything which constitutes respectability or happiness in the world, as it most unquestionably was in the case of Harry Hoffenden when he found his way to the gaming-table.

Nothing but the society of her child could possibly have enabled Jane to support herself against the evils of her position, and for its sake alone she clung to the man who had been the bane of her young existence. Alas! things have come to a sad pass between man and wife, when some extraneous circumstance like that is the only bond that holds them together, instead of that affection which was first lighted up in their inmost hearts.

But, if we look around us upon the great world, how many persons shall we find, wearing to society at large smiling countenances of apparent contentment, which are but the false masks that hide bruised and almost broken hearts? And although the consciousness of suffering by no means diminishes its individual excess, or can impart any consolation to a sufferer, it is nevertheless but too common.

And now, how she tortured herself to think what mystery it was that evidently hung about her husband's conduct, and why it was that she received not so much communication from him now as she used to do before their removal. Had, she asked herself, the exhortations of Andrew Ewert been of no avail then?

It will be remembered that he had told her of an appointment that he said he had with her cousin, and from that appointment she had hoped much. Oh, how she would have shuddered if she had known the reason why, on one side, at all events, it could not be kept by any human possibility. But no; she could not think the man she had loved and taken to her heart could be guilty of murder—that most horrible of crimes.

But how could she account for the apparent inconsistency in the mode of action of Andrew Ewert? Why did he go so suddenly, and so strangely, without speaking to her when there could be no possible occasion for slighting her feelings in such a way? I he had made an appointment with her husband, why not tell her of it himself personally, and, at all events, why not come afterwards to speak of the matter which had before so deeply interested him?

All these were queries which she put to herself, but which she found it much easier to put than to answer, for she could not satisfy herself upon any one of them; and her anxiety of mind, from the various causes of agitation, had really become most excessive. It was not till half the night had passed away that she dropped at all into repose, and then it was anything but a healthful, or refreshing slumber—for, on the contrary, her mind was haunted with all kinds of disagreeable images.

At one time she would fancy Hoffenden to be in some great danger, which would, with the inconsistency of a dream, then suddenly shift itself to her child, and then to herself until at length she thought she was flying through a thick wood, and was pursued as fast as feet could fall by the detestable Murdo. She thought that her feet failed her, and that she could proceed no further, when he cried out her name.

At this sound she awoke, for it was a real sound that mingled itself with her dreams, and she could hear distinctly and clearly a voice from the outside of her apartments calling to her.

She found that it was broad daylight, and that the voice was that of a female, who said—

"Madam, there is a gentleman who wishes to see you."

The hope that it was Andrew Ewert, and her dread that it was Murdo, held for a time about equal sway in her mind, and she knew not what to say. After a moment's hesitation, however, and the statement that she was wanted had been repeated, she said—

"Show the gentleman into the adjoining room, and say that I will be with him shortly."

Now this adjoining room that she mentioned was, in reality, the one in which she had fallen into sleep, for she had not gone to bed, but on a chair had dropped into that uneasy repose we have mentioned; and when she heard the voice calling to her, she had passed into the bedroom, at the door of which it was, in order to hear it more plainly.

She thought that if the visitor were shown into that room first, she should have a better opportunity of ascertaining who he was.

She heard that her orders were executed by the landlady of the house, and then she waited in breathless expectation to ascertain if she could, whether or not, if it was Andrew.

She heard a slight cough from the visitor, but that afforded her no information, and she was resolved to satisfy her doubts by a direct question, so she said—

"Is it you, Andrew?"

"No, lady; it is your slave, Mr. Murdo," was the reply; "but do not believe that I should have intruded upon you, if I had not come with a message from your husband."

Jane was so shocked and alarmed at finding it to be the very man she so much detested, and had so much reason to detest, that a feeling of absolute faintness came over her for a few minutes, and deprived her of the power of making any reply to what he said. At length, roused by the absolute necessity of saying something, lest her silence should give a kind of tacit consent to his presence, she spoke.

"If you have any message from my husband, although I regret his choice of a messenger, you can speak it now at once."

"Nay, Mrs. Hoffenden, I ought surely to be allowed the poor privilege of speaking my message personally to her to whom I promised to communicate it."

"As you speak now with a view of my understanding you," replied Jane, "you can surely have no difficulty in speaking to me the words with which you say you are charged?"

He was silent for some few moments, and then he said—

"I made your husband a promise that I would tell you that with which he charged me personally. I should much regret that I should be compelled to go back to him with the news that you so much slighted his message, that you would not see his messenger."

"You know," said Jane, "that that is a false view in which to place the subject—you know that well, Mr. Murdo. Speak at once that which you have to say, and you will by so doing go some distance towards assuring me of the truth of your promise that I should not again be annoyed by you as I have been."

"A hard condition; but I dare not trifle with my word to Hoffenden. I must and will now return to him to explain why I have not delivered my message."

She heard a movement of his feet, and the wife's affection triumphed over all scruples She did make her appearance at the door of the room, and with a face on which wa. some expression of anger, she said—

"Now, sir; in obedience to what you say are my husband's commands, I am here What have you to say to me?"

There is surely something about the very presence of real virtue which makes the guilty shrink and tremble; for bold as was Murdo, even he for a moment shrank back .

"You have done me the honour of appearing," he said, with hesitation.

"I want not one word more from you, sir, than will suffice to enable me to comprehend my husband's message."

"Most true. I am myself a man of few words, lady. Your husband's message will keep a little; but for myself, do you think I could fail to embrace such an opportunity as this for craving your pardon for what occurred when last I was in your presence alone?"

"I do not," said Jane, "I cannot believe that this affected humility is other than a piece of your hypocrisy; but if it be other, I can only say that an allusion to that circumstance can answer no beneficial purpose. I ask but the gratification of your absence."

"Cold and harsh words. But when you shall chance to see again, madam, the excellent young man who took your part in so gallant a style, present him with my compliments, and say that I now bear him no malice, but am abundantly satisfied."

There was something in these words which made Jane shudder; she knew not why, for they were in themselves simple enough, and did not seem to be calculated to convey any strong feeling of danger to Andrew Ewert; but yet the blood ran cold to her very heart as she heard his name pronounced in those strange, mocking accents of Murdo.

"You are satisfied?" she said.

"Oh! quite—quite. Most abundantly satisfied," was his reply.

"Your message, sir—your message. Speak it and be gone."

"It is, then, to the effect that business calls your husband from you, perchance for a day or two; but that as soon as may be he will be with you."

"Is he in London?"

"He is; but the fact is, an importunate creditor, from the pressure of whose demands I am endeavouring to do my best to relieve him, so far threatens his personal liberty, that he thinks a voluntary confinement preferable to an enforced one. But I doubt not of being able, in a short time, to restore him to you."

"That is all, I presume?" said Jane, keeping up as much show of indifference as possible before that man.

"Except that I can only tell you it is for your sweet sake I so act; and that although you shall not have to complain of anything from me in the shape of persecution, I love you."

Jane turned at once, and passed into the apartment, on the threshold of which, during this brief interview she had stood, and made an attempt to close the door; but Murdo was too quick for her, and held it open, saying with an earnestness which left a most painful impression upon her mind—

"Listen to me; admiring you as I do, I find it quite impossible for me to come into your presence without betraying, by word, look, or gesture, that admiration; and you will be tempted, some day, when you fancy your husband's heart is not so much alienated from you as it has been, to get him to make some promise of a nature that will produce ill-blood between him and me. Now, I say to you, Jane Hoffenden, beware, for I know a something, which you so little dream of, that if you were, you would consider it the wildest vision that ever crossed your imagination; but which, by the utterance of a few short words, enables me to destroy Hoffenden."

"Destroy!"

"Aye; to stamp indelible disgrace upon his name—upon you—upon his child. Beware, then, I say, that you make no ill-blood between us."

"I defy you, and all your base insinuations; and I should despise myself were I capable, for a moment, of allowing fear so far to get the better of me, that I should stoop to the endurance of insults from you, from any alleged danger. Leave this house, or I will make an alarm, which shall surely bring some stranger to my assistance, who will not see a helpless woman persecuted by a ruffian."

"If," he said, "I really thought that you threw down to me the gauntlet of defiance, in earnest, I would pick it up. But the consciousness of power keeps me calm; I know that I can utter words that would crush your spirit, and you know it; for there is a divinity about truth from any lips, which unites it with an air that may not be mistaken. We shall meet again; and, in the meantime, I leave you to ponder over what has passed, and the words I have uttered."

So saying, he turned and left the room, and she heard his heavy footsteps descending the staircase, with a feeling of great relief.

She sank upon a chair, with a deep sigh, exclaiming,—

"Oh, Harry! Harry! What have you done? What have you attempted, that gives this man a dreadful power over you? What can I think? In what quarter can I bid my fancy range, to gather conjectures with regard to such a dreadful subject. You, my husband, in the power of such a man as Murdo. Oh, no—no! it surely cannot be; for—for if it be, destruction is certain. Can such a man have power, and long refrain from exercising it? Oh, no—no—no."

She remained for a considerable time in a state of mind of the most painful description, and it was only the necessity there was of attending to the wants of that little one, who knew so little of the attention and the tone of a father, that roused her from such an apathy, and such a sad hopelessness of feeling, that had she not been blessed by the presence of that dear child, heaven only knows to what extent despair might have driven her.

But food was to be got for the child. Its wants must be attended to, come what would; and it was with a saddened heart, indeed, that the young mother tried to smile in her infant's face.

CHAPTER XII.

FOXLEY HAS NO OBJECTION TO THE PROPOSITION OF MURDO,—THE SECRET.

MURDO considered it of such first-rate importance to conciliate Mr. Foxley, the officer, as quickly as possible, that he went to him at the earliest opportunity, and finding that exemplary individual at home, he desired a private interview, which was readily granted.

No visitor of Mr. Foxley ever was asked to announce himself by name; for so many came who had a complete catalogue of names, that they might have been a little puzzled what to call themselves, and so, amid the multiplicity, might have hit upon one that conveyed no information to Foxley.

But that gentleman trusted far more to his own natural sagacity, in finding out who his visitors were, than to anything they chose to tell him upon that subject, and he, entirely from long acquaintance with human nature, had acquired a certain amount of tact that carried him on remarkably well.

It is a sad thing to think of, but a true one for all that, Mr. Foxley's experience of human nature should be so great, considering that his acquaintance with it had all been of a criminal character; but so it is, and there is no such thing as denying the allegation, that if we ever acquire a good idea of mankind generally we must do so through their vices.

But these two scoundrels, Foxley and Murdo, were well matched; for, probably, if London had been searched through, there could hardly have been found two who would have been their equals in villany and deceit.

Foxley was in his private room; as he called it, adjoining to that chamber in which, we have already shown to the reader, one unhappy wretch had lost his life; and it was there that he always received his visitors.

Upon the entrance of Murdo, he looked curiously at him, as if making an endeavour to recollect him, and then nodded his head with an air of one who would say—

"Oh, now I remember. It's all right; I have no doubt whatever about my man."

Murdo saw this look, and it disturbed him a little, for he began to think that it was just possibly it might bode him no good; for he could not exactly look back upon the last two years of his career, with a feeling that there was nothing to be called into question. He accepted the seat opposite Foxley, to which he was courteously invited; then, fixing his keen eyes upon the face of the thief-taker, he said—

"You are a man of business, Mr. Foxley?"

"I hope so, sir," was the cautious reply of Foxley. "You are a man of discernment But I presume you don't come here to pay compliments, or to listen to them."

"You are right, sir; I come upon real *bona fide* business; and I have been told, Mr. Foxley, that if any one come to make a proposition to you, that you always act honourably by them, and make the failure of the negotiation no pretext for any personal interference with those who make it."

"You have heard no more than the truth of me, sir, at all events," said Foxley, "whoever told it to you. I conduct all my business upon honour, or else I am quite certain I should not be able to conduct it at all. And now as we so well understand each other upon these points, suppose we proceed to business."

"With all my heart, sir. A-hem! In Adam-street, Adelphi, an uncomfortable circumstance has taken place."

"Ay—a murder, committed by a young man, named Harry Hoffenden, upon Andrew Ewert."

"Exactly."

"And one of my men has lost his life, too, in the matter. It's rather serious."

"It is; and that's what I have come to talk to you about, Mr. Foxley. You and I are men of business, and thoroughly understand what we are about you know. Of course, you know that an affair of this sort is worth so much, and no more; and, if that worth is doubled or trebled, why, of course as a man of the world, you have no objection."

"Look you, sir," said Foxley, "this is no ordinary piece of business. At present the thing is snug enough; but how long it may continue so, is another matter. It's a good £100 to me when the rope's round his neck; and the idea of his escaping me is out of the question."

"So I told him."

"Then, as I said before, you are a man of discernment. What's your proposition?"

"Why, the whole affair was just this,—Hoffenden came home and found the young fellow in his wife's room; and, on the impulse of the moment, he put a knife into him."

"Oh."

"He died, and Hoffenden is sorry; and, by some means or another, if the thing be kept quiet, he can produce £300."

"Hump! make it £500; that's my price; and then I'll warrant him as free as air from all consequence. I know all about it, and now the matter is completely in my own hands."

"Done. It shall be £500."

"Sir, the promptitude with which you do business, does you immense credit. When and where am I to have the money?"

"To-morrow, here, and at this hour."

"Good. You, I presume, will bring it to me; for the fewer there are in such an affair the better, as a matter of course,"

"True, sir; I will bring you the money, you may depend, without fail, at this hour; and I can only say that the manner in which you have met me on this little business, has inspired me with the highest esteem."

"Gammon!"

"Sir!"

"Oh, that's only a way I have of complimenting a visitor. But, remember, I will, within twenty-four hours, lodge Hoffenden in Newgate, unless the money makes its appearance. Understand me; I won't be trifled with."

"Nobody in their senses would attempt it, sir. I have the honour of bidding you good day, and shall have the pleasure, as well as the honour, of meeting you to-morrow."

Murdo left Foxley, and it is not going too far to say that, as far as he could admire and reverence any human being, he did the thief-taker, whom he considered to be the very perfection of that character which to him was an object of admiration—a clever rogue.

"This won't be a bad affair for me," he muttered, as he proceeded to Hoffenden's; and then, suddenly pausing, he said, "It was very forgetful of me not to think of asking Foxley what they had done with the body. He must have had it removed very quickly and secretly; for there has been no inquest, nor has anything reached the public ear upon the subject. I wonder, now, how he has succeeded in managing that so nicely?"

This, indeed, was a point connected with the whole affair that deserved especial attention, at the same time that it showed how perfect all the arrangements of Foxley were, that he could depend upon his men in the removal of a dead body, and have not a word said about it all the while; but this Foxley was a great man.

"I don't see," thought Mr. Murdo, when he had dismissed from his mind some of the uneasy thoughts about the body with which he was encumbered—"I don't see but what I ought to make something handsome by this whole affair now. It's running a great deal of risk, of course; and it will be just as well for me to tell Hoffenden that Foxley wants a thousand as five hundred pounds."

This was certainly a reasonable enough proposition.

"It is a large sum of itself," was Hoffenden's reply, "but compared to what it is said I am now worth, it certainly is not much; so, of course as personal safety is now a firs consideration, he must have it, Murdo."

"Yes, I took upon myself to say that I would be with him to-morrow, at the same hour, with the cash, you see; so it will be necessary for you to go to the lawyers' and get an advance."

"You think they will let us have it?"

"Of course they will; nothing is more common under the circumstances. You can say that you want a couple of thousands to clear off some incumbrances, and they will let you have them quite in the way of business, as a thing of course."

"And can I get there with safety?"

"That I think there can be no doubt of whatever. Foxley, or his agents you have only to dread; and I have no doubt on earth but he will keep his word. Nothing could tempt such a man to break faith with you, but somebody going to him and offering him more money to do so."

"Well, well; I will go of course. Shall we send for a coach?"

"Yes; that will be the best. Ah! how soon, Hoffenden, you will roll about London streets in your own carriage; but just for the present little exigency, a comfortable hackney coach will answer; and then, in case of any hitch in the business, you had better come back here at once, you know."

"If I must I must; but I hate the sight of this place."

"It's safe, that's it's grand requisite. It don't pretend to be ornamental at all; but it's safe, you may depend upon that; and, with all his knowledge, and all his daring, I doubt even if Foxley could get you out of this house of refuge, so long as you stick to it in defiance of all trickery to get you away from it."

"I could hardly have believed it, if I had not the proof of it that my own residence here has given me, that there was such a sanctuary as this in all England; but there is no fighting against the fact. Here it is, and probably it has saved me."

CHAPTER XIII.

THE ADVANCE OF MONEY.—A LITTLE ALARM, AND SPECIMEN OF FOXLEY'S ABILITIES.

THE hackney-coach was procured, and Murdo, with Hoffenden, proceeded as quickly as that species of conveyance could take them to Gray's-inn, in order to possess themselves of a sum of money, larger in amount than the most sanguine expectations of either of them had ever led them to believe they would be able to become possessed of.

Nothing happened *en route*, requiring any attention or comment. Hoffenden was rather nervous, but that, in consequence of the peculiarity of his situation, was quite to be expected, and Murdo took no notice of it, thinking that it was best to let such a feeling go off at its own leisure, and not attempt by reasoning to dissipate it.

Both the partners of the legal firm were in, and while Murdo remained in the coach, Hoffenden entered the office. Upon giving his name, he found that there was quite what the French newspapers call a sensation among the clerks, and that he attributed to its right cause, namely, a knowledge of the fact that he was the owner of so large a fortune.

He was not kept long waiting, but was introduced to the private room of the attorneys, who received him with cold civility. It was the little one with the bald head and spectacles that spoke to him, saying—

"Mr. Hoffenden, you are too like your lamented father, whom I knew well, and respected, for me to have the least doubt myself of your identity; but you will have to go through some legal process to prove that fact, before you can get the fortune which is yours, and the principal part of which is in India stock."

"I will submit myself to your direction," said Hoffenden.

"Very good, sir. But you will quite understand that we decline being your men of business."

"Very well."

"If then, Mr. Hoffenden, you will give an answer to some questions, which one of our clerks before you go shall write down for you, and come again when we send for you, the whole affair can be settled."

"That is all very well," said Hoffenden; "but in the meantime, I am harassed out of my life by all sorts of liabilities, and what I want of you is, an advance of cash on interest."

"We have no objection to advance a sum on your acknowledgment. How much do you require?"

"Two thousand pounds."

"Indeed! this is a large sum, Mr. Hoffenden. You must be aware that such a sum as that withdrawn from any one, is extremely likely to disturb some investment, and therefore, we shall require you to pay legal interest for that amount."

"Charge what you like," said Hoffenden, "only let me have it; for I tell you candidly, that unless I do, I shall not know what to do; I run a risk of my liberty by going through the streets now."

"Well, well. Be it so—be it so. You will have to pay five per cent. for the amount Mr. Hoffenden."

If they had said fifty per cent., Hoffenden would have consented to it, in his present embarrassed condition; and it was only fortunate for him, among so many black sheep of the law as they are, and he succeeded in getting hold of a firm so honourable as was the one which managed his late brother's affairs, through their Indian agency.

It was the bitterest comment they could make upon his conduct, that they should actually decline doing any business for him more than was necessary in the due discharge of their duty; and even he could not but feel keenly what a state his own extravagancies had brought him to.

He was compelled, however, by the exigences of the time, to swallow his chagrin as best he might; for he did not doubt a moment, from the aspect and manner of the little bald-headed lawyer, that, upon the smallest amount of provocation, he would order him to be turned out of the office; and he, Hoffenden, had two much at stake just then to risk a failure in getting the cash he so particularly required.

He gave the required acknowledgment, and his hand shook again as he found himself for the first time, in possession of a cheque for two thousand pounds, minus interest at the rate of five per cent. He was now anxious to leave, in order that he might realize as quickly as possible some of his golden dreams; and as no one there had any particular wish for his conversation, no attempt was made to detain him, and he was bowed out as quickly as he pleased.

The pleasurable agitation in his countenance, as he reached the hackney coach again, at once convinced Murdo that he had been successful, and that he was actually possessed of the sum of money which, of itself, a few days before, would have been considered as something positively brilliant, and great to have.

But now what was it? Something not much over a hundredth-part of that colossal fortune, of which there could be no doubt whatever, and which a few days would probably place entirely within his grasp.

Truly had Hoffenden become one of fortune's minions, and from the moment that his fingers closed upon the cheque that the lawyers had given him, he felt as if he were a new man.

He sprung into the coach, and ordered the driver to take them to the banking-house at once on which the cheque was drawn; and then the man, as he touched his hat, to the intense astonishment and a little of the dismay of Hoffenden as well as of Murdo—

"Mr. Foxley, gentlemen, told me to say he was afraid he would be engaged at the hour Mr. Murdo was to call upon him; but he will be at home for the next two hours, if convenient, or any time after nine to-night."

"Mr. Who?" said Murdo.

"Mr. Foxley. I am one of his men."

"Why—why, you drive a coach."

"Oh, dear, yes. We do all sorts of things to make ourselves useful, Mr. Murdo, I assure you, or we should not be able to get up the amount of information we do. So if you like, gentlemen, I will drive you to Mr. Foxley's, or I will take any message you like to him, and he will write a note to Mr. Hoffenden at the house in the Mint."

"The devil!" muttered Murdo, partly in dismay, and partly in admiration of the tact and talent of Foxley. "I think, Hoffenden, we could not do better than go to the bank first, and then to Foxley's. What say you—eh?"

"As you please—as you please. I am too much confounded to think for myself. Take me where you like, so that it be not——"

"To Newgate," added the man, as he closed the coach door. "All's right. I understand, gentlemen. All's right—all's right."

Hoffenden sank back with a groan.

"Am I betrayed?" he said. "Good God! am I betrayed?"

"No, no, no," said Murdo. "Foxley knows he will get the money. He would not get a tenth of the amount by having you driven to Newgate, and, therefore you are quite safe. Cheer up—cheer up. You are more pusillanimous, by a great deal, than ever I thought you could possibly be."

"I—I will hope for the best. But remember, Murdo, you are, in the eyes of the law as guilty as I am."

"Content. Only you know that the law's eyes wink at him who has been, perhaps, accessory only, and lets him go upon his turning evidence against his principal. That, you will perceive, is a little advantage I have, which you have not. But what folly it is for us to talk in such a strain. All is well, and all will be well."

Hoffenden recovered a little of his courage when he found that the coach stopped at the door of the banking-house where the cheque was payable, and he requested Murdo to get it changed into notes and gold, which that individual did most willingly; and, when he returned, he said to the coachman—

"We will go now to Mr. Foxley's at once."

"Very good, gentlemen," said the man, and the vehicle rattled off in the direction of that worthy's house.

They were not long in reaching that place, and, as the coachman had said, Mr. Foxley was at home; but on the road, Murdo began to think it was rather an awkward thing, if Hoffenden should find that he, Foxley, had agreed to take £500, while he, Murdo, had, pitched the sum at £1,000.

When, therefore, they got close at hand, he persuaded Hoffenden to remain in the coach while he transacted all the business with Foxley; and Hoffenden was really in such a

HOFFENDEN'S TERROR OF CONSCIENCE.

state of agitation, that, on the whole, he would much rather remain where he was, and escape the interview altogether; so, he readily enough consented, and let Murdo go in alone, a little circumstance which made £500 difference to that individual, as we are well aware.

"It's very seldom I alter an appointment," said Foxley, when Murdo was with him; "but I am, to some extent, at the command of others, and I know I shall be occupied all this evening."

"It don't matter, there's the money, sir; and now, will you tell me what has become of the dead body of Ewert?"

"Oh, that's my secret."

"You will not tell?"

"Certainly not. Mr. Hoffenden may rest completely satisfied that he will hear no more of this affair; I make it my business to dispoe of the body."

"You are a wonderful man, Mr. Foxley; but if you won't tell what has become of the body, you won't; so, with profound respect, I have the honour of wishing you good——"

"That's all very well, but you have quite forgot yourself, you must be aware. Mr. Murdo, I am surprised at you, really."

"Forget myself, Mr. Foxley; why, what do you mean by that? You speak in riddles to my poor comprehension."

"Oh, no," said Foxley, "it's you; that's the way, and pretend you don't understand me. You have paid me for Mr. Hoffenden, but not for yourself, and if you don't put down £500 for yourself, you will be given into custody to-morrow, if you were to bury yourself in the very bowels of the earth. You know me."

Murdo saw that he was taken in, and, from the manner of Foxley, he felt convinced there was no chance of escape. He did, however, say—

"Won't you take £120? I cannot afford it."

"I could not think of insulting you," said Foxley, "by naming a less price for you, than for Hoffenden. If I did, you would have just ground of complaint against me, which I should really, after the prompt and proper manner you have behaved, be very sorry to give you."

Murdo knew, in his heart, that all argument was waste of time, but he did cling yet a little to the other £500, before, with a groan, he placed in it the hands of the thief-taker and felt that it was gone from him for ever.

In a few moments he left the house, but, as he crossed the threshold, he turned and, muttered such a curse, that the man who let him out, looked a little aghast at it, although he was not used to the most refined language in all the world from Mr. Foxley's visitors.

CHAPTER XIV.

TWO YEARS HAVE ELAPSED, AND A GREAT CHANGE HAS TAKEN PLACE.

Two years have passed away! How easily are the words uttered! and yet, what a world of thought and of action two years may contain! What a round of joys, and yet what indescribable sorrows!

In two years the child springs up almost to a new existence. The girl may become a wife, and the wife a mother—perchance a widow. Over how many graves of those who have walked and moved about, having—

"A local habitation and a name,"

in the records of existence, may, in the short space of two years, be like the bleak wind's whistle! How many hearths may be rendered desolated in two years! How many hearts may be broken! The strong may be bowed down by sickness. The prattle of infancy may be heard no more, and but a sigh may awaken the sad echoes of the tomb.

The loving and the loved may alike have passed away. Kingdoms may have been shaken—dynasties destroyed! Alas! in the twenty-four revolving months comprised in that space of two years, how much moral mischief may be in this great world accomplished!

But the picture has another aspect. There is sunshine as well as gloom, or it would not be a just epitome of human nature as it is.

In two years, then, there may be much happiness diffused, and—

"Hearts that have been long estranged,"

may meet, and smile again. The loved one may be smiling with conscious happiness beneath a husband's roof. The child may be born that is to form the connecting link of love between two human beings for a long life. Feuds may be healed—sickness may have passed away like a vapour before the sunlight of health; and those who may have been repining under the cruel garb of poverty, may have become prime favourites of fortune, and be all that, in their wildest dreams, they had dared to wish themselves.

And this brings us back again to the Hoffendens. Let us see what two years have really done for them.

* * * * * * *

No. 10, Portman-square. That is the house to which we wish to call the attention of the reader—and a mansion replete with all taste and magnificence it is, indeed! It is one of the most costly in the square, and, as the time is night, and all the blinds are not closely drawn, there is an opportunity of catching a glimpse of the interior of some of the rooms, even from the street.

And what a glorious glimpse that is to any one who can look on without something of a pang at the wealth and the show of others!

Through those lattices might be seen the gorgeous resplendence of many lights, glaring upon, and borrowing a beauty from the rich and rare gildings on which they shone.

There were hangings, too, of the choicest fabric, most delicately shadowed, and arranged with all the skill that art could practise or call to the aid of wealth. And fair forms might be seen flitting to and fro, attired in all the glittering panoply of luxury and ultra refinement.

The time is eleven o'clock at night; and the din and rattle of carriages seem to be wending towards that spot. Yes; they approach the door of that splendid mansion. There is to be that night one of those late reunions of the fashionable world, which are so distasteful to the thoughtful and the reflective, as being a combination of all the disadvantages of a large collection of persons being associated together, with none of the pleasures. '

There is all the parade, and all the twaddle—all the petty jealousies and annoyances that can be imagined; and then an end. But still Fashion, with her imperious sway, seems to hold these people in such perpetual bondage, and they continued, year after year, in the same frivolous round of what is called fashionable life, and miscalled pleasures.

Now that side of the square on which this house is situated is full of carriages, and the blaze of light that comes from the open doors, illuminates the pavement for some distance.

The rattle of carriage-steps was incessant, and occasionally a pole would come into rather close proximity with a panel, producing a concussion highly favourable to coach-makers, but to nobody else.

And the reader will naturally ask what is the meaning of all this bustle to our story, and to whom does this house belong where so much gaiety and so much frivolity are going on hand-in-hand? We will tell him, and, with our usual great aversion to secrets and mysteries, we will tell him at once.

The splendid mansion, then belonged to Harry Hoffenden! Yes, to the Harry Hoffenden we saw at the gambling-house—the Harry Hoffenden whose progress we traced homeward, until, visited by a demon in the shape of the villain Murdo, he did the deed of blood which in its remembrance should, and surely even then, when he was surrounded by all the pomp and luxury of his new position, did embitter every moment of his existence.

It is easily accounted for how he came to be in his present situation. Foxley was bought off, as Foxley made a trade of always being bought off by the highest bidder; and consequently Hoffenden had come into full possession of the large property that had been left him by his brother, without hindrance from any quarter but—his conscience!

It was then his time, he thought, to show the world what he could do with ample means, and he set about it at once; perhaps he had a hope, too, that, by surrounding himself with so much magnificence, he should succeed in completely drowning all reflection.

Do we think he will succeed in that? Oh, no. Who ever did succeed in stifling those pangs of conscience, which, of all other pangs, are those that remain the most fixed and indelible upon the imagination.

A more wretched man than Hoffenden was not in the world. A perpetual curse hung over him—such a curse as is sometimes detailed in wild legends as comprising all that is baneful in all situations.

But it is now of Jane Hoffenden that we wish to speak.

The mode of life she was now compelled to lead was distasteful to her, for a variety of reasons. In the first place it was contrary to her tastes, for she much preferred the quiet, sober beauties of trees and flowers, to all the garish splendour by which she was surrounded in town, and there was not one among the motley crowd that came to the house that she could dream of making a friend of.

Then, again, the mystery that hung over the disappearance, so strange and so inexplicable, of Andrew Ewert, affected her most sensibly, and perhaps the more so, as there was no one to whom she could unbosom herself upon the subject.

It was true, that casting aside all false feelings, and firm in the conscience rectitude of her own conduct, she did boldly, to all appearance, ask her husband if he knew what had become of Andrew; but the consequence of so doing were such as did afford her no encouragement to mention his name again.

It was evident to her that the moment she uttered the name of Ewert, her husband was seriously affected—a sort of death-like pallor came over him, and that gave way to and accession of ungovernable rage; but whether that rage was real or assumed, she could not well make up her mind. It was sufficient, however, in its result, to prevent Jane from ever again recurring to the subject that had produced such an ebulition.

And then she had a third ground of uneasiness, and that consisted in the almost constant presence of Roderick Murdo at the house.

He aped now, too, more than he had done before, the man of fashion. Previously he was slovenly in his attire, and had about him a recklessness of appearance which he now studiously sought to conceal.

But his taste was a vulgar one; for he was bedizened out like a Jew on a holiday, with large trinkets of blazing colours, and his apparel was always in an outraous style.

And he likewise tried hard to conceal the vulgarity of his manner by an affectation of style in his discourse, which he now interlarded with as many long and fine words as he could; and, in short, he considered himself quite a man man of fashion, and, as far as that goes, he did quite as well as such, as the empty-headed fools who usually go by that designation in society at large, and who think themselves such fine fellows.

But all this was most especially disagreeable to Jane, who was forced to endure the presence of such a man in the same room with herself now on many occasions.

But the time had as yet been too short to allow Murdo to commence his designs. He was willing for a time to revel in the luxury that surrounded him, and to rest from the cares of life—to grow bloated and full of high feeding; then the loathsome wretch would begin to carry out the projects that found a home in his brain.

And what a constant horror must the continual presence of that man have been to Hoffenden—what a constant source of annoyance to find that he was compelled to endure the presence of one, who not only always reminded him of the past by his presence, but practically likewise continually did so by calls upon his purse. If he had dared to attempt the deed, he would many a time have aimed at the life of Roderick Murdo.

But the chances of failure in doing so deterred him, and the consequences of the revenge of such a man he knew might be fearful. Murdo might at any time fly to the continent, and there, in perfect security himself, send such particulars to London of the crime which he knew Hoffenden had committed, as must hurl him to destruction.

There was only one thing connected with the whole transaction that he, Roderick Murdo, did not know, and which puzzled him exceeding, and that was as to how Foxley had succeeded in so cleverly disposing of the body of Andrew Ewert, so as to leave no traces of its presence.

But although this was a subject of wonder and some speculation to him, he did not suffer it to molest him much, for he had a profound appreciation of the talents of Foxley, and had no doubt but that he had managed the matter with his usual skill, and that consequently no more would be heard of it.

This, then, was the situation of parties at the house of the Hoffendens; but the reader is not to imagine that Foxley rested quite satisfied with what he knew of the affair, and what he had made by it. On the contrary, he kept a most vigilant and wary eye upon Hoffenden, as well as upon Murdo, and as plenty of money was going, he thought it would be quite as well if he had his share of it.

But Foxley was cunning, and he had his own reasons for not being in a very violent hurry about the business; he knew that he could afford to wait a little, and he did. Besides, it happened just then that his own affairs required a good deal of his attention and consequently he threw into them all that vigour of intellect which he undoubtedly possessed, and which it was a great pity happened not to be associated with any amount of honesty of purpose.

The party at the Hoffendens appeared to be going off with great eclat, which consisted in the fact that everybody was crowded to death almost, and that many of the guests could not get farther than the staircase. That is fashion; but it seems to us, and doubtless, will seem to our readers, to be a remarkably long way off comfort.

And Hoffenden was there, arraying his face in smiles, which were no reflex of the feelings that lay hidden at the bottom of his heart; pretending to be completely master of himself, and well enough pleased, while in reality he was a prey to the most dreadful state of suspense in which any human being could be placed; but we have no pity for such a man as he.

There were some among his guests who, perhaps, had knowledge enough of human nature, and tact enough to detect the inward disquietude that lurked beneath the smiles of Hoffenden; but these few could only see the phenomenon, without being able to come to the least conclusion as to its cause.

And the female friends, as they called themselves, of Mrs. Hoffenden, were not slow in noticing the sigh, and the sudden catching of the breath, which she could not always suppress, and which convinced them that she, too, had her sources of grief.

But what was that to them? The *soirees* at the Hoffendens were brilliant. The *petite soupers* superb: and it was well known that they had money enough to stand all that, and much more, for report had multiplied every thousand of Hoffenden's property into three

---

CHAPTER XV.

THE INSULT TO JANE HOFFENDEN BY MURDO.

WE have said that Murdo was in no hurry to attempt the perfecting of those designs with which he had charged himself, nor was he; but he had, in a propensity of his own, one great cause of indiscretion, and difficulty in keeping any prudent resolution whatever,

The propensity was the love of good wine—an article which Roderick Murdo had not been always able to procure, but which he had in such great abundance at the house of Hoffenden, that he was tempted so exceed the just bounds of moderation much more frequently than one would have expected from a man with a head full of such scheming as his was.

On the night of this grand party he committed that species of discretion: Do not let it be supposed that Roderick Murdo got so far intoxicated as to lose possession of his faculties; but he drank just enough to drown his usual perception of caution, and to make him do what he really, in his cooler moments, meant to do, but not so soon.

It was twelve o'clock, and an elegant repast had been laid in one of the noble rooms of Hoffenden's house, for such of the guests as chose to partake of it; and it was done well, for there was no ceremony of sitting down to table, but those who chose could go to the refreshment room, where servants were in attendance, and get their wants satisfied in a few minutes.

Thus matters went on pleasantly enough, and not unfrequent had been the attendance of Murdo at the *beaufet* on which wine was placed.

On one of these occasions he encountered Hoffenden, to whom he spoke, saying—

"Why, I have scarcely met you all the evening. Are you aware that Creckton opens his new house to-night?"

"What? His new gaming saloons?"

"Yes; the getting up of the thing, they say, is splendid. Could you not steal an hour to go and have a peep?"

"I dread it."

"Dread it? What is there to dread? You say you have made up your mind not to play, and therefore, what have you to dread? You go merely, under such circumstances, as a spectator."

"True: but—but we may be tempted."

"I will tell you how to avoid that. Play a little, but total abstinence won't succeed. I used to drink too much. You know the time well enough when both you and I were rather out at elbows, and I tried the total abstinence plan. It was too great an effort, but I found that to drink no more than would do me good was not so. Now, you can play, but you must not play deep."

"But I doubt if any play will do me good."

"Psha! you cannot live in the world if you don't. I tell you, Hoffenden, if you would get rid of a grisly spectre, that I am sure comes sometimes too close to me to be agreeable, you will engage a little in all those pursuits that can draw your mind from its contemplation.

"A spectre !"

"Yes; you don't want me to name him ? If you do, I——"

"No, no—oh, God! no. And—and so it haunts you, too ? I thought that I only had that horror; and I see him everywhere. In my chamber I see him; alike in darkness as in light. I see him at the festive board; and if I look into the wine cup, his is the face that meets my gaze in the ruddy pool, instead of my own. I sometimes fancy that he dogs my footsteps; and, when I turn rapidly, it seems as if I almost caught a glimpse of the shadow of something."

"Pleasant, certainly."

"Maddening—most maddening ! and if such horrors continue, I shall go distracted !"

"Drink," said Murdo, filling up a glass of wine—"drink, and don't look into the glass this time before you do so."

Hoffenden made a faint opposition, as if he would put the glass from him; but it was very faint, and he took it almost at the moment that he seemed to be refusing it.

"Come, come," said Murdo, in a deprecatory tone; "such thoughts and fears won't do any good to either of us. You won't sleep to-night if you give way to them, I can tell you."

"Sleep, said you ? When do I sleep ? The fancied repose of a whole week to me does not make up the sum of one, when healthy, night's rest. No, no—I cannot sleep."

"Then Crockton's is the place for you to-night. All the world—that is to say, all the world of fashion—will go there; and as you wish some night to see it, why not to-night, when it may assist to drive away the uneasy thoughts that harrass you at this juncture. On my soul, I never saw you so thoroughly down."

"I am oppressed to-night—I own it; as if some impending evil were about to take place. I do fear that something will occur of a serious character; and—and I think I will go."

"Well spoken—the last three words I mean. As to the former part of your speech, I look upon it but as ill-omened croaking, meaning nothing, and not worth consideration of any character. Take another glass."

"No, no—no more wine. I dread what an indiscreet word might give rise to if I were to indulge myself too much. No more to-night."

"You have turned as temporate as an anchorite, lately, upon my word; and formerly you were one of the jolliest dogs in all the circle of my tolerably wide acquaintance."

"Yes, but formerly I was not haunted by that spectre you talk of; that pale face with the spots of blood upon it; those accusing eyes; those lips quivering in the agony of death."

"Hush! some one comes; and by degrees you have been raising your voice. You will attract the attention of the servants if you be not careful."

This admonition had all its effect upon Hoffenden, and he was alarmed into silence but the look of terror that had taken possession of his face, as he conjured up to himself the aspect of his victim, remained for a time, in spite of him, and he whispered to Murdo—

"Shall we go at once ?"

"No, not yet ; it's rather soon. But if you feel that you would rather not meet your guests in your present state of mind, you can find somewhere to go to, and I will meet you at Crockton's at half-past two."

"Be it so. You will be puuctual ?"

"To the minute, if possible ; but if anything should prevent me from coming to you quite so soon, you may fairly expect me within a quarter of an hour of that time. Be off with you, for you look like a ghost in that strange guise of countenance you wear."

"Do I look very bad ?"

"You do, indeed. Go and look at yourself in yonder mirror, and you will have no difficulty in coming to a full and correct conclusion, with regard to your appearance."

Hoffenden did go and look in the glass, and he was rather terrified at his own appearance; he looked so pale, and wan, and haggard. He saw the propriety of adopting Murdo's advice, and leaving the place as quickly as he could; so, without a word of apology to any one, he did so at once.

And, in the meantime, how kindly the dear friends of lady visitors were speaking to Jane Hoffenden ; and yet what absolute hollowness was at their hearts! It is, indeed, a fearful picture of human nature, that such society presents to any one who looks at it with a philosophical eye, and will not allow himself to be deceived by the shallow tinsel of show and glitter, by which it is surrounded.

"My dear Mrs. Hoffenden," said one, "how charmingly you do arrange everything !"

"Yes," added another, "most charmingly; but then the dear Mrs. Hoffenden has such a taste !"

"Ah," said that a third, "it is a delightful thing to be blessed with such a judgment. It's beautiful!"

Jane smiled, but it was in a sickly fashion, for she had observed what had passed between her husband and Roderick Murdo could not be of an agreeable character. Although she did not hear the words they uttered, she saw how Hoffenden's hand trembled as he raised the wine-glass to his lips, and she thought,—

"Alas! well I know that there is some fearful secret; but I am not quite aware that it was shared with that bold, bad man. Why cannot he trust one who really loves him, instead of one who preys upon him, and I am certain, makes a victim of him ?"

And then the kind friends of Jane whispered together saying,—

"Oh, it's all very well, as far as appearances go; but you know there must be something behind the scenes that nobody knows anything of but themselves; that's quite clear. Did you see Mrs. Hoffenden's looks?"

"To be sure," said two in a breath; "to be sure we did."

"And then, again, did you see what a miserable attempt at a smile she put on just now ?"

"Yes; and how she looked after her husband."

"Ladies," remarked another, "just step this way, if you please, and I will tell you all that I have heard, and all that I think about the Hoffendens; and I believe I can surprise you a little, rather."

So saying, this chronicle of evil led her acquaintances into the recess of a window, where she might, with more apparent effect, relate all the scandal her prolific imagination could suggest, relating to Jane and her husband, whose guest she then was.

The latter circumstance alone ought to have sufficed to stop the current of malevolence; and in a better state of society it would have done so; but we must recollect that we are talking of what is called high life, which is quite a different thing from all that is just, honourable, or feeling.

There was one thing, however, which Jane had managed that all her guests should, directly or indirectly, be made aware of, and that was, that she had no desire for the company of any of them after one o'clock in the morning, a rule which was sadly at variance with the dictates of fashion, which have a great propensity to turn night into day.

We are of opinion, ourselves, that this love of candle and gas-light, in what is called high life, must have originated, and must be kept up by those old *roue* women, whose yellow and debauched complexions will not stand the contact of daylight, which, with its truth-telling glare, would have the effect of exposing the pearl powder and rouge with which they plaster themselves up for evening parties.

But, for all that, it was difficult to stay in anybody's house after the time they had themselves intimated they liked visitors to leave, and by about half-past one, Jane had a clear house.

On the evening to which we have drawn the attention of the reader it was so, and never, probably, had Jane felt so thankful, as when she could seek the quiet and retirement of her own bosom.

But she had one comfort in the midst of all this—one crowning bliss, which stood in lieu of a thousand disagreeables, and that consisted in the affection she cherished for her child. Yes; she had that little one yet to cling to, as a glimpse of heaven itself, in the midst of all evils and all trials.

CHAPTER XVI.

THE MOTHER, THE CHILD, AND THE LIBERTINE.

It is two o'clock in the morning, and Jane is walking, with a quick step, towards the chamber of her little one, which she has had situated in a part of the house as remote as possible from the noise and bustle of the parties which it is the will and pleasure of her husband to give continually.

She suspects, but she does not quite know, that all such company was seen by Hoffenden with the hope that, in the giddy whirl of pleasure, he may succeed in losing recollection of that which might otherwise affect him even to distraction itself.

She suspects that he has committed some crime, but she cannot think that it is anything but a crime against property, committed, perchance, when he was very poor, with the knowledge and at the instigation of the villain, Murdo. Oh! if for but one moment her thoughts had wandered, with anything like plausibility, to the likelihood that it was murder which her husband had committed, what additional pangs would she have suffered! But she was spared that.

The nurse—who was extravagantly paid to take charge of the infant, who in its young life had already, in consequence of its father's vices, actually wanted food—knew well that Jane would not retire to rest without visiting the infant, so she was up when the young mother entered the room.

The child was sleeping.

"Oh, me'm," said the nurse, "you may believe, or you mayn't; but if you was to chop of my head, me'm, this very moment, I would say it; because, me'm, I'm Joan Blunt, and says what I thinks, and I do say, the more I looks upon this blessed infant, the more I gets reminded of a angel."

Jane stooped gently over the couch, and kissed the little slumberer, paying not the smallest attention to the too evident gross flattery of the woman, who continued,—

"And what's more, me'm, I do say, and I have got two mortal human eyes in my head, and so ought to know—I do say this little creature, me'm, is the image of you."

"How long has it slept?"

"Since ten, me'm. Oh, to look at that little creature, and to——"

"Thank you. Good night."

"I wishes you a uncommon good night, me'm, very. Well, that's the manners of some people; stopping you short off in the middle of what you are going to say, with a 'good night.' Oh, the stuck-up wretch! Well, if I do hate any one thing more than another, it's a beggar on horseback."

At this moment the child, who so much resembled one of the angelic host, slightly moved, and the nurse, who had found out that heavenly comparison exclaimed,—

"Oh, you little odious wretch! if you disturb me to-night, I do think I shall have to wring your neck. Will you be quiet? Oh! you are still, now, are you! Of all the little, troublesome brats that ever I came near, I do think you are somewhere about the worst!"

So much for Joan Blunt, who says what she thinks!

But Jane, of course, did not know that one of the consequences of her wealthy position was, that her child should be treated with unkindness. How much, if she had had the least suspicion of such a fact, would she have wished back again poverty, even with all its horrors! If there were now any tie whatever—now that she felt and knew that the affections of her husband had gone from her—that could blind her to the world, it was that child, and she hugged the belief to her mind that it at least was happy.

But it is only the children of the educated middle casses of society who have a fair chance of a happy childhood.

The children of the rich are given into the care of ignorant, selfish, and, in many cases, wicked and inhuman domestics, and the children of the poor are neglected altogether. We are really not quite sure that the latter are not the better off of the two. In one of the celebrated " Tales of a Physician," an appalling picture is drawn of the miseries that a servant may inflict upon a child. If we do not mistake, the tale is entitled " The Morleys," but it is in the first volume of that work.

After, then, having, as she considered, left her child in peace, and safety, and happiness, Jane went to her own room, and, sitting down upon the first chair that presented itself, she let her head and face rest upon her hand, and felt that she was very wretched.

As was but too usual, she felt certain she should not see her husband until, perhaps, the middle of the next day; and, although heaven knows that his society was none of the

THE REMORSE OF THE GAMBLER.

most agreeable when he did remain at home, yet there was something very painful in the fact of such utter neglect.

As she looked up, as she did after a time, she chanced to see herself reflected in the cheval-glass that was in the corner of the apartment, and the glitter of her jewels, which she wore on account of the entertainment, presented a sad mockery to the gloom of her heart.

"What baubles !" she said, mournfully, "do such things as these become, when the heart is surcharged with grief?—what an absolute mockery !"

As she moved, the diamonds shot their scintillating rays in all directions, and, with a deep sigh, she rose to divest herself of those glittering appendages.

Notwithstanding all her means, there was one thing as an appendage to it that some people would have thought indispensable, that Jane never would have, and that was what was called an own maid. She could not bear the fawning sycophancy of such creatures, and accordingly she had merely a civil, quiet girl, who came to her when she was sent for, and not on any other occasion.

But to-night Jane had given her leave to retire to rest early, for she could very well divest herself of those gaudy trappings that she wore, and, moreover, she felt so heavy at heart, that she did not like to run the chance of the natural and simple question from the girl of what was the matter with her.

She accordingly turned the key in the lock of her bed-room door, which likewise shut out the whole house from a snug and pretty little dressing-room that lay beyond it, and which was her's exclusively, containing, as it did, all the little things that she valued.

"Oh!" she murmured, as she removed the jewels from her dress, "how many persons would envy me the possession of these gems, fancying that they ought, and must constitute happiness; and yet how grievously disappointed would they be if they had my feelings to contend with."

When she had taken off most of the jewels, she sat down again, for she really had not the heart to undress herself, and burying her face in her hands, she told herself that she would calmly review her position, and try to think if there was a possibility of bettering it.

But how true it is that there are some subjects of contemplation, that the more they are thought over, the less are we able to come to calm and rational conclusions concerning them. The imagination dresses them up in the most frightful colours, and they gain in terror and in enormity the more thought is wasted upon them.

Of such a character were the cogitations of poor, unhappy, yet wealthy Jane Hoffenden.

And she had no friends now to turn to. All who had known her, and upon whose sympathy and attachment she thought she could have relied, had left her upon her marriage with a man not esteemed, and whose vices were better known to every one than to her.

And now that Andrew Ewert, whom she thought at least she could have confided in, had deserted her to all appearance, she felt that she was utterly lonely.

Heaven only knows what, in the despair of her heart, she might have been prompted to do, had it not been for the constantly recurring remembrance of the child—that was what saved her.

"And what," she asked herself half aloud, "what is to be the end of this? What is to become of me, and what is to become of him whom I feel convinced has now again commenced the career of gambling, which I hoped he had forsaken for ever? What wealth will withstand that dreadful mode of squandering it? No amount of means can withstand such a vice, and poverty will again come back to us. These glittering gems are but a mockery to me—they are like the false glitter of the serpent's eye—gleaming but to betray."

She was right—perfectly right. No amount of wealth can withstand that most fearful of all vices, gambling. Any other vice may damage a fortune, but that absorbs it completely and for ever. At a throw of the fatal dice, an emperor may lose a country. Well might Jane tremble to find that Hoffenden again went out from his home at night with Murdo.

And what could she do? Was she not very, very hopeless, and helpless? Did not that very tie—the child which prevented her from utterly despairing, likewise have the effect of making her dependent upon one who otherwise she might have left.

Surely, had she been alone, she could, by some honest course of industry, have found for herself a support; but, alas! not with that little one in her arms did she feel justified in leaving any home; and, besides, would he not pursue her? Yes, he would have a fair ground for so doing, if she took the child? And could she go without it? Oh, no. The mother's heart might be broken, but she could not part with that much-loved one, who had so dear, and so sacred a claim upon her love.

"God help me," she said, "God help me! I know not what will be the frightful end of all this; but a something seems to whisper to me that it will be terrible."

She walked into the adjoining room to look at a time-piece which was there, in order to see the hour. It was a sort of mechanical movement, more in consequence of habit than anything else, for Heaven knows it mattered little to her what the hour was.

She had, however, for so many and many a night sat up for Hoffenden, and had got so in the habit of looking at a clock to note the weary march of time, that she now did so although she had no hope of his return; and, if she had heard his step, he might for all she knew be flushed with wine.

It was but a few minutes to three.

"I must seek rest. For my child's sake, I must seek rest. I cannot think further to-night upon the dreadful possibilities of the future. They are with Heaven."

She had taken two steps towards retiring to the bed-room she had just left, when a strange noise, like the rattle of a key in a lock, struck upon her ears.

CHAPTER XVI.

THE NIGHT OF TERROR.

JANE was not quite certain that it was a movement in the lock that came across her ears. There are so many noises in a house that assume different aspects; but she trembled excessively, as she listened for a repetition of the sound, be it what it might.

For a time all was still; and she began to think that she must have been deceived by some accidental creaking, or movement of a piece of furniture, which might have been occasioned by a sudden admission of air from a crevice, or from any of the one thousand of accidents to which noises may be attributable.

"It can be nothing," she said, "but my own imagination that makes me feel so very fearful—nothing else, nothing else. How lonely the night is—I wish I had brought the dear child to keep me company."

She advanced another step towards the door, but she trembled so that she could get no farther; for, although she could reason with herself correctly enough, she could not conquer her fear wholly; and the tremulous beating of her heart was such that she was compelled to pause.

She leaned for support against a table with a top of veined marble to it; and, after a time, she did manage to get a little reassured, and to blame herself much for giving way to such absurd fancies.

"It is the time of night," she said, " and the nature of my previous feelings, that have made me fancy all sorts of terrors. Where is the courage that has supported me so long and so often? Where is the power of endurance that has carried me on so far as the present time? Have I turned so weak that an accidental noise in my chamber jars upon every nerve in my system, and produces the greatest alarm? Courage!—courage!"

There was a raised step between those two rooms, from the smaller to the larger one; and, as she placed her foot upon its softly carpeted surface, another slight sound, like the rustling of clothing, came upon her ears.

A faintness seized her; she felt now most positive that some one was in the chamber, and that, by that fact, she was cut off from communication with the rest of the house; for the room had no means of egress from it, except through the outer and larger apartment.

For a moment all objects whirled round in the mind's-eye of Jane, until they lost all similitude of form or substance, and she thought she was falling; but happily this dangerous condition passed away, and although she felt a death-like faintness still upon her, she did not absolutely faint.

She contrived to walk to the dressing-table, on which was some eau de Cologne. A portion poured into a glass of water, that fortunately was at hand, and hastily swallowed, sufficed very much, by its slightly stimulating power, to restore her to something like consciousness and courage.

She knew now that there was danger, and she had to nerve herself to face it. In a drawer, in the bed-room, she likewise knew that there were arms, for it was a fancy of Hoffenden's not to sleep without having pistols handy to his grasp, if he should chance to hear any alarm in the night.

But, how, admitting that she understood sufficient of those weapons to use them, and had courage to do so, was she to get possession of them? That was the question, and a question of no small moment was it.

Then, again, she asked herself, who it was that could thus have penetrated to her chamber, and with what motive could it have been done. Was it a thief, and would he, if so, content himself with what plunder he there found, and not seek to penetrate into the next apartment where she was?

Oh, what a world of anxiety was compressed into a space of not more than five minutes of time !

It would have been a great relief if she had heard some sounds conveying more unequivocal testimony to the fact, that there was some one there, than what she had heard already ; but the deathlike stillness that had reigned since the last alarm, gave a frightful rein to the imagination.

Yes, all was still—still as the very grave itself. Not the slightest vestige of a sound disturbed what might be called the solemnity of repose that reigned in the next chamber.

There was no bell communicating with the room in which she was, or else she would have rung it, and so brought some assistance to her aid ; and what might be the consequence of calling for assistance from the window, or otherwise, and so shewing she was alarmed, she knew not. The man, if man it was, that was in her chamber, might, for all she knew, murder her for such an act.

How cruel was her situation, so full of peril, doubt, and dreadful uncertainty.

But surely this was a state of things which could not last under such circumstances. It was a state of things too maddening to continue many minutes longer, for if anything more than another is calculated to drive the reason from its throne, it is really the suspense of fear.

And that was what Jane Hoffenden experienced now ; so, recommending herself to the protection of Heaven, she made another effort to move from the smaller apartment into the larger.

It was an effort—such an effort, as, before she made it, she could have scarcely thought it possible she could have made; but with the light trembling in her hand, she did ascend the step, and stood upon the threshold of her chamber. She held the light as high as she could, so that it should cast its rays in as diffused a manner as possible, and not bewilder her eyes.

Our readers may imagine the immense anxiety with which she cast her eyes around her, and after her alarm, they will likewise be able to comprehend how it was that the not seeing any one was no relief. That fact did not tend to appease her fears. It only taught her to think that some one was still there and hiding.

But she could not now retreat. She had commenced an onward movement, and she would persevere with it. Her object was to reach the fire-place, at each side of which hung a bell-pull.

After the first glance she had cast around the apartment, and seeing nobody, she gave up the idea of herself instituting any search, but thought that she might receive assistance to her aid possibly, if she reached the bell-pulls unobserved ; but with what agony was every step performed.

She knew not a moment when some rude hand might seize her, or when the knife or the pistol of a ruffian might be levelled at her life.

But, no, no—she is unmolested. No one disturbs her, and all is well. She is half way to the fire-place, and there is no stop put to her progress. A feeling of joy almost takes possession of her. Yes, she will soon now have help—she will alarm the household. Even at that time of night her ring will be answered. There is a hall-porter. He will hear it, and summon some of the servants to her assistance.

And now she has reached the fire-place. Yes! she treads upon that soft, yielding rug, that feels to the foot like a band of fresh fallen snow. Another step, and all will be well. She has placed her light upon the mantel-shelf, and then she turns to the bell-pulls.

Oh, horror! There was but wanting the discovery she now made to convince her of the reality of all her danger. The cords are cut far above her reach, and she is helpless!

She saw herself in the glass that was above the chimney ; and Hoffenden was not so appalled at his own ghastly appearance, in the mirror in his saloon below, when asked to look by Murdo, as was Jane at the terrific paleness of her own face, as she observed it now.

It was destitute of every particle of colour, and the very lips seemed bloodless. She was now suffering from the certainty that her forebodings of evil on that night were about to be fully and completely realised. Oh, horrible conviction ! What could she do—what was to become of her ?

It was well she had placed the candle upon the chimney-shelf, for her nerveless hands could not have held it, and she was compelled to lean upon the marble slab herself for support, or she must have fallen in the agony of that most terrific and bitter moment of misery.

An impression that her last hour was come crept over her. It was an impression she could not banish—a terrible idea that she stood, as it were, upon the grave's brink, and that she should never again look upon the sweet sunshine of Heaven, or even the eyes of her child—a sweeter sunshine to her. Oh! what would she not at that time have given but for the privilege of holding that young and beautiful being in her arms a moment, and of imprinting upon its little lips a mother's last kiss.

But she had no hope. Death was before her. She knew that some one was in the apartment. That suspense had passed away to be replaced by the more terrific question of—

"Where was the intruder hidden ?"

There were many places about the chamber in which more than one person could be easily and effectually hidden ; so that, when Jane set her imagination to work to answer her last question, it had a wide field to range in.

And after a time came the thought that she must summon courage enough to make a dash towards the drawer in which she knew Hoffenden kept his pistols, and with them defend herself against all aggression. But, then, that drawer was at the further end of the apartment, and how to get at it without interruption was the question.

But, after all, if the person hidden in the room was a robber, would he not be glad of an opportunity of escape? Perhaps he was as fearful now of her as she of him? What if she were to make an attempt to leave the place by the proper entrance, and so, leaving the door open, probably ensure her own safety by ensuring the escape of him who had given her so much alarm ?

The more she thought of this plan, the more feasible it looked ; and she, accordingly, summoned all her energies to her aid to carry it out. She left the light where it was, for it was in a position sufficiently to illuminate the whole room by its rays, and then, with a slow step, she moved towards the door.

No interruption—she reaches it in safety—but it is locked, and the key is gone!

Good God! what is she to think? Was all this like the conduct of a housebreaker? Why should he take the pains to lock himself in, so as to make his escape only the more difficult? It was dreadful now to be thrown back upon conjecture to know what were the intentions of her enemy.

There was a chair close to the door, into which Jane now sunk, for she found herself exhausted, and scarcely able to walk. She could see around the room tolerably well, and now she felt quite certain that a few moments must proclaim to her the real reason of all the strange precautions that had been taken to keep her within the verge of those two apartments. It surely was not Hoffenden himself playing her a trick. The idea crossed her mind, but there was too much hope in it to enable her to entertain it.

She heard a clock strike the chimes past some hour, and, when the sound had died away, it was succeeded by another. There was a rustling of one of the curtains of the bed, and a voice—the voice of a man—said, in low tones,—

"Jane Hoffenden, you have no cause for alarm. It is a friend, if you choose to make him so, who now, with all the wish to do so, addresses you!"

CHAPTER XVII.

THE DISCOMFITED VILLAIN.

As these words sounded on her ears, such a feeling of dread came over poor Jane, that the latter part of them was scarcely audible to her ; and then, as memory brought back to her the remembrance of the voice that uttered such words, the natural indignation that she felt made the warm blood rush to her heart, and from that again to her face and brow which it flushed with a roseate hue.

In another moment the curtain was thrown on one side, and, as she suspected, from the tones she had heard, Roderick Murdo stood before her.

"Yes! it was that villain who had had the unparalleled audacity to penetrate into her chamber, and to fancy, for one moment, that, by terror or by entreaty, he could induce her to encourage his criminal designs. He surely must, with all his tact and all his talent, have had but a poor capacity to judge of character.

But bad men, it will always be found, have a poor opinion of female virtue, until, by experience, they are convinced of the contrary.

To the reader the whole of the proceedings of Murdo will now be quite clear, as regards the events of that most dreadful night to Jane Hoffenden.

He had, when he had taken wine enough to produce the effect of banishing caution, concocted the idea of getting Hoffenden out of the way, under pretence of a visit to Crockton's gaming-house, and in that he had succeeded. Then, in the bustle of the departure of the guests, he had managed, instead of going down stairs, to go up; and, being tolerably, from the terms of great intimacy he was on with Hoffenden, well acquainted with the house, he had secreted himself in Jane's chamber, and there awaited her coming.

It was his locking the door after she had gone into the adjoining room that had at first produced in Jane's mind the feeling of alarm we have described, and his hiding himself in the ample drapery of the bed curtains occasioned the rustling sound that had, a second time, made her believe that some one was there.

It will be seen how he had, by cutting the bell-ropes, taken every possible precaution against surprise by an alarm being given, and now the bold-faced villain had the effrontery to face the piece of virtue and innocence he had so outraged. But what amount of audacity was too great for Roderick Murdo?

Jane did not scream, for there was a feeling of pride about her that forbade her to let him see or fancy that he terrified her; but she looked into his face with an expression of such indignation, loathing, and contempt, that, had he retained one spark of human feeling, would have shamed him.

But, because she did not, by her cries, immediately raise the house, he considered that his principal difficulty was over, and he spoke to her again, saying,—

"No doubt, Jane Hoffenden, it is a little surprise to you to find me here. But, knowing, as you do, the passion with which you long since inspired me, you can have no difficulty in ascribing my presence to its continued power over all my actions. I love you!"

Jane stepped forward a step, and then slowly turning, she mutely pointed to the door.

He knew what she meant. He showed that he did so by his reply, which, however, was not couched in quite such confident tones as he had at first spoken in. There was that in her aspect which terrified him a little, and made him have his doubts.

"I understand you," he said, "you would have me leave; but can you be so cruel, when you consider the danger and the difficulty I have gone through, to be able to tell you, that, notwithstanding all that has passed, I love you with an undiminished passion? Yes, I love you with a passion exceeding all that you can imagine."

Jane still pointed to the door.

"Nay, let me implore you to look with more favour on one who would willingly risk his life to be yours."

She saw that to preserve silence was in vain. She had hoped that she might have been spared the pain of uttering one word to him, who had thus desecrated what might be called the sanctity of that apartment; but now she found that she must speak, so she did so fairly and intelligibly.

The tone in which her words were uttered, was a strange and altered one. Had Murdo not looked upon her and saw her lips moving in unison with the sound, he would not have believed it possible that one, so quiet, so kind, and so musical as her tones usually, could throw such force into a few words.

"Leave this room," she said; "I have no words to tell you how I loathe and how I detest you. My husband cannot be so dead to all sense of honour, but he will avenge this insult. Roderick Murdo you are more abhorrent to me than the vilest thing that ever crawled upon the earth's surface!"

It was not so much the words themselves, although, Heaven knows, they were stinging enough, as the manner in which they were uttered, that made this speech tell with effect, even upon such a man as Murdo.

"You are mad," he said, as his countenance turned of a ghastly paleness with passion.

"I should be mad not to loathe what is loathsome. Leave the room, taking with you the detestation and contempt of one who will take care that you are punished for this most unparalleled audacity."

"You threaten."

"Yes, I threaten. I have never yet, in my whole life, threatened aught human. I do not look upon you as human; you are not of the category of God's creatures. You should be, and you shall be, crushed."

"D——n! do you think that I am the sort of man to be ridden over by a few words from an angry woman? I tell you, Jane, the principal dream of my life has been to hold you in my arms—to rain kisses upon your lips—to tell you how much I love you."

"Begone, I say, begone."

"No—no; you cannot mean what you say. Of course, I expected resistance. The conquest even of such charms as yours would be in my eyes valueless, if accomplished too easily."

"Begone!"

"Not yet, most charming of women; charming even in your anger. I swear to you, that he who is now suing to you, never sued to living woman before. But you have inspired me with a passion that knows no bounds. You must and shall be mine."

"The consequences of my alarming my household be upon your own head. If I do alarm them, I shall demand of them that they detain the midnight thief, whom I discovered in my chamber."

"Thief!"

"Yes; it is as a thief you shall be prosecuted, and if you think it will serve you to allege that you came here with a worse purpose, by far, than to possess yourself of my jewels, you can do so; I give you another minute for reflection. My husband's indignation shall be properly aroused, and you may be handed over to the police beforehand, or not, as best suits you."

This was a matter-of-fact way of putting the question, which certainly Murdo neither expected, nor liked, and for some moments he looked amazed at the self-possession of one to whom he had given no credit for such a quality, and the boldness of one whom he expected to overwhelm with terrors.

All the specious arguments that he had ready for the occasion, he felt convinced would be worse than useless, and already that ruffian might be considered as thoroughly discomfited.

"Leave at once, I command you," exclaimed Jane, as she found the advantage she had gained over him, and that he was cowed, and astonished at her boldness.

"No," he cried, as if, by a sudden effort, shaking off the kind of lethargy that the surprise he experienced from Jane's conduct had brought upon his faculties. "No; your conduct and bearing to-night have but increased my love for you. You show yourself all that I can admire, and I will not leave."

"Then I call help!"

"Hold. Beware what you do. Bethink you of the tale that will be told. A man, a friend of the family, in Mrs. Hoffenden's chambers, at three o'clock in the morning, when it is known that she retired to rest before two. What will the world say? Why, you will be condemned by universal opinion, and all I need say is, that we had a quarrel, which being a little too loud, reached the ears of the servants, and so for the first time the intrigue was found out."

Jane shuddered, but she did not shudder so much at what he said, as at the thought that there should be such a villain as he was in the world. It shook all her confidence in human nature, and almost her confidence in Heaven itself, that it should create such demons in human shape.

"You perceive," he continued; "you perceive that you will get no credit for your affected virtue. You will incur a far worse penalty, than as if you were absolutely guilty. Oh! I see you will be more reasonable; and, at your most particular request, on giving me room to hope along with the request, I will leave you now."

"God of Heaven!" said Jane, "can this be possible? Roderick Murdo, I am merciful even to you. Oh, say that you are not the demoniac being you would make yourself out to be. Tell me that you are not that being; and go home and pray to heaven to forgive you."

"I never pray."

"But pray now; heaven's mercy is boundless."

"Pshaw! I did not come here to be preached to. You are mine, Jane. I tell you that your husband will not interfere to save you from my arms."

"Will not ?"

"Dare not, if you like it better. Stop! You are about to raise a cry for help. Beware how you do so, for I can hang Harry Hoffenden. Yes, hang him—bring him to the scaffold—not figuratively, but actually, I can hang him. If I choose to open my lips, he has no chance of escape. You may have wondered at my strange influence over him, while he hates me, for I know he hates me. And now, I tell you why it is. It is because I hold the secret in my hands that can hang him."

Jane sunk on to the chair, from which she had risen, and turned as pale as death itself. The only movement she made was a slight one with her hands; and the only word she uttered, was the name of God.

"You perceive," he added, "that I have calculated well; and again and again I tell you that Hoffenden dare not say an angry word to me, any more than he dare hold a knife to his own throat."

Jane could not speak. This dreadful piece of intelligence did indeed account for much; and although it came from the lips of such a man as Murdo, yet, somehow or another, as it was the truth, it seemed to carry a weight with it, which is an integral portion of truthfulness, and which no falsehood, however specious, could possibly mar.

The pause which now ensued, and which lasted several minutes, was a dreadful one. It was a pause that, in its concentrated agony, added years to the life of the unhappy Jane.

Oh, how she wished that she were dead!

CHAPTER XVIII.

THE CONTEST, AND DEFEAT OF MURDO.

MURDO now thought indeed that he had got the better of the argument. He certainly had not intended to have recourse to such an argument as that which now he had used; but it was a knowledge that he had it in his power that gave him boldness enough to conceive and to go through with such an adventure.

Had he not been able to say to Hoffenden, "I defy you; I can bring you, if I please, to the gallows," doubtless he would not have ventured into the chamber of his wife; but he knew he could say so much, and he knew the dread that Hoffenden had of such a result, and that emboldened him.

But if he thought that he was a bit nearer his purpose because Jane was horrified at what he had told her, he was much mistaken. Horrified she was at the thought that such a man as Murdo should have such a power over her husband, bad as that husband had behaved to her; but she was not at all disposed to save him from such a doom at the sacrifice of virtue.

No; she felt that she had much to grieve for—much criminality to mourn over in others; but she was not willing to add to that by any action of her own. She might mourn, but she did not see that she was called upon to be self accusatory.

The silence was broken by Murdo, who said,—

"You now understand what you need certainly not have been troubled with; but you forced it from me. I tell you that your husband has committed a crime which, if known, will bring him to the scaffold; and I can say no more than that in consequence, as I am the only person who can denouce him, the vengeance you have threatened me with I can afford to laugh at."

He paused again; but Jane could not answer him—she had not power to do so.

"You perceive," he added, "that I have all the power I said I had, and that by yielding to my affection for you, you will not only preserve your husband's life, but your own fortune; for the law would take all the property of a convicted felon. Perhaps you know that."

"God help him !"

"Ah, well, that's all very well in its way. But you see the propriety of making no disturbance with me, because of the consequence. You have sound, good sense enough to perceive all that, I am quite sure."

"Alas—alas! and has it come to this ?"

"Yes, it has. You are getting, I perceive, as reasonable again now. Oh, I knew we

should understand each other well enough in the long run. It will be all right, of course. Come—come, Jane Hoffenden; you have altered your mind, and don't feel that such a vast amount of indignation is at all called for, or indeed correct, under the rather peculiar circumstances of the case."

Truly, Mr. Roderick Murdo seemed to think that he had the game in h's own hands, and was getting everything his own way, in a transaction so unexampled for its infamous character. He still knew little, or, we might almost say, nothing of the real character of Jane Hoffenden.

Could she have passed out of the door, it is probable she would have done so at once ; but that was locked, so that she could not do so ; and to the surprise, mingled with some amount of consternation of Murdo, she rose, and in a vo:ce which he felt quite certain must reach some friendly ears, cried,—

"Help !—help !—help !"

"Curses on you !" he shouted. " Are you mad ?"

"Help !—help !"

The difficulty of stopping any one who chooses to raise such a cry, under any circumstances, was quite understood by Roderick Murdo, and he felt quite certain that his capture by the servants of the house would be inevitable, un'ess, by extraordinary vigilance, he should succeed in escaping before, at that hour of the night, they could be aroused from their beds. Had it been day-time, he would have had not the slightest chance.

But here another difficulty, of his own making, presented itself to him.   He had locked the door, and put the key in his pocket; but, in the confusion, he had no recollection which pocket he had put it in, so that he commenced one of those hurried searches which so frequently defeat their own object.

And now that Jane had once begun to call for assistance, she was not likely to leave off until she had procured it, or been by force stopped in so calling.   The latter was, when he could not find the key, what the villain, Roderick Murdo, sought to accomplish.

He rushed upon her, and tried to grapple her by the throat; but she eluded his grasp, and got past him towards the other part of the room.   Another quick movement took her to the drawer where her husband kept his arms, and when he again rushed towards her, the cold, steel barrel of a pistol touched his face.

Such men as Murdo are necessarily cowards, for courage is a quality of mind which is of antagonistic character to vice; and so he flung himself back, till he came to the wall, crying, as he did so, in a voice that proclaimed his alarm,—

"No—no!   Don't fire!—Don't fire!"

"And why should I spare such a man as you are?" said Jane, as she kept the pistol levelled at his head.   "You have already attempted an outrage that empowers me to show you no pity, and you have told me that you possess a dangerous secret, and that you alone possess it.   Why should not I, then, at once, by a touch of my finger, deprive you of the power of being further noxious—villain that you are?"

He crouched down before her like a lashed hound, as, with a whining, suppliant voice, he said,—

"Spare me!   Oh, spare me!   You—you would not surely have even my blood upon your hands.   Spare me, Jane Hoffenden! and I swear to you this scene shall not be re-peated!"

"Truly it shall not," said Jane.   "It seems to me that it must be the will of heaven that I should rid the world of such a monster as you are.   Why should I hesitate?"

"Oh! mercy—mercy!"

"Ask it of heaven, not of me.   You shall die!"

"Oh, no—no!   I will say anything—promise anything.   Only let me go, and never again will I come into this house where I know my presence is distasteful to you.   I im-plore you to show mercy to me.   You see how abject I am!   Spare but my life, and you shall never look upon my face again.   Oh! you cannot kill me till I have had some time to repent me of all my crimes!   You do not know—you cannot know what a life mine has been.   Oh! spare my life—my mere life—that is all I ask of you!"

At this moment there came a loud knocking at the chamber door, and Jane felt that help was at hand.   Of course, she never intended to become the executioner of Murdo, much as she felt he richly deserved such a fate; but she had succeeded in keeping him effectually in check until her cries had produced the effect she wished, and assistance had come to her at last in the shape of the aroused servants.

"Burst the door open!" she cried.

Some of the men servants of the establishment, who had been hastily roused from their beds, and had put on some portions only of their apparel, heard her voice, and they did not wait twice for such a command; but, judging that the case was urgent, two of them flung themselves against the door with a force that dashed the lock from its fastenings in a moment, and then not a little surprised were they at the scene which presented itself to them.

There was Murdo—whom they all knew well enough to detest for his arrogance and overbearing conduct, against which they knew they could get no redress from their master—crouched down in a corner, and looking the very picture of abject fear, while Mrs. Hoffenden stood by the drawers from which she had taken the pistol, looking very pale, but very determined, and presenting the weapon with a steady aim at the ruffian.

"Oh, give it him, me'm, please," said a footboy, who was of the party—"oh, do, me'm!"

Jane felt that now she was safe, and that there was no further occasion to hold a weapon presented which she did not intend to make use of.   She laid the pistol on the drawers, as she said,—

"You will give this man to the watch!"

"Yes, madam," said a burly footman of six feet high, pouncing upon Murdo, and pretending to fall over him, just to have an opportunity of knocking his head against the wall—"yes, madam; certainly, with great pleasure. Oh, you rascal!"

"Is he a resisting, John?" said another, as he laid hold of Murdo by the throat, and nearly throttled him.

"You will," added Jane, "give him to the watch. I found him here, and can only suppose his object was the robbery of my jewels. Mr. Hoffenden is not at home, but will see to the case in the morning."

"Beware!" said Murdo.

"Take him away; and be sure you do not let him escape among you."

"Trust us for that, madam," said one. "Oh, you are a nice rascal, ain't you, to go for to come for to get into missus's bedroom?"

"Beware!" again said Murdo. "Remember the secret!"

"Take him away."

The servants took Murdo out of the room and closed the door. Jane clasped her hands, burst into tears, and flung herself upon the bed.

"Come along, will you, you vagabond?" said the big footman. "I always thought what you'd turn out to be. Oh, you won't! Do you, William, give him a kick up behind."

"With all the blessed pleasure in life," said William, as he followed Murdo down the stairs, saluting him with a hearty kick every now and then. "Come, come, old fellow, we don't want any resistance."

"I am not resisting," said Murdo. "Curses on you all! I will have your lives for this!"

"Give it him again, William."

"Certainly. Here you goes."

In this sort of way they got the scoundrel down to the hall; and as by this time the whole of the men servants were assembled, Murdo found himself tolerably well hemmed in when he was there. Suddenly, however, before anybody could be aware of what he was about to do, he got a knife from his pocket, and made a desperate effort to inflict some injury upon his captors.

Fortunately he missed his first blow, which narrowly passed John's whiskers, and before he could make another, his hand was caught, and the knife was wrested from him; and then he found that he had not at all bettered his condition by such a savage attempt at maiming some of his captors, who, after all, were only doing a duty by seizing and detaining him under the circumstances.

That he had previously made himself so unpopular, that that seizure and detention was performed in the roughest manner possible, was altogether his own fault.

CHAPTER XVIII.

THE TROUBLES OF MURDO INCREASE.—HOFFENDEN'S RETURN.

IF any scruple had existed before in the minds of Hoffenden's servants, as to the amount of punishment they would inflict upon Roderick Murdo, the attempt he had made with the knife completely banished it.

They now considered, and with perfect justice too, that they had a good personal quarrel with him, and as they thought such quarrel would be altogether merged in his other offences, and that they should get no satisfaction at all for it unless they took it themselves, they naturally came to a conclusion that to take it now was the very best course.

The butler, who on more than one occasion had come into collision with Murdo, was appealed to, and after hearing all the facts, he said, sententiously,—

"As my lady has found out that the fellow is a thief, of course we must give him to the watchman; and as for ourselves, why, let me see—mind, I don't advise any of you to do so unless you like, but while you hold him tight by the collar, John, I shall kick him."

"Bravo! bravo!"

Murdo made all the resistance he could, but his opponents were too strong for him, and kicked he was by the butler, and then, as might fairly enough be expected, everybody else followed his example, while Murdo had the satisfaction of knowing that he had been well kicked by all Hoffenden's servants.

"Let us have a go," said the page.

"Oh! to be sure," said John; "kick away, Joe. Give it him."

"Take that," said Joe, who had to make an effort to reach. "Take that. You punched my head once, you know, cos I didn't hear you ask for some wine all of a minute. How do you like it? Let's give him another. My eye, was there ever such a jolly lark? Oh, lor, I shall die o' laughing, I shall! Oh, my eye! Look, how blue he does look."

"Now, gentlemen," said the butler, "I dare say Mr. Murdo is in no great hurry to get into the hands of the watchman?"

"Let me go, and be d—d to you all," said Murdo. "I'll cut every one of your throats some day."

"You hear the gentleman. He don't want the watchman just yet; but as he seems rather worse, I think we ought to try and do something for him. Now, mind you, I don't advise anything   All I know is, that exactly opposite this door there is a pump. Now, don't mistake me, I don't say pump upon him within an inch of his life. I don't say it would serve him right."

"So it would," said John, "and break no bones—so pull him along."

"Good God! are you all out of your senses?" cried the alarmed Murdo. "I will pay you well to let me go; and you may depend that Mr. Hoffenden, upon a complaint of mine, would discharge every one of you."

"Oh, dear, no," said the butler, "that's too good. Mr. Hoffenden didn't know you made your way into his wife's bed-room. I suppose Mr. Hoffenden is a human being, and if he finds fault with us pumping on you for that, why, he's no man, and that's all I can say. But mind, I advise nothing."

"Come on," said John; "what's the use of making any more fuss about it? Come on, will you? Kick him up a little behind, William; you can't think how that makes him go."

Despite his protestations, threats, promises, and entreaties, he was dragged out to the pump, which was, as the butler had said, just outside the door by the curb-stone, and, to the astonishment of a chance passenger, John held him under, and kept turning him round and round, like a piece of meat roasting, while the pump-handle was most vigorously plied by the others, until Murdo was completely drenched.

When he tried to say anything John held his mouth under the torrent, and that effectually stopped him; and all the while the butler stood at the door rubbing his hands, and saying,—

"Dear me, what can they be doing? God bless my soul, what's it about?"

"Why, don't you see," said the chance passenger, "don't you see that they are pumping upon a man dreadfully?"

"Pumping!" said the butler, as he looked up and down, and right and left—anywhere but at the pump; "pumping! God bless me, I can't say I am aware of that."

"None so blind as those who won't see," said the passenger. "However, it's no business of mine, so I'll be off."

"A capital joke, upon my life," laughed the butler; "and, by all that's good, here comes a watchman. Oh, this is glorious above a bit."

As he spoke one of those poor old miserable watchmen, who used facetiously to be called guardians of the night, made his appearance round a corner of the square, and the light of his lantern, and his white coat, made him visible for a considerable distance off; so that thieves and evil-doers had no trouble whatever in getting out of the way of such guardians, whose only use really seemed to be to awaken people in the middle of the night by bawling the hour, and appending to that piece of information a remark regarding the aspect of the night.

When he got near enough to the pump to be aware that something unusual was there going on, he quickened his pace from a half mile an hour to a whole one, and reached the place.

"Hilloa! hilloa! Come, come, now," cried the Charley; "what's all this about? Move on? Don't break the king's peace, or I shall have to take you all into custody."

John laughed as he said,—

"You had better begin with the pump, Charles, for you won't be able to hold tight of the fellow we have got for you."

The watchman construed this into a dreadful threat, and immediately began springing his rattle furiously, and it was quite curious to note the effect produced by that nocturnal alarm.

In about a minute an answering rattle was heard, and then another, and then another, like a number of clocks striking the hour, and only slightly varying in their notions of the duration of time.

But this springing of the rattle certainly produced an effect, for in the course of about five minutes there came hobbling towards the spot a number of the white-coated guardians, until an overwhelming force was established, so that it was considered to be quite prudent to give up Mr. Roderick Murdo.

"Come along," said the original guardian, who, by virtue of being first on the spot, considered the charge to be his; "come along, and don't resist authority, cos, you know, if you does, we shall have to knock you on the head."

Murdo knew very well that this was no idle threat, for the old watchmen, feeling their own inability to run after a prisoner, invariably adopted the plan of stunning him if they suspected that he meditated an escape; so that when they did get a man to the watch-house, the charge of resisting the authorities was generally complicated with the original one for which he was apprehended.

"What's the charge?" said the watchman. "What's he done? Has he been trying to steal the pump?"

"No," said the butler; "he has only taken possession of a lot of the water, that's all. But you can take him in charge for being found on the premises with a felonious intent. Mrs. Hoffenden suspects him of a wish to steal her jewels, so off with him, and Mrs. Hoffenden will no doubt appear against him in the morning."

"All's right," said the watchman, as he poked Murdo in the back with the end of his cudgel. "Now, will you go on, and not give us all this trouble? Will you, I say, go on, old fellow?"

Murdo seemed to be upon the point of saying something, but, after the pause of a moment, to give it up. Perhaps, if the servants of that mansion had known him, as well as we know him, they would have thought it possible enough that something odd might eventually accrue from his feelings of revenge against them.

But they did not know sufficient of him to dread him, as he might well have been dreaded; and the boisterous glee they all felt at being enabled to have such a signal revenge upon a man whom they detested, quite delighted them.

"I say," remarked the watchman, into whose rather thick head an idea seemed to have wedged itself—"I say, this sort of thing won't do. Somebody must come to the watch-house and charge him, you know?"

"Oh, bother," said the butler; "nonsense; you don't expect a lady to get up out of bed for the purpose of going to a watchhouse, do you? Be off with you. Here's half a crown to drink among you, and you can say, of course, that Mrs. Hoffenden will come and prosecute in the morning."

"Oh, that alters the matter altogether," said the watchman, as he dropped the half crown into a capacious pocket; "I see it's all right. You need not trouble the lady at all about the matter, I'm sure. Come along, will you? Oh, it's easy to see what vagabond you are."

With this flattering opinion on his personal appearance, Murdo was pushed towards the watchhouse, but he learnt some wisdom from what he had seen taking place around him, and when he had got about two streets off, and his escort was reduced to three persons, he said,—

"It's all nonsense about the charge of robbery. The fact is, I went to the house on a love adventure, and they know it quite well, and only want to give me a night's lodging for it. Now, I have just five guineas about me, which you can divide among you, while I walk away down the next turning."

"You don't say so?" cried one of the watchmen; "I say, Wilkins, what a fine night!"

"Very. How the stars shine," said Wilkins, looking up.

"Uncommon," said the other, as he held out his hand, into which Murdo put the money.

" Dear me," said the third, " there's a light in that attic window opposite. I wonder if a blessed flue is on fire now, there ?"

And so two of them looked up at the sky, and the third at the attic window, while Murdo walked quietly away. When he was gone, the three guardians of the night laid their fingers on the tip of their respective noses and laughed.

" I'm afeard he's gone," said one of them. " He's a strange chap, or he would not have got away from us quite so easy, I'll be bound, would he ?"

" I should think not. But it's no use going after him, is it ?"

" Oh, dear, no. Come along. We shall find the Herring and Pickle Tub open, I shouldn't wonder, and there we can have a drop of comfort."

The three guardians extinguished their lanthorns, and leaving their three separate beats to look after themselves, they went to a public-house, where they knew that good entertainment was to be had at any time, and which they rightly enough, so far as the comfort of the thing went, considered very superior to stalking about in the cold, grey morning light, or even slumbering in a watch-box.

And we are rather inclined to be of opinion that, as regards the safety of the neighbourhood, that was much in the same state whether the watchmen were perambulating the streets, or indulging themselves with potations deep and strong in the Herring and Pickle Tub.

But we will now take a glance at the proceedings of Hoffenden at the new gaming saloon which was opened by the insolent and ignorant Crockton in St. James's-street, and to which he had repaired in the expectation of meeting with his companion Murdo at the hour they had agreed upon between them. Little did he, Hoffenden, suspect how Murdo was employed while he waited in vain for him. We will hope that all sense of ordinary manly feeling has not deserted even the gambler.

CHAPTER XIX.

THE GAMING-HOUSE.—AN INCIDENT.

It was in anything but an enviable state of mind that Hoffenden took his way from his own splendid home to the gaming-house in St. James's-street. On that evening he had suffered more than usual from the annoying reflections so necessarily contingent upon his condition, and he had but little even in the future to console him.

That one fearful secret of his past life, which he knew was in the possession of men who kept it not from any affection or pity for him, but precisely for what they could get, constantly harassed him. He felt quite confident that the day would come when he should be made a victim of by one or the other of them.

And what a sad state of mind was that to be in! To be for ever, as it were, standing upon the verge of a precipice, knowing that two grinning fiends, with hands uplifted, were ready to push him at once into the deep abyss below, was the nearest similitude to it that he could picture to himself.

But what could he do? For him there was no escape. He had done a deed the remembrance of which was horror—the consequence of which was disgrace, execration, and death. He was glad when he did reach the gaming-house—that abode of infamy in gorgeous colours, as it was; for, at all events, what he saw there had a tendency to withdraw his thoughts from more painful themes. The gilding, the rich hangings, the profusion of lights, and the whole character of the internal decorations of the place, made it more resemble a palace than anything else.

There were, too, crowds of well-dressed persons there—some as victims brought to be sacrificed on the altar of Mammon, and some as the victimisers, who might be likened to the high priests of so ungodly a temple. Is it not a surprise and a reproach that in a country like this there should exist such establishments, avowedly for the purpose of encouraging and perpetuating a vice which has made more homes desolate than war, or even religion, has succeeded in doing.

There is no vice whatever, be its character what it may, that may not be almost the companion, and invariably the follower, of gambling. All the most terrific and worst passions of human nature are aroused—cupidity, hatred, malice, envy—all are the gambler's companions; and many a deed of blood has resulted from that anger which the loser seems to think that he is justified in feeling towards the winner.

The cold-blooded speculators upon the products of such evil passions in humanity should become the scorn and the execration of society. The common hangman is, in comparison, a gentleman of repute and respectability; and yet he is shunned, and looked askance upon, while a man who sacrifices thousands by speculating upon that frightful love of games of chance which characterises all human nature, is looked upon, if he be successful, as quite a worthy gentleman.

But such is ever the case as regards the opinions of the world. It is success that is everything, not the means by which such success has been crowned. Show the world that gold has been the result of any course of action, and no matter how it has been obtained; then will be all the lip service, and all the cringing deference paid to it, as if it had resulted from the best of operations in the cause of humanity.

Hoffenden found that among the motley throng at the gaming-house, there were many persons, who were well known to him, and who were not a little pleased to welcome again to such a place, one who they knew, now, was worth the plucking again.

He was shaken by the hand familiarly by lords and honourables, who, if they had not been aware, as they were, that he had acquired money, would have seen him

"Deeper than plummet ever sounded,"

before they would have done him what they, perhaps, considered so much honour.

These scoundrels — strange as it may appear to any one having a veneration for aristocracy; not that we think there are any such among our readers—were extremely anxious that Hoffenden should play; but he excused himself, on the ground, that he was waiting for a friend.

But, for all that, they could see, by the eager eyes he bent upon the game, that the old spirit of gambling was reviving in him; and with mutual nods and winks the old hands at the game intimated to each other, that here was a rich pigeon come to be duly plucked.

But the hour came for bringing Murdo, according to promise, and it brought him not. We are well aware how very differently he was occupied. Now, certainly, one of the vices of that man was not want of punctuality; and, therefore, Hoffenden might well be surprised, when half an hour over the time named for this meeting had passed away, and Murdo did not make his appearance.

It was so very unusual a thing, that he felt certain something very serious must be the cause; but still he knew not what better to do than to stay where he was, for he was perfectly well aware that before he could reach his own home, even if he started at once, that would be cleared of all visitors; and, therefore, there was no chance of finding Murdo there; and if he, Hoffenden, left the gaming-house, he might miss him altogether.

The saloons now began to fill with company, and the play on that first night was prodigious, giving the proprietor of that den of iniquity a most encouraging proof that he had not made a miscalculation in laying out so large a sum to make vice assume a glittering aspect.

There were many too, who, like Hoffenden, came ostensibly only to look upon the proceedings who stayed to play, and did more on that one night to make their future lives miserable, than they could otherwise have done in twelve months. Among these, Hoffenden, himself, was shortly to be enrolled; although he certainly was wretched enough, without any new stimulus to such a feeling.

At length, however, wearied out by waiting for Murdo, he approached one of the tables, and staked a small sum, which he won. Of course he won the small stake; gamblers always do, that is the bait by which cruel fortune hooks the fools.

This amount, however, was so small, as to be a matter to him of perfect indifference, whether he won or lost it; and, although he continued his play, his whole attention was absorbed by the proceedings of another player, who was sitting nearly opposite to him.

This was a young man, who, by his fresh complexion and general aspect, seemed not long to have been a resident, or even a visitor of the metropolis; but as he played his look of health and vigour deserted him, and he became pale, wretched, and nervous.

His losses, whatever they were, evidently had, to him, reached a serious amount. God only knows what trust he might be betraying, or upon whose head he might be heaping misery by the wild recklessness of that one sad evening; but, certain it is, that as he played on he seemed to be nearly maddened by the chances of the game, as they went all against him.

His voice sounded strange and discordant, as he named his stakes; and, at length, with a laugh, that sounded more horrible than any shriek could have done, he threw his last portion of money upon the table, and waited with the most horrible anxiety the result of the throw.

What a strange contrast was the manner and bearing of this young man, to that of the imperturbable official, against whom he played, for he staked his money with the bank, as it is called. The moment's suspense was dreadful.

"Lost again," said the official, as, with a small wooden rake, he swept the stakes into the coffers of the bank. "You are rather unlucky to-night, sir. Try again; luck is sure to turn, if the game be pursued only long enough. To stop is the evil."

CHAPTER XX.

THE DEAD BODY AND THE WELL STAIRCASE.

THERE was a feverishness in the young man's manner, which he, in vain, endeavoured to conceal, but without success; he could not do it, and he paused a moment or two, unable to answer the words of the official who had spoken. He rose, and going to one of the side tables, poured out a large glass of wine, which he swallowed, and then again filled and swallowed. This he did three or four times, with the haste of one who does an act which he considers necessary, but not one which he takes any pleasure in.

During this pause, the official was coolly conversing with some frequenters of the room, of whom there were many, and persons whom he had seen before at other places; and the young man seemed to have recovered some degree of nerve, and he came back to his chair.

"Stakes?" said the official, looking at him.

"Yes," replied the young man, who had succeeded in attracting so much of Hoffenden's attention; and he at the same time named his stakes, and appeared to await the decision of the chance with more equanimity than he had before done; but this was mere appearance—a quietness forced—a terrible calm, beneath which was raging a storm of emotions which tore his breast.

The game was gone through in a short time, but the period it took might have been called an age by he who was thus watching with suppressed frenzy, a delirium, a madness; and yet he scarce shewed it to an ordinary observer.

And yet one who had been used to an observance of human nature in circumstances of difficulty—in cases where each passion was played off against another, would have observed that there was far more than met the eye, and that an internal volcano of passion existed, awaiting but for a time to break through some new barriers with more than usual terrific violence.

"Lost! lost!" he ejaculated, as the result manifested itself.

"Why, yes, sir, as you observed, lost again. Extraordinary! but still not so greatly so as you might imagine. I recollect once a gentleman who played on straight for fourteen hours, and had not won one stake the whole time; but then luck shifted like the wind, and the bank was broken in less than three hours more."

"Wonderful!" said a person standing by.

"Ay, he played for seventeen hours, and walked away with one hundred and seventy-five thousand pounds in his possession—a man of large fortune, then."

"It does not often happen, I suppose?" said the young man, bitterly, as he watched the official draw towards him the gold he had just lost.

"There are few who deserve it, sir. Where is there the man who could sit down and play for fourteen hours right to an end, besides three more hours to win? He deserved it, sir—he was, indeed, an enthusiast whom nothing could tire."

"Stakes," said the young man, as he again produced from his pocket the glittering dross, for whose sake he was literally undergoing a martyrdom.

The official again staked a similar sum to that produced by his antagonist, and they

then proceeded to settle the point as to whose it was to be. The player looked with a swollen eye and compressed lip upon the game that was going on.

Hoffenden looked on, and could not but feel interested in the game that was played. He almost felt the situation of the stranger as that of his own, and felt slightly nervous at each movement that was made, and strained his own eyes to watch the progress of the game.

Nor was he the only observer of what was going on; for although the *coup d'œil* was splendid, and a number of tables were erected in various parts of the place, yet there were so many present that there were groups of gentlemen conversing together, while others were walking about the rooms. Rich wines were to be had everywhere.

Altogether it was a beautiful place; but the object was one that was subversive of all that tends to human happiness. What could be done at such a place? To walk about and enjoy the glitter and the well-dressed throng would not be possible, unless you mixed occasionally with the players; and to do that would be but seeking a temptation that could not be resisted by any human ingenuity or strength of purpose whatever.

Men do not go to these places for such purposes. They go with the intention, and are expected to take their places at the gaming-table some time or other, and they would not dream of frequenting the rooms without doing so.

It was a fine sight, and those who went there for the first time, and never entered such a place before, without knowing the devilish character of the amusements, would have believed that such a place was the very elysium of fashion and amusement.

But Hoffenden's attention was again called to the table at which the young man had been playing. He had risen for a moment, and, going to a side table, poured out a large goblet of wine, drank it off without a moment's pause, and then returned to the table under an assumed appearance of calmness.

"Stakes!" he exclaimed, and naming the sum he drew forth from his purse, which he crushed up in his hand in a manner which showed he had entirely emptied it. Without waiting a moment, he named the stakes, as he placed them on the table with a desperation that could not fail of being noticed by Hoffenden.

However, the official took notice of nothing, save the stakes, which he immediately covered with the utmost coolness, and then proceeded with the chance, which it was not long in deciding who was the winner.

"Lost again, sir. Try again; your luck has deserted you—you deserve to have it back. Win the next, perhaps, though you've lost this."

"Ruined—utterly ruined!" he muttered, and going up to a wine table he drank glass after glass furiously, and then wandered about, heeding nobody, until he came to a door, which he opened, and rushed out.

"I will follow him," muttered Hoffenden; "there is more to come of this affair yet. I will see it out; he is mad from losses."

As he muttered these words, he walked to the door which he had seen him pass out of, and passed through himself; but, when he got through, he found that it was not the way out of the house, but led somewhere else.

"Well, here I am, and I may as well go on until I overtake him. I can hear him on ahead; he's going I don't know where, and I am not sure that he does."

However, he went on. It was very dark, there being no light; or, at least, he had been in such a scene of glitter and splendour, that the subdued light and almost darkness that was here, appeared like a total absence of all light to him.

The passage he had entered led to a staircase, which led upwards. There was no light here at all, but he thought he could hear there were footsteps above, which he believed to be the same he was following, and he accordingly followed on.

There was at the top a window, which looked out upon the backs of the houses all around, and some light came in here—very little, indeed; for the night was gloomy, and though the moon was up, yet the masses of clouds were so heavy that but little of her light came down, save a sort of diffused light, scarcely enough to come in at the window, though enough to enable him to see about over the houses around.

"Well, this, I suppose, is the private part of the house," Hoffenden thought; "but it is a very extensive place. I shall never get back as long as I live without some discovery; but I can go on till something happens. Where this fellow can have got to I don't know. Here's a room; I wonder if he's gone in here."

He listened at the door, to ascertain if it were safe to enter, and that nobody was there before him.

"Empty, I think. I'll venture."

He pushed the door open, and entered a splendid apartment—a kind of drawing, or reception room. The furniture was costly; at least, as much of it as he could see of it by the dim, uncertain light afforded by the clouds rather than the moon, for they appeared the means of diffusing the little light they permitted to pass through them.

The hangings were soft and thick—silky; the carpet like piles of velvet; the place was hung with glasses, girandoles, and chandeliers.

"Well, if this is not a fairy land," he muttered, "it is difficult to tell what is. I thought that they had exhausted all their wealth and taste below, but it appears that those rooms, splendid as they are, are by no means the only specimen."

As he was examining the place, he heard a loud laugh fall upon his ears, that caused him to start; but then he heard it again. It came from the other end of the room. Upon looking towards that spot, he saw another door, which was only partially open, where he heard the rattling of dice, and he made towards the door.

This he approached cautiously, though the carpet was thick, and gave out no sound. He could peep through the opening, which was several inches wide, and saw two persons sitting down to a table, playing at hazard. He watched them for a moment or two.

"Ha! ha! seven's the main," said one of them, as he turned the dice-box upon the table; "try your hand, and see if you can beat it."

The other seized the dice-box, and, with unsteady hand, rattled them, and turned them over, and, upon looking at them, exclaimed,—

"Five only, by G—d!"

"Lost again! But no matter; you can have your revenge. When shall it be?"

"I have not yet done," replied the other; "one more stake, and, win or lose, I shall leave the house. I have an appointment."

"Shall I throw, or will you?"

"I will take my turn first this time," he said, as he threw the dice, after rattling them, on the table, but he did not seem satisfied with the result, as he uttered an imprecation, and threw the box down, while the other took the box up with the utmost coolness, and, rattling the dice, threw them.

"Won."

"You have!—damnation! Curse the dice!"

As the person spoke, he arose hastily from the table at which he had been sitting, and rushed out of the room rather precipitately, giving Hoffenden no time to retreat; but the unfortunate gamester was by no means in a state of mind to notice him, but passed on, leaving him behind him; and he, Hoffenden, immediately turned to the room, where one only now was sitting at the table which the other had but just left.

"Ha! ha!" he laughed, softly. "He's cleaned out. I am the richer, and he the poorer. What matters! Money changes hands often in one man's life. 'Tis like the breath of the body—we receive it but to expel it again."

Hoffenden viewed him for a moment, and there was a demoniac glee spread over his face, as he put in his purse the money he had won, which consisted in part of gold and in notes; and, when he had done, he murmured,—

"And now for some other pigeon. He's off to his father for more. I know him, though he knows not me; but I will now to the general rooms."

So saying, he arose, and Hoffenden immediately hurried out of the room. He saw the other, who had preceded him but a moment, go down the stairs, when he immediately got upstairs, and then came to a room door. But he paused, until he heard the gamester coming out, and take another route, and was soon out of hearing.

Finding there was no sound issuing from the apartment, he tried the door, and entered it. It was unoccupied. There was nobody there, and he paused a moment or two, to listen. He heard no sound, and he was about to shut the door, when the report of a pistol came upon his ears with appalling distinctness, then a fall, and a groan!

There was no motion in Hoffenden for near a minute; he was petrified, though he had expected some event that would cause a sensation; but he listened attentively for more than a minute for some other sound, but none came.

He had heard too distinctly to make any mistake as to the direction in which the sound came from, and he determined he would make his way to the spot, and ascertain if the unfortunate man was yet living.

"Thus ends the drama," muttered Hoffenden, as he felt his way along the gallery in which he found himself. "It is senseless to commit such an act; but, then, he considered it necessary, and hence he might have passed years of misery; but now he is dead, and cannot more be the subject of painful thoughts and acts. He might have led a life of wretchedness and misery, and though the world would condemn him in public, yet few will, unless they have a fear upon them of death, condemn him seriously in private."

With that he entered into the next passage, and walked on until he came to a door, which opened as he laid his hand upon the lock.

The door opened, and he looked in, but was all dark, or nearly so; and he walked in to ascertain if there was anything in the place that would lead to a discovery of the whereabouts of the miserable man.

He had not gone three or four steps into the room, when he fell over something, and found he had stumbled over the body of the unfortunate man, upon whose face he placed his hand. He was not yet cold—he was warm, and there seemed to be a kind of muscular motion about it which could hardly be called life, and yet was not far from it.

He had placed his hand in the blood—in the warm ensanguined stream in which he lay on the floor.

"Good Heaven!" he muttered; "how horrible!"

He had scarce uttered these words, when he heard the sounds of some one approaching; he paused to listen; they were coming that way, no doubt, with the same object as himself, but he did not wish to be found with the body, for who was to say by whom the trigger had been pulled. It might give rise to awkward mistakes, especially as he had no business there, and that might be hard to explain.

At all events, one thing with the other would offer many an uncomfortable surmise, which would be hard to be met by any one whom it was convenient to accuse.

However, he determined to leave the place at once, but was deterred from doing so by the sudden flash of light that came from the candles of those who were upon the same errand as himself—that of seeking the unfortunate suicide.

"I cannot escape that way," he muttered; "I cannot escape them that way—I must go some other way—I must hide if I can't get away."

He looked up the other end of the passage, but that was blocked up, which effectually settled the question of it, and he immediately retired into the room, for he could see and hear those who were coming towards him.

"I think it must be this way," said one.

"Yes; I think the sound came from this place somehow or other—from some of these rooms, or those adjoining the passage."

"No doubt; who the deuce it can be, I can't imagine," said one.

"Nor I; but I suppose somebody has become tired of his life, and put an end to it. Well, if they are tired of it, I say that nobody has a right to call upon them to keep the ball up after all. The lights are put out, and the wines cleared away, and that is the case when a man's pocket is empty, I expect—what more would they have of him?"

"It saves his friends some trouble."

"So it does."

"And besides that, there is to be considered the troubles he escapes himself."

"He does so," said another.

They by this time reached the door, and at that moment the light fell upon the door of a closet, and he in an instant opened it, and walked into it, closing the door at the very moment the men with the lights entered the apartment.

"Here it is," said one; "I thought I was not far out, when I said the sound did not come far from this quarter. See, there lies the body."

"God bless my heart!" said another of the party, "so it is. Well, I put my foot upon it, even after you spoke—who would have believed it?"

"Why, seeing is believing, I believe."

"So it is; and if anybody sees that body, they can't say it isn't one. Ah! he's done for, and no mistake. Put the pistol in his mouth, and send the bullet out of the top of his head. Well, it was cleanly done—there's not an atom of a chance for any man who fires a bullet through the palate of his mouth."

"No, no, he meant what he did—there can be no doubt of it, none at all. He has been cleared out, I suppose, and there is no need to look into his pockets. We may take it for granted that everything has been done upon that score that can be done. He's lost his last shilling, there can be no doubt."

"Yes; but it's quite a pity he didn't go home and do it."

"And not come here to make such a mess. Lord, you know the carpet is spoiled; but what is that to the uncomfortable talk that such an occurrence is sure to produce all over the town, if this affair should get abroad."

"But we must prevent that."

"That must be our care; for to have such an affair as this staring us in the papers, would be a decided mischief, and an injury to us."

"Yes; and only think of the questions of a coroner's jury. They'll ask more than it's convenient to tell; and they'll contrive to keep the game alive by summoning every one of whom they can get the names; and there will be adjournments, and all that kind of thing, and indictments, and every other infernal machine that can be invented, to stand between a gentleman and his amusements."

" We must dispose of the body—that can be easily effected. Nobody knows of it but ourselves, and we must keep the secret."

" Decidedly—we must do so for our sakes."

" I am content. Indeed, I think it would be unwise to let such a circumstance as this come to light; it would play the devil with us all. A regular break-up would be the consequence, and many of the unplucked ones would be scared away."

" So they would."

" But what shall we do with the body ?" inquired one.

" Throw it over the well staircase, and there let it remain."

" But the stench, after awhile, will infect the house; there can be no doubt but that would lead to a detection. No, no ; some other means must be found of placing the body where it cannot be any trouble to us, and it can be safely forgotten."

" That is just what is desired. I tell you what we once did in a place in France, where another kind of affair happened."

" Where were you, then ?"

" In Paris."

" And how do they settle these things there ?"

" I'll tell you. We have a few minutes to spare, for we had better let the body bleed, else it will make us all in a mess, besides giving us a deal of trouble, and leaving traces of blood all the way there, which had better be avoided."

" Yes, decidedly."

" We will just move it on one side to let the blood drain away, else it will clod all over the clothes, and make it slippery to carry."

They dragged the body, which was yet warm and bleeding, though slowly, from the pool of blood, and then let it remain. As they did this, they all stood so that Hoffenden had a good view of their features, for the light shone full on them, and the closet door was several inches open. He was much afraid that he would be discovered, and felt quite sure that were he discovered, he might be pitched down the well staircase too; for they would less like the matter to become known after he had heard their conversation, than they would that a suicide should become known on the first night of opening such a place, which would be its ruin.

He remained therefore perfectly motionless, with suppressed breathing, for he could hear everything they said, even their breathing ; and if he could hear theirs, they must have heard his, he thought. However, they were several persons, and no doubt they believed they heard each other's breathing.

" Well, what was this affair you were speaking of in Paris ?"

" This. I was with some friends in Paris ; we got up a house for obliging those that had some money, and wanted to get rid of it in a gentlemanly sort of way."

" Ay, ay."

" The house was going on well enough, and prosperously too, I can tell you ; we were making a good thing of it, and never hesitated in our course. We kept but a poor look out, as we used to say, because we had but few hands, but we adopted a very good plan. No one was admitted but such as were known, unless in the company of some one who was well known. This being the case, we were never disturbed."

" Well, you were more fortunate than many in this country."

" You are right. We completely baffled the police for a long time. However, we were well frequented, and at that time we used to have a count—he was an Italian refugee,— he used to come and play very high indeed, with varied success.

" That being the case, it was an acknowledged thing that he played fair, and every one was anxious to prove how far his purse would last out. He was to be plucked, that every one knew, for he was constantly a fair player, and always paid.

" Many people looked upon him as a mine; at the same time, the question of ' Where does his money come from ?' was one which everybody asked, but nobody could answer ; but, you know, a man with money is one whom nobody will slight, and they will very little trouble themselves about the means by which he acquires it.

" The possession of money is the great thing, and those who haven't got it, study how they can obtain it ; so the world may be divided into two classes—those who have money, and those who haven't ; and the one tries to get more, and the other to take from them for their own use ; and though everybody, when it is known, condemns his neighbour, he hesitates not to hit upon some worse plan of his own to compass the same end.

"They do that; there's nothing so bad but somebody else does something worse."

"You are right; but push along."

"Well, the count was a very polite and ceremonious man, and one who would put up with no lapse of etiquette; indeed, he more than once caused a bit of disturbance and an encounter; but he was too cool, and always came off conqueror.

"It was determined at length to make up a party, who were to play the count and run him down. They raised a subscription purse amongst them to pit against him, and they were all to share alike in the proceeds—that is, the winnings."

"We understand—it's often done."

"I cared but little about the success of the plan, but I should have something from it I knew; and yet the count was a very good customer of ours; but then, you know, we must do business among our own lot."

"Yes, we can do nothing without it."

"Well, matters went on very well, when the count began to lose, and then he began to play sharp and watch the game with more than ordinary interest, and the result was what might have been expected. The count discovered they were playing him false, and detected one in the commission of the trick.

"Sir," said the count, "I thought I was playing with a gentleman, and not with a cheat."

"If you apply that to me," said his antagonist, who was no chicken, and had more than one encounter; "if you call me that, I shall call you liar."

"I say distinctly, I saw you cheat—you are a mere swindler, and I insist upon a return of the money you have had of me."

"You may insist as long as you please."

"Will you give it up?" said the count, in a towering passion.

"I will not," said the other; "if you repent having played, you may return home and repent at leisure. I have fairly won what I have got, and shall keep it."

"You are a rascally cheat," said the count, and he struck his antagonist a blow in the face, that he caused him to stagger; but recovering himself, he returned it, and gave the count a blow, and called him a coward, as one who dared not settle a quarrel in a gentlemanly way, but who chose to proceed in a manner more suitable to a porter than any one else, because it is not so dangerous as the mode a gentleman would pursue.

"I cannot fight with you—it would be a disgrace."

"I am your equal in honour and in station."

"But a mere cheat."

"Not so; you accuse me, because you have lost, and expect your money should have been in your own purse; and you quarrel with the hope of regaining it."

"I do not. I will fight you. I demand instant satisfaction."

"And you shall have it."

There was an instant commotion, and it was agreed, after some words, that the room should be cleared of all impediments. Two swords were given them, and lights were held around them, and fixed in every quarter of the room, where it was convenient for the combatants, and to throw as little shadow as possible.

"How was that?"

"Easy enough, when the light comes from all sides, there is no shadow, and you can observe what is going on in your adversary's face. Well, they took their coats off, and tore off their right arm shirt sleeves, so that they should not be any impediment to them.

Every one present, and there was not six in all, saw that it was a serious affair, and the probability was, that the life of one, if not both, would be sacrificed in the affair, so desperate did they both appear, and so cool and determined; though they both appeared to be in the greatest passion previous to this time, but they had cooled to become more deadly.

Their swords were placed in their hands, and the seconds retired at the same time; they crossed their weapons, and then fought cautiously; but they soon warmed, and a desperate fight took place. They were both first-rate swordsmen, and fought with skill and desperation.

But it was a long contested fight, and the candles burned dull as they fought so long; the seconds began to think of some accommodation, when the count suddenly made a desperate pass at his adversary, which the other found the greatest difficulty in parrying; as he did so, he returned the thrust, and with such good effect that he passed his sword through his right breast, and out below his left shoulder blade.

The thrust was a fatal one—the wound was mortal, and the count fell heavily on the carpet, and never moved more.

"What did you do with the body?" inquired one.

"That is just the question that was asked by those who had witnessed the affray.

"What can be done with the body?" inquired one and all.

"That I will undertake to get rid of," said one of my friends; "if you will all keep your own counsel, I will dispose of the body."

"How?" was the general inquiry.

"I have some cellars below, where, if you will all aid me, I will bury the body; below we shall be compelled to use the pick—what do you say to my proposition; are you all willing to aid and assist me?"

"We will," said everybody; "anything to get rid of the body—we don't want to be had hold of by the police—anything but that."

"Well, then, do you take up the body among you, and follow me. I will lead you to the place where you will be able to put him out of sight decently and in secret. That, I take it, is a great point—wherein we can pave him over."

Well, they were all well-enough pleased with this, and resolved to follow him, and we did. It was a large, old, rambling place, in which there was no end to the odd, out-of-the-way places, and where there was plenty of room for concealment, and where a dozen men could be buried without it ever being suspected.

After much turning and twisting, we came to a gallery and a long staircase; down this we pitched the body, and went after it, and carried it into the cellars; and then we dug up the flooring of one of the cellars—one that had never been used since it was built, and therein made a grave, and pushed him in and covered him over.

"Now," said the man, "if nobody splits, we shall be safe a hundred years hence, for we should never be suspected."

They all swore to be true to one another, and we left the cellars and came upstairs again; and I am sure I could not have found my way down stairs again to the same place in which the body lay, so rambling and intricate was the place. However, we had a good supper, and plenty of wine; and then we parted for the night, not in the clearest state of mind a human being could be, certainly.

"Well, what became of the affair?"

"Oh, we never heard any more of it. We were all true, and the count was never named, and was never inquired after by any one."

"Then he disappeared, nobody knew how."

"Exactly; but now, I think, we had better look to our own affairs, and put this corpse out of the way, so that it will not be any further trouble to us; for it would be the devil to have any unpleasant circumstances to cause us to decamp hence."

"Oh, it's not to be thought of."

"By no means, by Jove," said one; "I now recollect myself seeing this young fellow playing in the room below. He lost continually. I saw he was much agitated, and unable to play well, though he tried hard to appear unconcerned."

"Ay, he made up his mind to win all or lose all."

"It was quite evident from the first that he meant it. Well, he had a bold run for it; but it was of no use, he has paid the penalty of his rashness. It is his own act, and therefore he can complain of no one."

"None at all; but we are idle; we must stir ourselves. Come on, and we will pitch him over the well staircase, and that will save us from carrying him down some eighty or a hundred steps, and that is anything but agreeable."

"All this is very much like body-snatching, only it is not so pleasant by a very great deal; you see it's unpleasant to have anything to do with a dead body, and that dripping with blood; but this can't be helped; so now, then, lend me a hand."

Hoffenden could see them take hold of the body and lift it up, while the others held the lights, and then they left the apartment by the door at which they entered; but it was some moments after they left that he recovered himself, and felt that he was safe.

"I am safe," he muttered, as he drew a long breath; "yes, I am safe; but it was a very nigh chance for me; but I will follow and see where they put this body; it may be important to know something more about this affair."

Hoffenden was conscious that if he were discovered the consequences would be disastrous to himself, and there would be no mercy shown him, because there would be no security to the men who were now about to conceal a dead body.

He crept out cautiously, and, peeping out, saw them proceeding along at a very slow pace before him; but he followed them almost close enough to hear every word that was spoken by them; he followed close in their shadow.

" It's very handy," said one, " that this staircase should have been constructed in the manner it is.   A man might be accidentally pitched over, and his death is easily accounted for; though it is not at all necessary to account for it when you have stowage room beneath the house.   Come on; don't be all night."

" We are here—this door."

They went through a pair of doors, which swung to with a loud bang.

Hoffenden paused to consider whether he should pursue this matter any further; he had seen the body of the party, and he had heard them all speak, and therefore knew them well; he knew very well what they were about to do with the body.   To go on was fraught with danger, but yet to stop short was to place it in the power of several unscrupulous men to destroy him, and conceal his body in the same manner they were about to conceal the one they had with them.

" I will follow them," he muttered; "my knowledge of this affair will be quite complete, if I do so, and, being complete, it may be useful some time or other."

Having resolved to do so, he immediately followed them.   It was easy to do so, for their voices were enough to direct him in his course.   He opened the door and listened; they were not far, for he could see the reflection of their light, and he heard their voices.

" I shall be there in time," he muttered; " they are not so far but I can overtake them. It will be very strange, but I will see the whole of this drama from the first to the last act.   I shall know all."

He soon came up with them as near as he dare; but he could overhear all that was said by them, as all was quiet, and the distance only a few yards, and the men spoke plain and unreserved enough.

However, they passed through several places and then through a door which led to a long gallery, into which they descended by means of two steps.

Here he was compelled to be cautious, because the place being bare and naked, with nothing but the bare boards to walk upon, gave out a clear sound; but, as there were several feet and several persons talking, the few sounds that arose from his footsteps passed unheeded by, and, after going about a score yards, they paused.

" Here is the well staircase," said one.

" I'm not sorry," said another.   " I'm tired of him, for my part; it's no joke carrying about so much human clay; it feels uncomfortable."

" Ha! ha! ha! he's beginning to be afraid, as sure as I'm born."

" Not a bit, any more than I should be afraid of a dose of medicine.   I don't like either; but, at the same time, I don't care for either—it's a matter of like and dislikes. As for the mere fact of human carcasses, I have known them sold to a butcher rather than waste them."

" And what did he do with it?"

" Oh, I can't tell.   I only know the fact; but then he didn't buy it for the sake of losing by the transaction."

" Oh! well, over with them."

" Just help me to put it on the ledge here, and then we can push it down, which will save our time and labour—heave up."

The men lifted the body up, and placed it upon the ledge of the iron railing, which run along on one side of the gallery, and which wound round the well staircase, which was a spiral series of steps, like the thread of a screw with the centre drawn out, or like a staircase wound round the sides of a well.

" Here we are—push him over."

" With all my heart.   Here goes."

As the man spoke, several of them pushed the body over the rails gently, and it fell with some sounds as it descended, as if it had struck heavily from side to side; and, then, after a minute had elapsed, there was a dull, heavy sound, as if the body had fallen to the bottom.

The men had all leaned over and listened to the dull, heavy sounds that escaped in the descent.

" Well, he's gone down though."

" Yes ; I almost expected he would have stopped on the road; he didn't seem well balanced, for he ought to have gone down head first."

" He would have done so, but he had lost his brains, you know ; they are in the room we have just left."

" You had better go back after them, since you have made the discovery."

" Ha, ha, ha! a very likely thing; go after a man's brains that hasn't got any ; that will never do—come on, we mustn't waste more time.   By Jove, we may be wanted elsewhere, and we have work enough to do, I know, before we leave off."

"Will it be hard?"

"I'll warrant the flooring of those cellars will be as hard as we can desire them; they'll want a pickaxe to loosen them."

"Why, they must be wet, surely."

"They are tolerably wet for that matter; but you see they would be hard, even if they were wet. There is no reason why a wet soil should be softer than a dry one; indeed, I am inclined to think a wet one will be worse to work than a dry one."

They now descended the staircase, which wound round and round for some distance, till they came to the bottom of it, when it terminated in a long passage, and a number of cellars, that branched away in different directions.

Hoffenden followed them down until he came to within a dozen or two steps, and then he crouched down, and looking below, could see all their movements and features. There were the men all standing round the body, which had fallen in a heap on the earth, and was terribly crushed and broken with its fall.

"Well, now, bring it along."

"Where to?" inquired another.

"Just where this cellar is," pointing to one.

"That's not far; lay hold of his head while I take the heels, then we shall have done with him, I hope."

"I recollect burying one man at York who was not really dead."

"Aye, how was that?"

"Oh, we had got into a fray, and a man intruded who had no business in our circle, and appeared to take too much notice of things that were going on around him; and one of our side struck him a blow which brought him down as senseless as a log, which you know was not quite agreeable."

"Well, being settled in that manner is, I must say, rather summary; but I suppose you had very good reason for so doing?"

"Indeed we had; he had seen enough to transport some of us, to say the least of it; and we were not anxious that there should be any in our secrets but ourselves, and he was brought down as if shot."

"It was sudden."

"It was; there was no time for deliberation, and if it had been put to the vote, we might not have agreed to it; but it was done, and there was no use in thinking about it. What was to be done? was the question.

"' Put him under ground, and say nothing to nobody,' was the answer.

"' But I don't think he is quite dead,' said one.

"' Nor I,' said another. ' But it strikes me uncommonly forcible that he will be, if we put a few score pounds of clay over him; that will be the best thing we can do; if he gets round again, it will be the worst for us.'

"' So say I. He will never forgive us, and we may depend if he would not have done it before, he would do it now. He might have tried to use us, but there is no mercy to be shown now he's got that knock of the head.'

"' Besides, it will be just the same; he's insensible, and will know nothing about it all, and there can be nothing felt. We can bury him, and he'll know nothing, and feel nothing.'

"' Hurrah! that will do.'

" In about five minutes more, we were merrily digging the earth up, and had prepared a large hole, just suitable, when he began to open his eyes.

"' In with him!' cried one.

"' Hit him on the head!' said another.

"' Put him out of his misery!' cried a third; and in a second he received a blow, and was then tumbled into the hole we had made for his reception. Well, do you know, we tumbled the earth in after him, and a scene took place I shall never forget."

"What was it?" inquired one.

"Why, as we tumbled the earth in, he recovered his senses, and, though we had covered him over several inches deep, he began to get up, and move about.

"' Jump in,' said one, to the man who had knocked him down, ' and tread him down, else he'll be up in another minute or so; and if he gets away now, it will be worse than all; we shall be all of us in a pretty state.'

"' I'm d—d if I can!'

"' But you must,' said one, and he gave him a push behind, that sent him clean upon the other, who was trying to get up. By a desperate effort, he got up on his knees, but then a struggle took place between him and the man who was in the hole with him.

"For some minutes, we looked on somewhat alarmed, to tell the truth, and didn't half like it, and I think that more than one of us had serious thoughts about running away; but the certainty that if we did, we should all be discovered, prevented us.

"'Help! help!' shouted both men in the grave; 'Help!—mercy!'—'He'll get out —help!—I can't keep him down!'—'Help!—mercy!—let me get out!—I'll never speak of this!'—'Help me to keep him down!—curse you!'—Help!—mercy!'

"This went on for some minutes, till one of our people gave him a slice over the head with a spade, and that stunned him, and he fell back; and then the man in the grave with him put his foot upon him, and jumped up.

"Didn't the shovels go to work! they threw the earth in again as if it were flying, and in a few minutes there was a covering of four or five inches of clay over the man, who showed signs of moving; but the other jumped in again, and stamped it down, and the earth continued to be shovelled in with such rapidity, that a minute or two sufficed to fill it.

"All was over, and we stamped it down; but we did not forget it. It spoilt our evening —that is the fact."

"Well, it must have been a rare uncomfortable affair, certainly; and it would have spoilt my sport for the evening, I must really admit."

"And mine, too."

"Well," said one of the men, who had been using a shovel, and wiping his hand across his forehead, as he looked around, "I think this is large enough to hold our man, at all events; I feel tired."

"Well, I feel tired too," said a companion, who had been using the pick-axe; "I feel as if it was time we were done."

"That is large enough. Now for the body; put him down as low as you can, because there will be less escape of gas when it putrifies."

They now drew the body towards the grave, and lifting it over the earth they had thrown over, they at once laid it down in the bottom of the grave, where it lay quiet and easy enough, and gave them no trouble.

"He lies kindly enough."

"Yes; he won't want knocking on the head to lie quiet."

"No; he has given us all this trouble to please himself, and not us, confound him; but he has paid for his pains. Now, then, shovel away; the sooner he's down tight the better; this over, and we have something else to do more comfortable than this."

They all set to work, and Hoffenden saw they were not long about it, and shovelful after shovelful of the rough earth was thrown into the grave of the unfortunate suicide, and he watched the whole proceeding with something like awe and interest.

The dark forms of the men, for they appeared so, save where the candle-light fell upon their persons and partially illuminated the arched vaults or cellars in which this deed was done, gave the dark, damp, and dismal place the appearance of the habitation of some loathsome beings who fed upon the vices of mankind.

How different was the scene here to that above. What a contrast! The dull vaults were a strong reverse of the picture above, where all was life and brilliancy; here all was dark and silent; the damp walls, moist with slime, were a contrast to the gaudy hangings and glasses above.

There were gay lights; life and fashion to its very height: here was a scene that was dependent upon that above, in the same manner that death accompanies life; it is the catastrophe of the other.

"Well, I am pretty well sure," said one of the men, "that this affair needs no more to complete it; what do you say? Can it be done better?"

"No; this will do; we had better put away our tools, and then return above stairs. I am really nervous; a goblet of Burgundy, or a glass of champagne, will be no despicable end to this adventure."

"The sooner we have it the better; I shall like it."

They now left the cellar, and Hoffenden found himself compelled to retreat into another cellar, where he again concealed himself until they passed.

This they did, and in a certain spot they placed the instruments they had used, and now sought the stairs, and proceeded upwards, without having noticed the presence of Hoffenden, who could not feel very easy and comfortable in the vicinity to such men, and could by no means consider himself safe; for if he were discovered, his life would be lost.

Such men, he argued, would take his life with the utmost coolness; and he would have no chance, either in resistance or in assistance; for his cries would be heard by none, and his attempts at self-defence would be unavailing, where each man would be equal to himself upon all ordinary occasions; but now he would be overwhelmed in a minute.

However they saw him not, and they proceeded up the well staircase; and, when half way up, Hoffenden stole from his place of concealment, and followed them cautiously, keeping as much in the dark as he could possibly do.

"Well," he heard them say, "we must now take what measures we can to erase all the marks he has left up stairs; but that might remain till the morning. I will take the key of the door, and then we shall be able to keep all intruders out, for there is no occasion for more than are present to know anything of what has happened."

"Certainly not; it would be madness to do so."

"It would," replied the principal speaker; "and we had better be careful not to let our confidence outrun our discretion, and so play the fool, and be hanged for it, which will be the most natural result of such folly."

Hoffenden was still on the staircase, and followed them slowly and cautiously, until they went to the end of the passage; then he walked rapidly after them, but he missed them; they must have gone through some door which he had not observed. However it was, they were gone, and he could not trace them, or hear them at all.

"Well, it matters not," said Hoffenden to himself; "I have seen and heard all I can, and must now seek my safety by getting out of this labyrinth. Once out, and I know I am quite safe; here, however, I am not so safe—by no means so safe. Now, to get out is the great point. If I knew my way back, I should be all very well; but I don't. I know no more my way back than if I had not been at all. I was too much intent on my own personal safety to think of marking the way in my own mind."

This was the fact. He had been too stunned by the event, and the character and manner of the people who had in that unceremonious style disposed of the remains of an unfortunate human being—a man who spent his last penny to satisfy the cravings of such men.

*   *   *   *   *   *

Hoffenden gave over thinking, and pushed onwards, in the hopes that he would presently come to a door that would lead him out of the private part of the house; for the question of "How came you here?" could not be very satisfactorily answered, and might possibly procure him more mischief than he was prepared to submit to.

He heard a door slam, however, and a flash of light shone in upon the passage, but not on where he stood, and he resolved to find his way down to it, and ascertain where he was, and if no prospect of escape could be held out to him.

He got down, but in a roundabout way, leading to the end of a gallery, then to a staircase, which also led downwards. This he descended, and in a few moments found himself in a passage near a door. He could hear people talking, and the rattling of the instruments of gambling.

"I am right for once," he muttered. "I know those sounds too well—much too well, to mistake them anywhere."

He pushed open the door, and saw he was where he thought he was—that was, in the gambling saloon he had a short time before left. He went to one of the side tables, found out some wine, and drank several glasses off at once without a moment's hesitation.

Then he walked up and down the glittering apartments, and found that all he saw there could not obliterate from his mind the scenes he had witnessed. The very lights appeared duller, and the lustre of the glasses had diminished, and he resolved he would leave the house, and walk through the cool streets, and attempt to shake himself free from the melancholy thoughts that now came over him. In a few moments more he found himself in the streets.

CHAPTER XXI.

THE SAD SITUATION OF MRS. HOFFENDEN.—THE COMING MORNING.

OUR readers may well fancy, without any elaboration upon our parts, what must have been the wretched condition of Jane Hoffenden after her truly dreadful night adventure.

The frightful act of audacity of which Murdo had been guilty, was of a character that never could have entered into her mind to conceive any one could have been guilty of. It transcended anything in the shape of daring guilt that she could have imagined; but, alas! she little knew the unscrupulous character of the man she was almost at the mercy of; and yet, while she would not believe the dread insinuation he had made, she trembled to think of it.

"Oh, no, no," she sobbed, "I cannot, will not think it possible. Harry is cruel to me, careless of my happiness, neglectful of his child, and weak enough to be led by others more crafty than himself into vice, but he is not criminal."

There was truly something to the young wife too dreadful in the idea of her husband being so far in the power of such a man as Murdo that he dared not resent an insult offered to his wife, and that an insult, too, of so very gross a character, that the poorest spirit that ever lived would turn against it. The thought was too humiliating for Jane to harbour it, and she resolved that she would not lose one moment in communicating what had occurred to him.

But when could she calculate upon seeing him to whom she had a right to complain? When could she say to herself, "I shall have an opportunity of seeing my husband, and of telling him how I have been insulted?" She knew not. Days might elapse ere she looked upon the face of him whom she had sworn to love, and whose first words of fondness had wakened in her heart the pure spirit of affection. She was a gambler's wife, and she had no hold upon her husband's affections to be compared to the hold which that fascinating demoniac vice had obtained.

How could she hope to fight against such an unholy passion? It was not to be done; and, insulted as she had been, she felt that she must wait for an indefinite period before she could pour her complaints into the ears of him who ought, by every sentiment of honour and of justice, to attend most particularly to them.

And how could that young mother—for a young mother still she was—have borne up for one moment against her sorrows, had she not been sustained by one circumstance— the sweet memory that she was a mother; and that, in proportion as Hoffenden forgot all that he owed to his child in the way of affection, she ought to make an effort to supply his place.

In the caresses of that little innocent she would for a time forget the sorrows that preyed upon her heart; and many a time she had wept some griefs away by the bedside of her child.

And what a glorious resource that was upon this occasion, and with what hopefulness she made her way yet in the darkness of the night, to the side of that couch which contained if not all she loved, at least all that she fully believed loved her.

The child was sleeping; its little hand lay outside the coverlet of the bed; and oh, what earnest, passionate kisses of fond affection the mother poured upon that hand!

"My own, my child, my beautiful!" she murmured, "may you never know the griefs that have weighed down the spirit of your poor mother to the earth. My infant! may Heaven's choicest blessings fall upon you!"

"Yes, ma'am—certainly, ma'am," said the child's nurse, making her appearance in the room; "if ever there was a little angel, it is this dear child, ma'am—ahem!"

Mrs. Hoffenden never liked this woman. The gross flattery she was accustomed to indulge in was sure to be distasteful to so pure a mind as Jane Hoffenden's; moreover, the woman had an odd habit of spoiling the effect of what she said by a short dry cough at the end of it, which always involved the preceding speech in a world of doubt.

"Oh, are you here, Elizabeth?"

"Yes, ma'am, I am here. I am always here, ma'am, if you please. It's many a time in the night that I gets up and comes out of my own precious warm bed, to see what the little angel is a doing of. Oh, it's the apple of both my eyes, ma'am."

"Well, well; I am glad you are fond of the child."

"Fond of it, ma'am? Wouldn't I lay down my life, ma'am, bang, any individual mo-ment, if it was only to save it from a pain in its blessed innocent stomach?"

"Thank you, thank you; that will do. It sleeps soundly, I think."

"Like a lamb, ma'am, as has swallowed a whole quart of soothing syrup, ma'am, I can tell you. There never was a baby in all this here world as could sleep half so well, ma'am; and though I says it, perhaps, as oughtn't, I do say that I makes myself a perfect slave to this child, ma'am, early and late, and late and early. I dreams about it all the while I'm awake, and I thinks about it all the while I'm asleep, ma'am, I assure you."

Jane Hoffenden could only, by a great effort, endure the garrulity of the nurse. It was almost too great an effort for her, but she did manage it in some way for a time. She then kissed the soft cheek of the child, and bidding the nurse adieu, she went gently back to her own chamber again.

It was still dark, although the hour of sunrise was sufficiently near at hand for her soon to expect the coming of a new day.

She sat down, and for a time resting her head upon her hands, she gave herself up to painful reminiscences of the past, such reminiscences as brought with them many a pang, because they were in such great and startling contrast to the present.

She remembered when first Hoffenden had breathed to her the words of fond affection, and when she had truly believed that that affection would and could know no change. Alas! how different were her impressions now of the constancy of the heart she had thought all her own, and of the endurance of those vows she thought at one time all equi-valent to promises from Heaven!

But the theme was too agonising and powerful a one to pursue for long, and she was compelled to seek for some resource by which to shake off the agony of such recollections. That resource was in the pages of fiction. Yes—there the wounded spirit found a resting-place. There the dove from the ark of the mind found an olive leaf. To possess herself of a book was her present resource.

*   *   *   *   *   *   *

Trimming, then, her night lamp, for it was yet not day, Jane opened the volume, and commenced reading as follows:—

The good City of York was always a place famous for the residence of wealthy Jews, but more so in former ages than in the present time; for it is of too quiet and dignified a character, and has too little business, for these people to reside in, in any numbers; but in former ages this was not so, for the City of York afforded them shelter and refuge which they could not always find in the country, or even, at times, in the largest cities in England, or even in Christendom.

The population of England were particularly averse to the Jews; but this arose from religious notions, in the first place; and the habits, which persecution had rendered necessary and habitual to them, in the second. They were confined to commerce, and married but with themselves. They were the only people who carried on trade, and in whose hands were to be found money in any quantity.

True it was, that at a later time, the citizens of London rose to eminence; but much of the wealth of that class was to be attributed to the residence of foreigners—the Lom-bards and the Jews.

However that might be, in ages gone by, there lived at York a rich Jew, whose name was Ben Shemai. He was wealthy, and was one of those who looked upon the degra-dation his people suffered, as one of the greatest and most grievous misfortunes that could have happened as a direct infliction from Heaven. He wore the usual Jewish dress, and that of not very fine or new materials; for he was well aware that to appear rich, was to incur danger of being considered enormously wealthy, and that would bring down its appropriate species of oppression.

Ben Shemai had a daughter. A pearl she was herself, if considered in her own person; and a very diamond, if her wealth were taken into consideration. Rebecca was one of the most beautiful women of her nation. She was scarce eighteen summers old. She was accomplished in the accomplishments of her people.

Her father came home each day as early as he could, for he did not deem it at all safe to be out in the city late in the day, because there was much greater probability of vio-lence being done him, and robbery, than at any other.

"Oh, Rebecca," said the old Jew, when he had wiped his brow with a silken handkerchief, apparently much aggrieved about something, "these Nazarene dogs will not permit those who would remain at peace, to be so, without suffering all the indignities that it is in their power to inflict."

"What, my father," said the Jewish maiden, " have you suffered more vexation—do the Christians still pursue you with their hatred?"

" Ay, Rebecca—thou image of thy mother—they—they do."

" Would that our people were more warlike!" murmured the maiden, thoughtfully.

" More warlike, Rebecca!" said her father, suddenly; " more warlike! dost thou not know they are not warlike at all? and had they been so, there are not enough of them to right ourselves. I see, daughter, the last tournament has turned thy head, and thou thinkest of nothing but trumpets, and lances, and battle-axes; and hath lost thy love of peace, and of ingots of gold and of silver."

" No, father. I have not acquired the one, nor lost that of the other; but, at the same time, I should like to see our people in security. I should like to know that you could walk the streets in safety. Our people, in the olden times, were victorious in many battles, and they conquered numerous hosts."

" Ah! they did, child. They fought, and conquered, till a greater power than theirs overthrew them at last, and the Roman triumphed on the walls of Jerusalem. All that is left us is—wealth and our national type."

"But what have you suffered to-day, father?"

" Suffered! I have been defiled by every dog that comes past me. The people of this place appear to wax more and more dangerous every day, and I have heard that there have been risings in several parts of the country, in which many of our people have suffered from their violence."

" Indeed, father; and are we safe here?"

" As safe, I suppose, as anywhere else. Our doors are strong, and we might resist some violence; but I fear that we could not resist all that might be done. But give me some of that wine, Rebecca. It will cheer my heart. Those Christians will take our moneys, and have not honesty enough to return them. They do not love paying debts; I am sure they are naturally dishonest."

" But, my father, have you been disappointed to-day in getting your own?"

"Yes, I have, Rebecca. I have not received the money from the Christian merchant, Locksley. He has not paid me; and, worse than that, he has not been at his house during the hours of business."

" But he has been here," said the maiden.

"Ah! to borrow more money. I see how it is. He has not means to pay the original debt, and yet he would induce me to lend him more. No, no; Ben Shemai knows the value of money too well to dream of it."

"No; he has not been here for that purpose, I think, father, if I may judge from what took place. He paid the money down, and interest; he, at least, is just, father. He would have paid to you on demand, at his own house, as agreed upon; but he had to take a journey, and the party he joined was to leave early."

"Ah! Rebecca, 'tis well we have something more than mere disappointment to encounter; we have sometimes success. But this money is mine own; I had lent it to the good merchant, and the interest he gave me was my only gain. What I gain here I may lose there; but we have no other occupation now. But where is the money, Rebecca?"

"Here," replied Rebecca, placing a strong box on the table.

"Ah! I will count it. Hast thou done so, girl?"

"No; I have not counted it, father. It is as he left it with me."

"Daughter, have I not told thee never to trust these Nazarine dogs—never trust them; always count after them, and see they defraud thee not."

Rebecca made no reply, but watched her father, as he sat down and counted the golden pieces, one after another, as though they were the most precious things in his estimation that human nature could possibly set its affections upon.

" But, Rebecca," he said, when he had finished counting, "there is another merchant who has not paid, and he is a week past the time. I must enforce the law, Rebecca—I must enforce the law—men will not pay me, the law must compel them; 'tis not I who made their bargain—they must pay, or suffer the extremity of their bonds."

" But, father, he hast lost, too; he says that one of our tribe has been a defaulter to him; he received merchandize for which he never paid."

" Am I answerable for other men's sins, as well as my own, Rebecca?—I would answer for none but myself. If I am bond for any one, I am answerable for him, but not otherwise; and, as for this man, I have nothing to do with him. I expect him to pay my debt, and that by to-morrow, or else I will see what the law will do."

"He, too, has been here."

"Eh? Rebecca, eh? did he bring the money—that is the main point; that is what I want—the money, Rebecca, the money?"

"Yes, father, I know that; the money he will have ready, but not yet."

"Not yet, child—not yet!" exclaimed the Jew, testily—"not yet! Then I must do something, since he will not. When did he say it would be ready?"

"He prays your forbearance for three months farther, and says ——"

"Hark ye, Rebecca, never mind what he says—never tell me. I will not listen to it; it is scandalous, and not to be entertained. I will wait no three months—the money must be paid, or he must suffer what others would be glad to make me suffer. They make us suffer enough; our people are made to suffer all that, as men or animals, they can suffer; their bodies tortured, and their substance taken from them."

"We are oppressed, father, and the character of our oppressors is hateful; let us not imitate them, but show mercy."

"I showed mercy, Rebecca, when I lent the money."

"Need you cease to do so?"

"Yes; but it is no oppression to seek for what is our due; but I will say no more to thee, child, upon this matter. I shall have a visitor presently, whom I will have treated with such respect due to one whom I most honour."

"And he shall be so treated by me as my father's honoured guest deserves to be treated by his daughter."

"Yes, Rebecca, I know that; but—but Ben Nomai is to be my future son-in-law. He is a worthy man, and has much wealth—a worthy man, Rebecca, and one who will make you happy—one who will protect you better than your aged father. The time is coming, girl, when nature will cease to be, and I shall be no more; and when, without such protection, you will be but the sport of Jew and Christian."

"Woe to them that would hurt the fatherless, be they Jew or Gentile, father!" said the maiden. "But we will not think of what must happen."

"As you please, daughter; but Ben Nomai is to be my son-in-law," said the old Jew, as if he had spoken about this matter; but the tone was one which expressed determination to be obeyed.

The maiden gave a look of deep sorrow towards her father, who seemed to be much irritated at something—apparently her manner of receiving this intimation; for he presently said to her, with some bitterness,—

"I have not only the injustice and the open robberies and violence of the populace to bear with, but I have a division in my own house. May Abraham look down upon me! I have no comfort—even in my own family I am opposed."

"My father," said the maiden, "you have been crossed to-day. I do not murmur that you should be angered, or that I should be the object; but I am not disobedient, father. I am ready and willing to die for you. There is but one matter I beg your indulgence in; and if you persecute me, where shall I fly for refuge—the unfortunate daughter of a persecuted race—persecuted within and without."

"I wonder why I was born!" muttered the old Jew. "I wonder how Abraham offered up Isaac as a sacrifice; and yet, I dare say, there were reasons enough. He might have been crossed, and the sacrifice could not be great on his part. It does seem to me that there is no comfort in children—do what you will, you are certain to be thwarted in whatever you do for their advancement."

"What would you of me, father?"

"Obedience."

"You have but to command me, and it shall be found that I am obedient."

"Then accept Ben Nomai as your husband."

"Well, father, Ben Nomai is much older than I."

"So much the better, Rebecca."

"He is mean and spare—the counterpart of fear and care. Rich, I grant; but poor in all that makes a man a happy husband."

"And what more can you desire than Ben Nomai? He can keep a good house, and has means of protecting you."

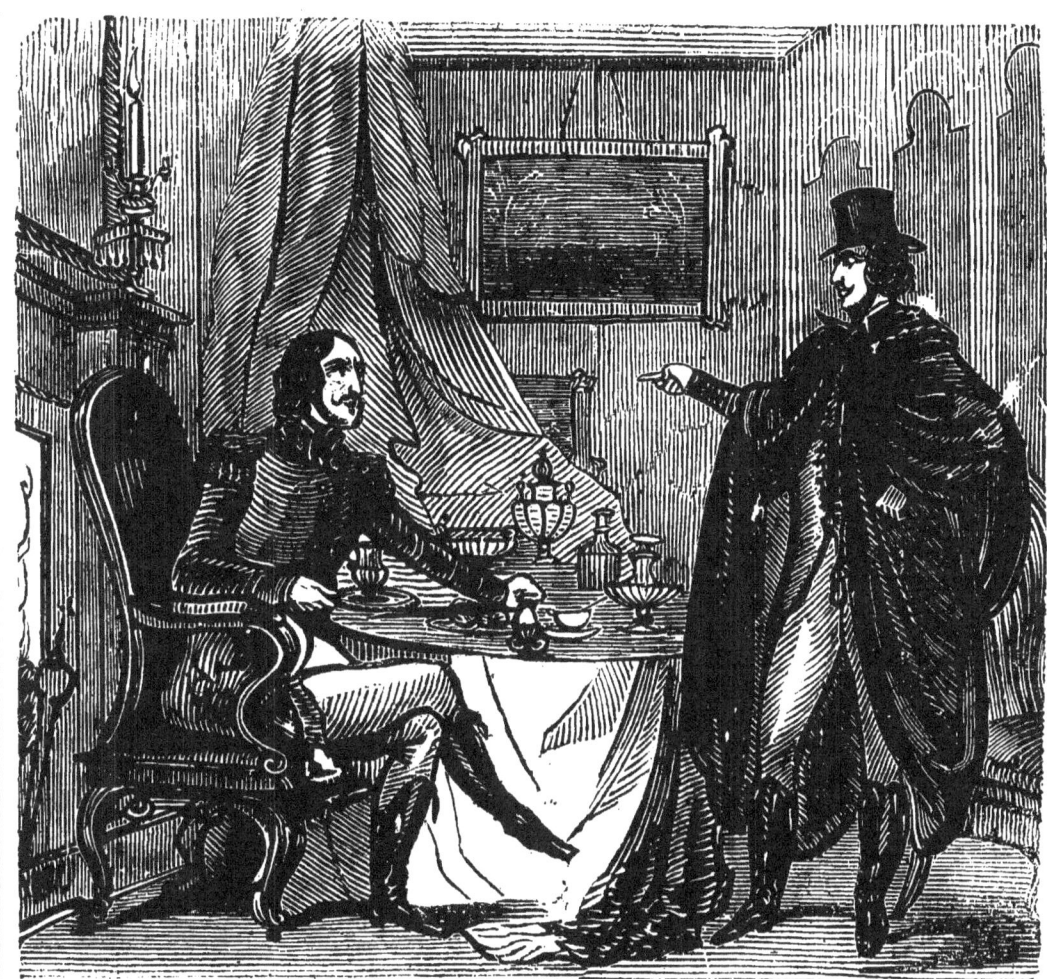

"Well, father, Ben Nomai shall be, since you desire it, my husband."

"Well, that is a proper and sensible obedience.   You will make my heart glad. I shall then be happy in seeing you happy."

"I shall be miserable.   You may be glad, but my heart will be stone cold. I shall not be sorry when the time comes that will lay me by the side of my poor mother. Death will be welcome, since all have failed me—my hopes for the future and my happiness in the present.   I can only remember her words."

"Her words! and what were they?"

"'That there was little happiness here below—we might expect it; but it always fleeted before we could reach it.   The grave was a resting-place against man's oppression, and the bitter disappointments of life.'"

"Well, am I now doing what will help to turn aside all the shafts of fate?"

"Rather, father, you are doing all you can to make me as wretched as you can do; but you must be obeyed, though it cost a daughter years of unhappiness to do so, and that can be nothing in comparison to the hardship of being thwarted in your pleasure to the disposal of another's happiness."

"It may be so, Rebecca; but here is my friend Ben Nomai."

Rebecca clasped her hands in despair as she heard the demand for admission; but there was no help now, and though her father saw the act, and heard her words, yet he was as far from relenting as ever; indeed, an obduracy of feeling was produced, and he resolved that, whatever happened, he would be obeyed.

"It is all useless waste of precious breath," he would say; "she may think what she says, but she will soon get the better of all that kind of thinking, and she will soon adapt herself to circumstances, and be as happy as she imagines she would be under any other circumstances of her own choosing."

Thus thought the old Jew when his friend, Ben Nomai, entered the room, and greeted both himself and daughter. What a picture did the new comer present for a wooer! He was tall, and over thirty years of age, or verging on towards forty; thin, meagre, and miserly; a long face, of the Jewish caste, with a high but narrow forehead, and a black, twinkling eye, as if he were on the look-out for a chance of some character or other, in which he could benefit himself.

The evening passed away in an entertainment of no mean character, for the wealthy Jews exhibited their riches in their homes, and in the costliness of their entertainments; as they dared not show them at other times, lest they should excite the lawless love of plunder in the people, who would think it a meritorious act to despoil a Jew of his riches, which was a deed often done.

"I think," said Ben Nomai, "that there is a very uncomfortable spirit abroad; the people look upon us with louring brows."

"I have noticed it myself," replied Ben Shemai.

"It bodes us no good, I fear," said Ben Nomai. "I never saw such things but once before, and then the people wore the same ominous, scowling brows, and then it preceded an outbreak and massacre of our people."

"It is the misfortune of the captive to bear with the insults of the victor," said Rebecca; "we are a submissive people."

"And could we be otherwise?" inquired Ben Shemai, suddenly.

"We cannot be otherwise than what we are," said Ben Nomai; "we have our place fixed for us, and we cannot help ourselves."

"And yet we have been a conquering nation," said Rebecca; "Arabia and Egypt can testify to that truth. We have had men of war, war-chariots, and the hosts that went forth in battle array."

"Those days are gone," said her father, "and we have now only to do with the present; for one scattered remnant of the tribes they could do nothing, amidst the rage of contending hosts of Christian warriors."

"Besides, our home is in the hands of the Infidels—the Pagans and Christians are alike our enemies. We have no friends—none who would aid us; and, if we had, we must await the appointed time till the ten tribes shall again gather together under the walls of Jerusalem."

*   *   *   *   *   *   *

Rebecca stole from the room; she had seen and heard enough for the night of her father's choice; but it was not her own. And, though she had promised, yet her young heart rebelled against her own sense of duty. She sought to calm the agitation of her spirits by walking in a small enclosed yard, in which she was safe, because it had high walls to surround it.

Here she paced up and down for some time, and tears coursed down her cheeks. She sobbed and sighed bitterly as she walked about, and yet she was much better, she thought, there than in the same apartment with the man her father had destined for her husband.

"What will become of me?" she sighed. "I shall lead the life of a prisoner—a wretched and miserable being. Ought my father to have asked this much of me? He ought not. And if he ask, am I in duty bound to embrace the fate he has proposed for me? Custom almost says 'yes;' and yet my heart tells me it is too much to require from any human being."

As these thoughts passed through her mind, she heard her own name pronounced from the wall. She started, and beheld the form of a man descending by means of a rope, and in another instant he stood by her side.

"Rebecca," he said, "I am here; pardon my intrusion."

"Herbert, you ought not to be here. You know you would be a sacrifice to my father's anger and that of his people."

"I know they carry long knives, and will use them; but I wear a sword, Rebecca, and, moreover, I am a belted knight, and know not what fear is; and I hold myself able to make head against more than two with only such weapons."

"Alas! you know not what enraged men you have to deal with; they are very tigers when brought to bay. The spirit of their forefathers animates them; and the descendants of those who fought and conquered Palestine, will be found, in the hour of need, to equal their ancestors."

"'Tis well said, Jewess," replied the young man; "and you have more of the spirit of a Christian in you than your race. I have loved you, and now bow my knee before thee, and implore you to leave this country with me."

"Oh, Herbert, that cannot be !"

"And who should say so but yourself? I care not what the world says—I care for no human being. I am willing to give up all the world's glory—all my hopes of wealth, and every chivalric notion in which I have been born and bred. Say but the word, Rebecca, and I am your slave."

"My father destines me for another."

"Can you be happy—can you look in the face of the fallen slave, the man who can see his people writhing under oppression, and not even turn to oppose an enemy ? Can you look at the man proposed, and be happy ?"

"I cannot," murmured Rebecca.

"Then why, for one moment, should you make the attempt to render what may be a long life miserable—a scene of wretchedness and repining? Why should you do this? You will be making life a burden, and a reproach to your Maker."

Rebecca sighed, but she said nothing, her heart was too full.

"Then, again, dear Rebecca, who knows how long you may have the protection of even a husband, or a father ?—Popular outbreaks occur every day, and yet there is every chance of these things going on.'

"So my father hinted, and Ben Nomai."

"Think then of all the misery that must ensue to yourself. Can you love, Rebecca ? Can you love—and if so, do you love? Your silence confesses it; you would not then admit another heart to your own. You would not commit such a perjury as that, surely. I am convinced your own rectitude of conduct would tell you better than that—fly with me from these climes to where we can both live in safety and happiness."

"Begone. I hear some one coming; your life would pay the forfeit of this intrusion; hasten, and quit this place while you may."

"But, Rebecca, will you consent ?"

"No—no; begone—for your life.''

"Nay, one kiss." As he spoke, he pressed her lips to his own, and whispered something in her ear, and then, with great swiftness, he seized the rope and sprang up the high wall, and was speedily over the side, just in time to escape the old Jew, who entered the place in search of his daughter.

"Rebecca," he said, calling Rebecca; "where have you got to? Ben Nomai is awaiting to bid you farewell for the night; I am disgraced by such conduct; he is to be your husband; come in, I command you."

"I come, my father, I come," said Rebecca, as she followed her father into the house, and he then closed the door with ponderous fastenings; for the Jews in those times made their dwellings as secure as they could, because they were so liable to violence, that all means were resorted to to secure their dwellings from outrage and robberies, which were very frequent.

Rebecca was compelled to re-enter the apartment, and enter into conversation with the man she most disliked—with whose timid and rapacious habits she each day became more and more disgusted.

The young Christian had saved her from shameful violence, and, by his sword alone, he had kept at bay two or three men who had already despoiled her of her jewels, one evening, while she was coming home under the care of her intended husband, who had run away when he saw so much danger.

This was one reason why she disliked him; and, then, when she compared him to the frank, open, athletic form, and the manly bearing of the young Christian, the difference was so manifest that the most uncomfortable comparisons were drawn between them, and the result was injurious to the Jew.

Besides, Rebecca had read in her own literature of the deeds of her tribes in the land of her fathers—how they fought and conquered in foreign lands, and how they secured a land to themselves, and drove out the original possessors of the soil; but how fallen were they! They were but as slaves; they had wealth, it was true, but, at the same time, they were covered with obloquy—they were accursed, and the hand of Heaven was against them.

Many thoughts crossed her mind, and she could not but think that this was not an unjust punishment, because it came from Heaven. It was inflicted by the only power that could make it so universal; and what could the great crime have been that had caused such an infliction upon them?

These and many other thoughts often crossed the mind of the Jewish maiden, and all that her elders taught her could not do away with the impressions that forced themselves upon her mind; but an incident occurred in a few days after the above, that precipitated her choice of life.

The discontents that had arisen against the Jews in the city of York were augmented at that time, in consequence of a partial dearth which affected the population, who attributed all to the presence of the Jews, who, they said, had got all the wealth of the country.

The outbreak had in some measure been feared and provided against by the Jews, many of whom had retired to other places for safety, and some depended upon the strength of their habitations and the support of the military.

However, the outbreak came at last, at a moment when it was believed that day had passed, and when some, who had feared the outbreak, and had quitted the city, had returned to it just in time to suffer by it.

There was a great outcry in the middle of the night, and a shout of " Down with the Jews—down with the Jews!" was heard from all quarters of the town, and great bodies of men were seen moving about by torch-light.

"Rebecca," said Ben Shemai in the middle of the night, " Rebecca!"

" Well, my father, I hear. What would you have of me?"

" Do you not hear that horrid shout?"

" I have heard a great tumult, father, in the streets. Something has happened to set the populace up in arms."

"And, as usual, whatever may be the cause of the outbreak, the Jew must suffer—he must lose—he must suffer."

" Aye, father, there is a curse upon our people."

" Never mind about that, Rebecca; that is beyond your understanding; but, if there be a curse upon us, at all events, curse upon the dogs who will not let an honest man enjoy in quiet the produce of his own skill and industry."

"Well, father, the noise comes nearer and nearer. What shall we do? Where shall we fly? To stay here will be dangerous—they will murder you!"

' Aye, girl, they may."

"Then why not fly, father?" exclaimed Rebecca, with much earnestness.

" Because the cries come from all quarters; and to be discovered out of doors now, would be certain death, and there is no chance of safety in flight; all that we may have to suffer must be suffered in our own habitation."

"Merciful God! what will become of us?"

" That, Rebecca," said her father, " I know is not to be escaped now. I would we were on the raging billows of the ocean, rather than in a Christian country—rather than I should be in a country where they preach of peace, good will, and good faith."

" The Turks and the Pagans treat us better than these people. Why not again travel to the East, and live in security?"

"I would, could I escape; and yet I am old now, and should never survive the journey. Hark! Rebecca, hark! they come—they come!"

They came each moment nearer, and loud shouts and menaces against the Jews, and a loud knocking came at the door, and at several other houses at the same time.

" The doors are strong," said the Jew, " the doors are strong; and there are many bolts and wooden bars. I have thought of that. I am sure that the doors will not very easily yield to force. But I fear they will exert themselves too long and too much; and yet they may be deterred by too much time and trouble being spent in the undertaking."

"Hark! how they beat the door!"

"And it will stand all that, and much more," said the Jew, listening.

" But their angry shouts are terrible to hear. They ring like death notes upon my ears. I would we were elsewhere."

"Aye, Rebecca, aye; but we are here. Hark! those heavy blows shake the foundation of the house—the door cracks, the bolts and bars strain—they will all give way with such force."

It seemed as though the populace were bent upon destruction, for they battered the door with great preseverance and energy, until, at length, the door began to give way beneath such a continued and heavy battering, and, with many curses and execrations the mob contrived to force open the door.

" Hurrah !" shouted the mob; "hurrah ! now for the Jews—down with them—burn them—hurrah ! hurrah ! Death to the Jews !"

Rebecca clung to her father for protection when she heard the execrations of the mob, and the sound of their feet upon the stairs.

" God of our fathers protect us !" said the old man, as he stood watching with intense anxiety the approach of the rioters. He made no effort to escape—none. He stood, with his daughter cowering at his feet, as if for protection.

The rioters were no sooner in the house than they made all possible haste to throw all the furniture into the streets, where it was immediately broken into atoms and burned by those below.

" A Hebrew, by St. Mary—a Hebrew ! You take the old crow, and I'll have the young dove," said a big, brawny fellow who came towards them.

" Have mercy upon the aged and upon the woman !" said the old Jew. " You are men, and have fathers and sisters. We stand here pleading for our lives—spare us ! —take all we have. Our whole worldly wealth lies before you—take it, but spare my daughter—spare her for mercy's sake !"

" Hark at the old man preaching ! Take him below and put him on the fire."

The men advanced to do as they were bid ; but the old Jew would not part from his daughter, and one of the men cut him down with a sword, saying—

" That is the best way to settle his business."

" Now for the young girl," said another, attempting to seize her ; but a young man half-armed, drew his sword, and stood forward, saying—

" Back—back, ye dogs ! I will not see this maiden ill-used. By my sword, if ye dare to lay a hand upon her, I will chop that hand off !"

" Who are you, that should stand between us and a Jew ?"

" I am a knight, and sworn to protect the helpless—ye worse than heathen dogs—I am ; and by my knighthood, I will dye this floor with your blood, and there shall not be a man among you who shall escape."

At that moment two squires stepped forth, and, drawing their swords, presented such a formidable front, that the rioters were overawed.

" Will you see her in safety ?" gasped out the Jew.

" I will. She shall not want for protection whilst I hold a sword, old man."

" May Heaven bless you ! Rebecca, be grateful—farewell—I—I——"

The old man could speak no more—life was fled—the aged Israelite was dead. Rebecca had recognized in the voice of her protector the same that had spoken to her of love and happiness, before she saw her father fall, and she fainted in the arms of the young knight, who, aided by his two attendants, bore her away from the scene of tumult and danger.

*　　　*　　　*　　　*　　　*　　　*

In the Venetian states there resided a young knight, whose house no one hardly ever entered, though it was said that he had a beautiful wife ; yet no one ever saw her. Its interior was decorated in the most costly manner. The owner was the young knight, with Rebecca, who had saved much of her father's wealth, and, abjuring her faith, she lived in peace and happiness.

CHAPTER XXII.

THE ADVENTURE OF HOFFENDEN WITH FOXLEY, THE OFFICER.

WE left Harry Hoffenden in anything but an enviable position. It was true that he had escaped from the perils of the gambling-house, but he was in possession of a secret which it was, probably, as dangerous to reveal as it was to keep.

If he made use of the information he had regarding the fate of the young suicide in the gaming-house, and acquainted the police with the circumstance, he well knew that he should call down upon himself the vengeance of men who were perfectly unscrupulous as to how they accomplished their purpose, and who would not even stop at murder, in order to be avenged on any one who gave them trouble.

Then, again, if he kept the secret, he could not help owning that he ran some risk; for, although he thought it more than probable no one had seen him leave the saloon immediately upon the track of the young man who had so awfully put a period to his existence, he could not be quite certain upon that head.

He tortured himself by fancying how many accidents tend to convict sometimes a perfectly innocent man with some seeming crime; and, with a sensation of alarm, he asked himself if he had owed his escape from the gaming-house to the connivance of any of its officials, or to his own carefulness in keeping out of the way.

Hoffenden, however, was not a man of sufficient decision of character to put an end to any torturing and perplexing doubts by an energetic movement, so he slowly took his way towards his own home, much harassed, but yet not dreaming of doing anything to escape from the annoyance he felt.

He had not, however, proceeded above two streets' length from the gaming-house, when he became aware of some one following him with a quick step; and, had he been really the murderer of the young gambler, whose corpse he had seen so mercilessly disposed of, instead of a mere spectator of the scene, he could not have been more alarmed than he now was.

His first impulse was the natural one that he was sure to feel at the idea of being pursued, and he at once carried it out by quickening his pace; but a moment's reflection told him how utterly useless that was if any one were really determind to come up with him.

As soon as this conviction came over him, he rather walked slower than before, and, in a few minutes, he was accosted by a man, who said,—

"Mr. Hoffenden, various circumstances have hitherto kept us apart; but I think now that it is highly desirable we should know each other, as we have some interests in common."

Hoffenden turned, and looked upon the speaker in surprise.

"I do not know you," he said. "You must be labouring under some mistake."

"Not in the least. My pronunciation of your name ought to be sufficient to convince you of that. You do not know me, because, although you may, at times, have seen me, you would not know me now. I flatter myself that, unless I choose it, my most intimate acquaintance would not know me."

"Indeed."

"No. My name is Foxley. It is a part, and not at all an unimportant one, of my trade, to be unknown when I so please; but, you see, with great candour, I tell you who I am. I am Foxley, the officer."

The heart of Hoffenden almost died within him. He knew well how much he was in the power of this man; and that with Roderick Murdo he shared a knowledge of the dreadful secret which might, if it was so much as whispered, consign him, Hoffenden, to a dungeon.

"You—you are Foxley!" he faltered.

"Yes; but I don't know, Mr. Hoffenden, what real cause you have to be alarmed at making my acquaintance; you ought to have fully expected to make it some day."

These words had, to the ears of Hoffenden, a very equivocal sort of sound, and might mean, for all he knew, that Foxley had come to take him into custody.

There was an awkward pause of some few seconds' duration, and then Foxley said—

"Come, come, Mr. Hoffenden, we must understand each other better than we now seem to do. You will walk with me to my house, and I will explain to you why I now seek your acquaintance, after abstaining from doing so for so long a time."

"I—I was going home."

"Oh, pho! pho! this is not a time of night at which a man goes home. Besides, business must be be attended to at all times, so come along."

Hoffenden found himself completely in the power of this man, and he followed him like a child. Oh, what frightful humiliation has not guilt to pass through!

It was about twenty minutes' walk to Foxley's house, and very few words indeed passed betweeen them as they went. The officer let himself into his own abode with a latch key, and he stopped in the passage to light a small hand-lamp, with which he preceded Hoffenden to the same apartment in which we have before found him giving audience.

There was quite a free and easy off-handedness in his manner as he told, rather than asked, Hoffenden to take a seat; and then artfully placing the lamp so that the greatest amount of its light fell upon Hoffenden's face, he spoke with rapidity—

"I need not trouble myself, I am quite certain, to wrap up or disguise known facts, Mr. Hoffenden; you have done what the law would call a deliberate murder."

"Hush!—oh, hush!"

"Oh, you need be under no sort of apprehension here, I assure you; all is right. No one can overhear a word that is uttered in this room, and if they did, perhaps it would be all the worse for them; I say you have committed a murder. There are two people only who know of this."

"Yourself and Murdo."

"Exactly. Now Murdo is a man with no conscience. He is continually asking money of you; and of course, prompted by your fears, you as continually give it to him."

"That is true."

"I know it. While I, who am in possession of precisely the same means of doing you mischief, have held off from you, as you well know, and not made myself at all obnoxious or troublesome to you."

"You have, you have; but, but——"

"I know what you would say. You mean; am I going to begin now to make myself obnoxious, and I answer, I am not. You, however, are, as regards this man, Murdo, in a complete state of bondage, and you pay dearly for being kept in constant misery."

"It is certainly something very like it."

"I know it. Now, what I propose to you, is, to cut his throat."

"What!"

"Perhaps, when I say, cut his throat, you apprehend me too literally. What I mean simply is, that you should get rid of him by taking his life—a life only of importance to himself; and then you can deal with me with much more certainty as regards results, and I truly believe much more cheaply. At all events, you will know what you have to pay, which you do not know with Murdo."

"No, no; I cannot—no more blood, no more blood."

"Psha! You are unnecessarily squeamish, I think. Why, I would shoot down such a man as Murdo with far less compunction than I would a hedge sparrow. What is there in all his life, that should make you feel the least pang at killing him? It would be a good riddance to society, as well as to you."

"Still it is a murder."

"Yes; but only another."

"God of Heaven! that any man living should have the power of saying that to me!"

"Come, come; this milk-and-watery mood will pass away from you, and you will, in time, awaken to a far better comprehension of your own interests—you will find that it is absolutely necessary to do the deed; for, in plain language, I say I will be paid, and you cannot pay us both."

Hoffenden groaned.

"Indeed," said Foxley, "you are scarcely the man I thought you. I imagined you had courage, and now I find you full of fears."

"Let me go, now, and I will think; I do not say no, but I do not say yes—I must think. Let me go, now, Mr. Foxley, for your proposition has taken me too much by surprise, to enable me to give you an immediate answer to it in all its bearings."

"Now you understand me," said Foxley; "you have it in your power to do yourself a great act of justice, and to get rid of a great scoundrel. In comparison with the deed you have already not scrupled to do, it is quite a little piece of innocence itself."

"Is it—is it?"

"Yes; good morning to you. In half an hour it will be daylight; so be off, for it's just as well you should not be seen coming out of my house. You can think over what I have said to you, and let me know the result as soon as possible. I expect that, from a man of sense, there can be but one answer."

Stunned and bewildered by this interview, and the atrocious demands to which it gave rise, Hoffenden staggered from the thief-taker's house towards his own home, more like a man in a dream than one in his walking senses. And well, indeed, might he doubt if the rapid events of the last twenty-four hours were real; and yet he knew not all of them.

He found himself in that inexecrable state of confusion which he might well have supposed would have resulted from recent events, but which, probably, in the midst of the excitement he had experienced in lavishing his wealth, he had overlooked.

He found that that day of retribution he ought ever to have looked forward to had come at last, and that it would be impossible for him longer to hide from himself the distressing fact that, with all his wealth, he was a most unhappy and miserable man, and that he held his very existence on the frail tenure of the silence of other people regarding acts, the public knowledge of which would at any time hurl him to destruction. And yet how strangely familiarity with criminal considerations divests men of the horror with which they had at first regarded them.

As he crept along towards his own home, he caught himself thinking with much less of horror upon the proposition which had been made to him to murder Murdo, than he had first regarded it with. He found that the more he considered it, the more it assumed to his mind a strange shape of probability, and by the time he reached his own door, almost all that remained for him to consider was the means of carrying out what might be called a fixed suggestion.

CHAPTER XXIII.

MURDO AND HIS ASSOCIATE.

Most happily would it have been for those in whose minds innocence and virtue still found a home, if Roderick Murdo had taken his repulse as he ought to have taken it, and, finding how hopeless was his further pursuit of Jane Hoffenden, have dismissed it from his mind.

But he was an individual not formed of dissuasive materials, and every defeat that through life he had experienced had only tended to increase the natural villany of his disposition, and to induce him to adopt more stringent measures for the accomplishment of his purposes.

He was one of those men who had no belief in the reality of virtue, but who looked upon it as a thing collaterally dependent on other circumstances; thence, when he came, what he called, calmly to reflect upon his night's adventures, he assigned any but the true cause for his defeat.

Absolute rage at the treatment he had received for a time extinguished every other feeling, and he was unable to think of anything but the immediate means of revenging himself upon Hoffenden's servants, who certainly had treated him so grievously.

He thought over all imaginable schemes of bringing them to destruction and to ruin. Nothing would satisfy him but that they should individually feel the full weight of a terrific resentment; and although he just had sufficient sense left him to feel how impolitic it would be personally to interfere with any of them, yet he made up his mind thoroughly and entirely that he would not stop at any trifling sacrifices for the accomplishment of his deep and dire revenge.

But then, it was a favourite axiom of his, that revenge would keep, if no other emotion of the mind was of so durable a quality.

He soon, therefore, threw off these considerations connected with Hoffenden's servants, and he turned his whole attention to how he should humble the haughty spirit of her who had treated his advances with such contemptuous disdain.

"Does she think," he muttered to himself, "that I am a man whose passion is to be thus easily crushed? Does she so far mistake me as to imagine that I am an individual who, once repulsed, is for ever defeated? No: I have waded through much more intricate affairs than this; I have accomplished objects apparently beset with many more difficulties; but this time I will be slow and sure."

He had changed his dripping apparel, and was now in a more comfortable mood; and as he sat by the cheerful light of a fire, the wild storm of passion that had possessed him gradually cooled down, and, although none of his revengeful feelings were really suppressed, he was not so likely to do anything hastily or incautiously as he had been.

"Yes," he said, "she shall be my victim, I am quite certain of that; and all that

THE KNIGHT AND THE JEW'S DAUGHTER.

remains to be considered are a few of the careful preliminaries to the accomplishment of that object."

He rested his head upon his hands and strove to think; but the attitude was by far too quiescent a one for him to indulge in long, and he rose and paced the room with agitated steps, as he muttered to himself some of his future resolves.

"Yes," he said, "it shall be so. I can well conceive the mischief that prosperity has done to her. I can well understand how her haughty spirit has risen to absolute pride since she became rich; but yet she shall be mine. Shall I suffer myself to be crushed in what now has become the principal object of my life, because a woman has said nay to me? No; she shall fall from her high estate—she shall be poor again—despicably poor, and then we shall see how far her boasted virtue will stand the test."

Thus we shall easily perceive how very erroneous an estimate the villain made of the character of Jane Hoffenden, by supposing that she resisted his infamous and dastardly proposition because she was rich and surrounded by worldly comforts, and not from that innate spirit of virtue which she possessed, and which would have bloomed under any circumstances.

"She will complain to Hoffenden," he said, " of course, and he, perhaps, is not yet quite so deadened to all sense of honour that he may resent the injury. Well, well— let him do so—yes, let him do so."

He suddenly now paused in his uneasy march to and fro in the room, and spoke with more cheerfulness, as he exclaimed—

"A lucky thought—a lucky thought! I quite forgot my old acquaintance, Colonel Davidge. A greater scoundrel never lived. He and I fell out long ago, but certainly not on that score; now, however, he is the very man I want, and he will prove most invaluable to me in this transaction."

That was not a very seasonable hour to call upon any one ; but somehow or another, the friends and acquaintances of Roderick Murdo were not of that order of persons whose habits and actions are to be counted on like those of the world in general.

He knew perfectly well, even at that strange hour—for it was four o'clock in the morning—where to pitch upon Colonel Davidge.

And it may be as well that we inform our readers, at this juncture, who this Colonel Davidge was, which we can do very shortly, by stating, that he was an adventurer of the very worst class, that is to say, as regards villany, though not as regards appearance ; for he kept up a remarkably showy exterior, and lived at the rate of at least a couple of thousand pounds per annum, without having, apparently, the smallest available resources.

How the colonel managed these things was only known to himself and to a few of the initiated ; and probably, if he had been candidly speaking, and really wishing to inform anybody how he lived, he would in his own slang phraseology have said it was " by plucking pigeons," that is to say, robbing at play inexperienced young men of fortune who might happen to fall into his clutches.

He was well-known at most of the gaming-houses of the metropolis ; and the inferior hands at the fashionable pursuit of pigeon plucking were commonly in the habit of giving him due notice when a fresh victim appeared ; and trusting to his generosity, in which he was tolerably liberal, to give them a share of the spoil.

Roderick Murdo had frequently played this game with the colonel, but they had had a precious quarrel about a sum of money; and so, of late years, the former might be said to have set up in business on his own account, and consequently all communication had ceased between them.

The reader, by this casual mention of Colonel Davidge, will perceive what dark and disreputable scheme had found a home in the breast of Roderick Murdo. He had made up his mind to ruin Hoffenden for the sake of being revenged upon his wife ; but, as that was a transaction in which he could not himself very well personally appear, he thought it was just the thing to entrust to his old associate Davidge.

With such men, a quarrel is nothing, because it almost invariably arises from a diversity of interests on some points, so that a coalition of interests again easily cements the broken connection between them.

Under these circumstances, Roderick Murdo felt no difficulty or hesitation in calling upon the colonel ; and as he knew he should find him at a certain hotel in the neighbourhood of Leicester-square, where very high play was indulged in, he at once, with unflagging energy started to do so.

" I shall have no repose," said he, " until, at least, I have taken some step towards the procuration of my revenge ; and if I once set Colonel Davidge upon the scent, and tell him that he is to have my assistance in effecting the ruin of Hoffenden, instead of my opposition, that ruin may be already considered as a fact accomplished."

He threw over his shoulders a cloak, for the early morning air was rather inclement and the severe pumping upon he had got from Hoffenden's servants had by no means improved the tone of his system. Pulling his hat, then, over his brows, and muttering a most diabolical oath, as he thought of that treatment, he sallied forth into the street, and, with hasty steps, took his way towards the hotel where he expected to find his ex-friend, for whom he entertained just about as lively a regard as such scoundrels have for each other.

" I'm sure to find him," he muttered, " for he has the habits of an owl: he sleeps when other men are awake, and so at night he is full of life and spirits at the gaming-table, and feels but little exhaustion from what enervates the spirits of other men, and undermines their constitutions in no trifling degree—yes, yes, I'm sure to find him.''

CHAPTER XXIV.

JANE HOFFENDEN'S ACCUSATION OF MURDO.

WE have before talked of how Hoffenden crept to his own house, as if there was an ndefinable feeling on his mind that some evil had occurred, and some disquietude was to result to him when he crossed its threshold.

This feeling or presentiment wonderfully grew upon him as he approached the house, until, by the time he stood upon the actual step of his own door, he was in a state of great discomposure and nervousness.

He felt in all his pockets to see if he had a key that would admit him without the necessity of knocking; for he thought of the probability of Jane waiting in listening expectation of his return, and he wished, if he could do so, to enter the house without her knowledge.

He found, however, he had no means of accomplishing this purpose, so he made a very faint appeal to the knocker, which of course was nearly entirely disregarded by his servants, who were quite fashionable enough not to care for anything but a violent appeal to the street-door.

By repeating the summons, however, in a louder key, he did at length get some attention paid to him, but it was rather of a rough sort; for a half-dressed footman flung the door open, and placing his face within an inch of Hoffenden's, cried out—

"What the devil is it now?"

"Scoundrel," said Hoffenden, "what do you mean?"

"I begs your pardon, sir, I really thought it was somebody else; for the fact is, sir, we've been put a little out of sorts, and been obliged to pump upon a gentleman."

"Pump! did you say pump?"

"Yes, sir, that was it—pump was the word."

"And what was the occasion of this disturbance?"

"Why, sir, you must know missus found somebody in the house, and in course she wasn't going to put up with none of that nonsense, so first of all we jolly well pumped upon him, and then gave him into the custody of about twenty watchmen."

"And who was the insolent intruder—some thief, I suppose?"

"Well, sir, I can't take upon myself to say that; but, to tell the truth, sir, it was a most remarkable likeness of your friend. Mr. Roderick Murdo."

Hoffenden staggered back a pace or two, as he said—

"You must be mistaken—there is some mistake. Mr. Murdo, did you say?—Oh, impossible!"

"Yes, sir, it's very likely impossible, but it's true, for all that."

Hoffenden was extremely disconcerted at this intelligence; nothing that could have been said to him would have given him more uneasiness than this. In a moment many circumstances rushed to his mind to make it seem probable that Murdo must have had some very sinister intention on that evening.

He remembered the appointment that had been made with him, at a particular hour, at the new gaming-house in St. James's-street; and he remembered, too, how that appointment had been broken, although it surely would have been so very easy to keep it.

"The villain!" he muttered to himself, as he ascended the staircase, "the villain! has it come to this—and Jane has given him in custody, too—what will be the result of that? —I dare scarcely think what the scoundrel's evil passions may tempt him to do; he has my very life in his hands, and I am powerless. Heaven only knows what will ensue; and what dare I say to her of such a circumstance? Everything tends to convince me more and more that I ought to take the advice of Foxley, the officer, and have that man's life."

It would, indeed, seem now as if everything had that tendency, and Hoffenden, in this outrage of which Murdo had been guilty, began to find abundant argument for carrying out the dreadful counsel that had been given to him.

"Am I to be for ever," he thought, "the slave of this man?—have I sank so low that because he happened to be cognizant of a crime that I have committed, he is then to commit against me and mine every outrage which I should feel most particularly called upon to resent? Is all this possible, I say; and shall I, with the remedy as it were in my own hands, calmly put up with it? No, Murdo; your time will surely come, and you must die."

Hoffenden thought he would avoid his wife for that night at least, and he made an effort to shrink into his own chamber unperceived; but she heard the light footstep on the landing of the staircase, and, walking out of her own apartment, she confronted him with a face so pale and wan, and so full of suffering, that it was terrible to look upon.

Well might that guilty man shrink back with a consciousness of his iniquity, and of how undeserving he was of such a heart as that to which he had caused such a world of acute suffering.

"You have come home, Harry," she said, "you have come home—oh! how I have longed for you to come, for there has been a serpent in the house—a deadly serpent."

"What do you mean, Jane—what do you mean?"

"Step this way, and I will tell you; the story is sufficiently brief, and sufficiently terrible; this way, Harry—this way, and I will tell you all."

"Had you not better," he faltered, "defer until the morning that which—which you have to communicate to me?"

"No, Harry, no; it brooks no delay. I have waited long enough; besides, how is it that you talk of morning—is it not morning now?"

"But you're in such a state of excitement that—that you had better rest."

"No, no, I can guess your feeling, Harry—you understand it; you dread that which I have to tell, and yet I must tell it, were it ten times more dreadful—it must be told; it is a duty I owe to myself, to you, and to our child—it must and shall be told, Harry."

"If it must, then, be it so, I will listen to you, Jane."

He followed her into the apartment from whence she had come, and taking a seat in such a position as to hide his face as much as possible from the light, he prepared himself to listen to the tale of which he had already heard something, and which certainly was not at all calculated to increase his equanimity, or to render his position less embarrassing.

He drew his breath short and thick, and he felt the perspiration stand in cold drops upon his brow, as, in a few simple and concise words, she, his wife, informed him of the outrage that had been perpetrated during his absence.

She added nothing, but she extenuated nothing, and she concluded by saying—

"I summoned my servants, and told them to rid me of the villain who dared thus to intrude himself into my very chamber; they did my bidding, and I believe he is now in the charge of the police; but—but——"

"But what?—it would seem, Jane, that there is yet something to be told."

"There is—there is; the villain boasted that your—aye, even your very life was in his grasp. He said, Harry Hoffenden, that you dared not resent even what I now tell you—it is for you to contradict such an aspersion."

He was silent for some moments, but it was not because he was engaged in thought, but because he was really too much terrified to speak; and, when he did, although his words were those of defiance, yet the abject fear that was creeping over him was too evident to be concealed.

"Fear nothing—fear nothing," he said, "what can there be to fear? He shall answer to me for this outrage, be assured: the complaint has not been made in vain; and, were he ten times what he is—villain as he is—I would be avenged. My life—my life—did he dare to say my life?"

"He did, Hoffenden; but beware what you do; we have been estranged of late, and we meet but seldom; still I would not have you rush into peril, for I cannot forget, Harry, the happy days that we once have passed, and I would not willingly banish from my heart the sweet thought that these days may come again."

"Come again!" he said, abstractedly, "come again!"

"Yes, what should prevent them? Do you think for one moment that I believed the insinuation of guilt that the villain Murdo laid to your charge?"

"No, no—believe nothing—believe nothing; believe nothing that that man can say, even if he were to accuse me of—of——"

"What, Harry—what ?—he did hint at murder."

"Hush—hush! 'tis no such thing—'tis false—it is a bugbear—a spectre, got up to scare my imagination ; but he shall answer to me for all ; be at ease, be at ease ; he shall answer for all, say, the villain! thus to add the grossest insult to the grossest injury. But I will be avenged—yes, yes, I will be avenged !"

" Not personally, Harry ; leave the law to deal even justice between you and such a man as that ; promise me that you will not personally attempt anything, for, as I tell you, Harry, I still cling to the hope of happier days."

" I will be careful—I will be careful. I tell you again to be under no apprehension ; and—and—it is just possible that the happy days may come again."

" Oh, blessed words—blessed words ! let me hear you say them once more, Harry ; let me hear you say that the happy days I thought were buried in the tomb of the past will rise again—let me hear you say that I shall be so blessed !"

"Hush ! Jane, hush ! no more at present ; I must get some rest, for I am weary and vexed. I—I—have been out with some friends, that's all—merely with some friends, Jane. We will talk more of this a few hours hence—good night, good night."

" It is good morning, Harry."

" Morning, morning—yes, it is morning ; well, well, all shall be right ; I will exact an account of this Murdo, which he shall remember while he lives—just while he lives."

He took a candle from the hand of his wife ; for, although the streets were getting light and clear, as the morning was growing on apace, there was a dim darkness yet in the house which made a light, if not an indispensable article, yet an agreeable adjunct to an apartment.

He trembled excessively as he reached his own room, and as he set down the light and flung himself exhausted upon a couch, he said—

" Yes, it is now settled—quite settled that Roderick Murdo must die, and by my hand, too. It is very strange how many circumstances should now point with a strange and ghastly coincidence to that one object—death—death to Murdo !"

CHAPTER XXV.

THE INTERVIEW BETWEEN MURDO AND COLONEL DAVIDGE.—THE COMPACT.

MURDO did not reckon upon finding Colonel Davidge from any defective information. On the contrary, he went with a positive certainty that he should encounter him at the hotel where he resided.

This hotel, to look at it merely from the outside, was a quiet-looking, respectable-enough place ; but in reality it was a gambling-house, and the only connection it had was among those disreputable characters who had no fixed home, and who, having long before given up every notion of domestic felicity, lived within its walls, and were incessantly occupied in the practice of their favourite vice.

Colonel Davidge certainly had held the rank he claimed in the British army, but he had committed some act which had at once induced the authorities to inform him that his voluntary resignation of his commission would be by far the most graceful method of his leaving the army ; for if he did not do so, they would be compelled to institute such proceedings as would end in his disgrace.

After a little reflection, the colonel took the hint, and gave up his commission ; but he did not cease calling himself by his military title for all that ; and those who did not know his disgrace, conceded to him without inquiry, while those who did, called him colonel from habit, and cared nothing about it.

From the period of his leaving the army, he had turned his whole attention to gaming, and he found the pursuit in his hands not a little profitable, for his knowledge of society, his easy manner and address, and his consummate assurance, were enough to impose upon any one.

He was a welcome guest at any of the gambling-tables in the metropolis, for he was liberal with his winnings to the underlings, and he had that sort of manner about him which was calculated to attract the unwary into the frightful meshes of gambling.

Such was the man to whom Roderick Murdo now took his way.

Upon reaching the hotel, it had all the appearance of being closed, but in so obscure a corner close to the door, that no stranger would have noticed it, was a little bell handle, and this Murdo pulled, and then waited the result.

In the course of a few minutes the door was opened by a man who put his head out a little way, to see who it was that demanded admission, and when he observed Murdo, he said—

"Oh, is it you?"

"Yes, it is I."

"Why, what makes you come at such a time as this?—they have all gone long ago; that is to say, a good half hour at the least."

"I don't care about that; I want to speak to the colonel. He is here, I suppose."

"Most decidedly; but he has gone to his room; though I won't say he has gone to bed, for his coffee has just been taken up to him."

"Well, that's all right. I want to see him on particular business. I'll just run up to him at once, William—I know his room."

"Very good."

"What sort of play did you all have last night?"

"Middling, middling. By-the-bye, were you at Crockton's? Somebody whispered something here about a little accident that was said to have happened there."

"Indeed."

"Yes; a young man shooting himself, or cutting his throat—I'll be hanged if I can tell you which; but it certainly was talked of, though in a guarded manner. I thought you would be sure to know."

"Yes; and probably so I should have known if I had been there; but the fact was, I was otherwise engaged, and so missed the opening night at Crockton's, which I much regret; but I suppose I shall hear all about it in due time."

"Of course you will. You can go up to the colonel. You will find him in his room. The second floor, you know, No. 8."

"Oh, yes, yes; I remember, although it is some time since I gave him a call."

Murdo ran up the stairs at a quick rate, and soon arrived at the chamber of the colonel. He tapped at the door, and then, in obedience to the loud summons to come in, he turned the handle of the lock, and found himself in an elegant dressing-room; at a table in which, drawn close to the fire, sat the colonel, sipping his coffee, preparatory to retiring to rest, in order that in the evening he might be again fresh and ready to commence his gambling operation.

He looked for a moment a little surprised to see Murdo, whom he certainly had not beheld for a considerable time, but he could judge at once by his countenance that he came upon an amicable errand, and as that could only be one to the pecuniary advantage of the colonel, he beckoned Murdo to a seat, saying—

"Pray sit down. How have you been this year and a half?"

"No, colonel, we have certainly not met for some time; but I have been thinking that still we need not, on that account, hesitate to transact any business that may be mutually advantageous."

"Certainly not. That's about the most sensible speech, Murdo, you ever made in all your life. All I can say is, cut short the circumstances as soon as you can, for my bedtime has just arrived."

"I need not detain you, colonel, many minutes. You have heard, I presume, that Hoffenden, who used to play much at Lamaitre's, has come into large property?"

"Yes, and that you had taken him under your own protection, and so completely got him into your clutches by some means, that he was a pigeon nobody else could ever have a chance of plucking."

"That is not the fact."

"What is the fact, then?"

"Simply this, that I have come on the old terms, to offer his plucking to you, if you are not better engaged. I want him ruined, but I dare not set about it myself. Hark you, colonel, I am now getting as much money as I like to ask for from this Hoffenden, and it may seem to you something like killing the goose that lays me the golden eggs, to bring such a proposal to you."

"Rather," interrupted the colonel.

"But I have," continued Murdo, "thought of all that; I am willing, for good reasons, to do so. Remember, I am to have one-third down of all you get from Hoffenden."

"Agreed. But you must bring him to the scratch, you know. Do you think he will bite easy, or will he require much angling with before we have him fairly?"

"That I can hardly tell you. He is a strange compound character, and may give much more or much less trouble in the affair than any one imagines."

"Well, well; you know he could not fall into more experienced hands than yours and mine. I have no hesitation at all in saying, Roderick Murdo, that I regretted the infatuation that induced you to leave me in the way you did. You may depend it would be more profitable to you, in the long run, to work with me."

"Perhaps it would. But still, you know, by your own feelings, that there is a spirit of independence about everybody which induces them to do for themselves if they can."

"Very well. I have no objection."

"By the bye, as we have met, can you tell me what has become of young Harrowbridge?"

"Oh! the young farmer?"

"The same. If you recollect, it was about him, and the share I was to have in what spoil was got from him, that two such shining lights as you and I tried to put each other out."

"Bless my heart and life, Murdo, you are getting quite poetical. That's a devilish good idea of your's. We are two shining lights, and, like every other shining light, it is by night that we show ourselves in all our lustre?"

"True; but what became of the young farmer?"

"Oh, I plucked him."

"Yes, I guessed that. But what then—what then?"

"I can gather from your manner, Murdo, that you have heard something about it, and want to know if I will confirm it.—Pray hand me the cream—thank you.—Well, if you must know, he went one morning to Kensington Gardens, and shot himself in one of those little boxes there, with seats in them.—The sugar, if you please. I am sorry to give you so much trouble."

"Shot himself, did he?—Don't mention the trouble."

"Thank you.—Yes; the bullet from the pistol went through his head, and lodged in the woodwork at the back of the seat, where it actually remains now, for I saw it only a few days ago."

"And that was the end?"

"I suppose so. It ought to be the end, I think, when a man shoots himself through the head. It's generally the end, I rather imagine, ain't it?"

"Why, yes, to him, certainly. But, however, it's nothing to me. I was out of that, you know; and now, colonel, what house do you recommend that I should bring Hoffenden to?"

"This, by all means. It's most decidedly the quietest."

"Agreed. And now I must tell you that a little affair has happened which may, possibly, induce him to call me out. If so, I must go; but the matter must be managed so that no mischief ensues, and the only way I can get out of this scrape I am in with him is to take a shot from him if he insists."

"What do you mean by managed?"

"Why, his second must keep the bullet out of his pistol, and then he may blaze away at me as much as he likes, you know. Should he challenge me, will you act for him?"

"How can I, unless he comes to me?"

"You shall have an opportunity of throwing yourself in his way. I know he has no friends at all, and will eagerly catch at any one who will play the part of second to him. Promise me this much, and I will communicate to you all that is necessary for you to know, in order to enable you to act properly in the matter."

"Well, it's a little bit of amusement, and I don't care if I do. But what have you quarrelled about?"

"Hoffenden has a handsome wife."

"Oh! that's it, is it? Well—well; if a man is fool enough to fight about a woman, he must be just let do it, I suppose. You may depend upon me playing a character in the little farce you propose."

"Then, colonel, I may, I hope, congratulate both you and myself upon the t of our ancient friendship being again cemented."

"As you please. We certainly have interests in common. And now good morning to you; for my bed-time has fairly come, and I must have my systematic rest."

"Good morning!—you shall hear from me. He is quite as great a scoundrel as ever," muttered Murdo to himself, as he left the colonel's room.

"That Murdo," remarked the colonel, as he finished his coffee, and prepared himself for bed—"that Murdo is, I think, the greatest rascal unhung!"

CHAPTER XXVI.

THE MYSTERIOUS OCCURRENCE IN FOXLEY'S HOUSE.

WHILE these rascally manœuvres are going on, and so much is being done on all sides for the purpose of achieving revenge, as well as the gratification of other bad passions, there are some mysteries connected with Mr. Foxley and his abode, which we may as well not altogether lose sight of.

That gentleman, after he had parted with Hoffenden, to whom he had certainly given advice of an extremely practical character, sat for some time in perfect silence, apparently in deeper thought than he usually indulged in on most occasions; for he was rather a man who prided himself upon the off-handed manner in which he managed to settle everything in which he might be engaged.

"Yes," he muttered, to himself—"yes; my only chance of making a thorough good thing of this affair, consists in getting rid of the rascal Murdo; and Heaven knows my hands are full enough already, without undertaking the task of ridding the world of him. Besides, by inducing Hoffenden to do the deed, I have yet another hold upon him in consequence of that criminality which could not be gainsayed."

He paused suddenly, for he heard some one touch the latch of his room-door. In another moment the strange young girl, whom we introduced in the early portion of this work, entered the room.

"Ah! Maria," said Foxley; "you are early a-foot."

"I am. And yet would have been with you earlier," she said, "but that you had some one with you."

"Can I pleasure you in any way? Do you want money to go to Job Oakes's with, Maria?"

"No."

"Well, the negative is certainly boldly given."

"It is. But I will tell you as boldly what I want, and what I will have. That is, an assurance that the life of him who occupies No 2 will be saved."

"Hush! Maria—hush! You, and you only, are in possession of the secrets of this house. You know that I have four apartments, strongly secured, and seldom vacant, in which it is part of my policy to hold prisoners sometimes, until I have made terms with them for their release, or the authorities have offered sufficient to make it worth my while to surrender them to the gallows."

"I do know that; and in such transactions, base as they are, you know that I have not in any manner interfered; but the prisoner in No. 2 is not of such a sort."

"Pho—pho! Maria; we must not draw nice distinctions. He is of a sort to bring me money, and that is, surely, quite enough for me."

"Enough for you, but not enough for me; you mean to take his life."

"His life?"

"Yes; you find that you can do better with him dead than with him living. I know it, Foxley—I know it well. You cannot hide that fatal truth from me. Now I not only know that from symptoms that I have seen, but I know what your motive in taking his life is!"

"Indeed."

"Yes; it is to ensure his secrecy upon a matter which concerns him nearly; and I tell you, you need not prevaricate with me, for I know that such is the case."

"Well, and if you know that much, Maria, what follows in your mind contingently upon that knowledge, I should like to know."

"This much—that if I show you how to btain your object without committing a cowardly murder, you are bound to yield to me.'

"Go on—go on."

"You want the prisoner in No. 2 out of the way. I can get him to go voluntarily out of the way, and to keep the secret you would hide in the grave. Will not that much content you?"

"I must be well assured that it can be done."

"You shall be well assured; you shall have it proved to you by actual facts. Listen to me. I know, from what I have ascertained of his character, that his word is to be relied upon. I will prove to him, that, for the sake of one whom he loves better by far than he loves that vengeance, which, in his case, might well take the name of justice, he had better be silent."

"Can you fancy that promises are sufficient in such a case, to bind any one?"

"I do not fancy it, I know it."

"You are too romantic about this matter by far, Maria. What on earth can it be to you? Leave me, I beg of you, to act in this rather complicated affair as shall seem the best to me.   D) not mix yourself up in a matter that will, in the end, be surely most unsatisfactory to you."

"Do you know so little of me, Foxley, as not to feel that what I say I shall assuredly do?"

"But I would dissuade you."

"Did you ever know me to be dissuaded?"

"Now, really, Maria, is this like you?   You are possessed of much sound sense; you have acquirements far beyond your years, and yet you come to me with a proposition which must be quite inimical to that sound sense, and which certainly cannot be thought of."

"Very well."

"Stop—stop! where would you go?"

"To Bow-street, to make confession of some things that I know, which will make some sensation among the magistracy."

"Know you not that I could stop you?"

"I know you could stop me by taking my life; but I know, likewise, that you will not do so; that I know well enough. You will not do so, Foxley; there are some considerations which are powerful enough to make you hold your hand."

"But why will you drive me to such an extremity, Maria? You have done me good service on many an occasion. Why should you seek to cross me now?"

"Argument—reproach—solicitation," cried the girl, "all are alike vain; I am resolved, I tell you. You may, by complying, which you ought to do, and might do, with perfect safety, with my proposition, restore us to our recent friendly state as regards each other; but I tell you frankly, I will not have this young man sacrificed."

"Well, this is a most extraordinary fancy of yours?"

"Extraordinary or ordinary, it is my fancy. You shall suffer nothing in your views or you prospects, you may depend; and it is because I have that argument in my mouth that I feel myself so strong and firm."

"Well—well."

"You consent—you consent?"

"If you can show me good reason for believing what you say, as regards my views not suffering, I do consent."

"'Tis well; 'tis well; you have acted most wisely, for I had wound myself up to a pitch of desperation which would have stopped at nothing."

"By Jove! you have, as I well know, some fiery blood in your veins, that will yet, unless I am very much mistaken, lead you some day into serious mischief. You are by far too much a creature of impulse. You feel much more than you think."

"It is no matter. The strange circumstances that have prematurely developed my imagination are to blame. Let it suffice that I have, as you know, always been most faithful to you."

"I grant that most freely."

"Then, so far, my strange temperament does no mischief, and you need not comment upon it."

"Do not be offended, Maria. Remember, that I have yielded to you, when I would have yielded to no one else in this world. You should remember that, Maria; and set it down to the fact, that I have at least some gratitude to you for past affairs."

"And you remember," said the girl, "I know quite enough to be mischievous."

"Why, you are mischievous."

"But I can be more so, as you well know, Foxley. I don't want to cross you in any of your schemes, if I can help it; but when I tell you of a way in which a thing can be done, that is as good as your way, and not so violent or wicked, it shall be so, or I will do what you will repent daring me to."

"And what may that be?"

"Peach—peach. Do you understand that word?"

"I understand it well enough; but you dare not do so, I tell you. Nevertheless, in pursuance of the disposition you have always found in me to consult your wishes in all things, the experiment shall be tried, and, if it succeed, you shall have your own way."

"It will succeed."

"Very good; you need not be in such a passion, Maria; it is as much for your sake as my own that I act as I do. You will live to have the advantages."

"I shall not live," said the girl, as she hastily left the room. "You are mistaken; I shall not live!"

"Well," said Foxley, to himself, when he was once more alone, "this is certainly one of those affairs that are a little out of my line, and I rather doubt if the motives will be sufficient. Hang the girl, she is a troublesome piece of goods, certainly, as I have found before, to my cost; but yet she has been at times uncommonly useful to me—that I am quite willing to allow, and if she were not so plaguly romantic, she would be quite a genius."

He paced the room in silence for some time, and then he muttered to himself—

"No, no; hang it—hang it. I cannot touch her—I cannot do her any harm. There are some old recollections that ever have power to stay my hand. Maria, you are safe, and the experiment you insist upon shall at all events be tried; I can judge for myself of its success. All I want is that Hoffenden should be left alone."

It was evident that Mr. Foxley was not a man who was inclined to murder for the mere sake of murder, and he viewed the taking or the preserving of human life with an amount of philosophy which had it's sole basis upon his own interests.

CHAPTER XXVII.

THE QUARREL BETWEEN HOFFENDEN AND MURDO.—THE CHALLENGE.

HOFFENDEN rose on the following—morning, we were going to say—but it ought to be on the same morning, at about eleven o'clock, with his brain heated and bewildered. No wonder that it was so, for if ever any human being had, from conduct which he might and ought to have controlled, cause to feel bitterness of spirit, that human being was the wretched Harry Hoffenden.

What was there now for him to look back upon his whole career, that could give him any degree of satisfaction?—literally nothing. And, if, by chance, his mind did wander back to scenes of former days, when he was innocent of the deep and glaring iniquities that now he had committed, the contrast with what he was then with his present condition, only seemed to embitter the latter, and to render it less endurable.

He felt, at times, as if he was going mad.

Such, however, are the usual morning reflections of the drunkard, the gambler, and the profligate. It is not until the day has made some advances, that he can hope for equanimity.

And, in order to recover at all sufficiently to go through the affairs of the day without actually exhibiting the distressful feelings that possess them, these victims of the evil passions of humanity are compelled to resort to the most baneful stimulants; so was it with Harry Hoffenden. He partook of a large glass of raw spirits before he could encounter even the man who had injured him.

His intention most certainly was to leave the house without encountering Jane, and accordingly he opened the door of his chamber, and listened to hear if the staircase was clear, in order that he might step unperceived from his own house, as if he had been a felon.

Alas! that a man's own criminality should have reduced him to such a state that even beneath his own roof he does not feel that security and comfort which the poorest ought to enjoy, and not unfrequently do, far more than the wealthy, and the seeming great and happy.

All appeared to him to be perfectly still, and, as he could hear no sound of any voice, he thought that probably all the doors were shut, and that now or never was his opportunity to slip down stairs and get out of the house without any one perceiving him.

Accordingly, he cautiously left his own room, and reached the hall without encountering any one; but, as he crossed it, he saw through an open doorway his wife sitting by a table, on which was an untasted meal, and sobbing as if her heart would break.

In vain he tried to tear himself away from the sight; he felt as if spell-bound, and that he could not do so. It seemed to him, as if he were compelled, by some mighty and irresistible influence, there to wait until she should look up and encounter his gaze.

Truly Hoffenden suffered during the succeeding five minutes something like a mortal retribution, such as he had not before imagined the existence of.

Yes; thus waited that sometimes bold, and alas, now always bad man, until she, his much injured wife, should confront him.   He did make more than one effort to leave the place, but he could not; and at length, when Jane Hoffenden looked up, and saw him, she uttered a cry of dismay, for he looked much more like some evil spirit than what he really was.

"Good—good morning!" he said, as he moved towards the door. "Good morning; I must go."

She rose, and gently approached him; she placed her small attenuated hand upon his arm, and led him gently into the room.   There was a strange expression upon her face. He thought that her sorrows had driven her mad, and he shuddered to think that he was in the presence of a maniac, whose humour might be as uncertain as the winds.

"Jane, Jane," he said. "What do you mean?"

His voice seemed to have the effect of unlocking the springs of her tears, and she wept abundantly.   Oh, those blessed tears! Who shall say how many kind and loving hearts have been saved from madness by your chastening, yet soul-relieving presence.

She still clung to him, and still wept; while he shook like some criminal standing at the bar of earthly or of heavenly justice, to hear his doom.   It was some time before she spoke, and then she said softly—

"Harry—husband! It is time that we should converse together—it is time that I, your wife, should make to you a last—a loving appeal.   "Oh, Harry, you have turned from me when I have remonstrated—you have refused to listen to my prognostications of evil; but now it is of good that I speak to you, and let me implore you, for the love of the great God, who is now beholding us both, to listen."

"He trembled violently, and was compelled to hold by a chair for support, as he said—
"What is it? What would you say?"

"You will hear me? Thank Heaven for that. You will hear me, Harry? I have no reproaches. I know your fortune is a wreck—I know that there are those in London whose baneful society you cannot shake off—I know, Harry, that you are a victim; but listen to me—I have a scheme that shall end those sorrows. Oh, Harry, do you think there is yet a green spot in your heart that can expand so as to induce you to love the soft beauties of the fields and flowers, as once you did?"

"I don't understand you. Say on—say on."

"Then, Harry, you will hear me? Oh, you look, even in these few minutes, more, much more like your former self, dear Harry; and now, let me ask you, have you ever thought of escaping from the thraldrom that surrounds you?"

"Hush, hush! It may not be."

"It may—it may, and it shall, Harry. Listen. There may yet, surely, be snatched enough means for happiness from what the world calls ruin; surely that can be done. What, suppose now, we were, even with the small means that could rapidly be collected together, go to Switzerland, Harry, or the south of France—the sweet country of Languedoc, where there is nearly eternal spring? Oh, surely we might yet, in some such place be happy. Speak, speak, what think you of the scheme?"

"God! no—no; it may not be. Jane. do you want to drive me mad? I say, it may not be. Hush, hush, no more of this—no more of this. Oh, why did I listen to the possibility of such a dream! Peace, peace—oh, peace, unless you would drive me mad at once!"

"Mad—mad, Harry! Oh, do not speak thus! What have I said, what have I done to drive you to so much desperation? Do you not see, Harry, how that what I propose may surely be done?"

"Jane, Jane, you know not what you say! I did hope to have left this house without your knowledge, this morning; but as it is, Jane, I am glad to have seen you, for now I feel that, before I do leave it, I ought to ask your forgiveness for much of the past."

"Oh, no; not mine, Harry! You will in the future make up, and more than make up for every pang that the past has given me."

"The future?"

"Yes, oh, yes! Why do you repeat that word, as if it had some awful signification? The future will come to both of us; and it shall be a future of happiness. Why should it be otherwise, Harry?"

"Because—because——"

"Because what? Why do you pause? Is there really some horrible secret? Oh, do not let me think it possible that that bad man has spoken faithfully!"

"You mean Murdo, Jane—you mean Murdo. That name, by its very sound, has roused me to what I have to do. Oh, Jane, Jane! you do not know what you say when you talk of happiness yet to come. You do not know all, Jane. Let me go now; I have that to do which will not brook delay. Farewell—farewell!"

"No, no, no! my heart misgives me. You are bent upon some terrible purpose, Harry. Do not—oh, do not leave me!"

"What purpose do you mean? Look at me; am I not calm and collected? Ay, so calm and collected, that I will promise to think of your scheme of—of leaving England. Oh, if it could but be done after——"

"After what, Harry?"

"No matter—no matter. There must be a retribution in this world; I have felt it, and why should not another of much worse impulses than even I have? Oh, yes, yes! Farewell, Jane, farewell! I cannot remain now longer with you."

He tore himself away from her detaining grasp, and more and more did he feel determined to extract from Murdo an expiation for his offences towards him. With a full resolve that the villain who had been the bane of his existence should no longer live to boast of his deeds, Hoffenden left his home in search of that man who certainly seemed to have something demoniac in his disposition, for one could hardly believe any one simply mortal could be so desperately wicked.

"Yes," said Hoffenden, whose feelings towards the ruffian, who might be said to have been the destroyer of his peace, were by no means ameliorated by the interview he had just had with Jane—"yes; it shall now come to an end. He shall either consummate his villany by my death, or I will rid the world of one who is a disgrace to it."

It happened, though, that the time of day was not one well calculated to enable any one to find Roderick Murdo; for he was tolerably sure to be somewhere sleeping off the fatigues of the preceding night; and, as he had no fixed abode, it was no easy matter, even for one well acquainted with his haunts, to make sure of finding him.

Few men, however, listen to difficulties, when revenge urges them on; and, as Hoffenden could not bring his mind to brood over anything now but his projected punishment of Murdo, he was indefatigable in his search for him from place to place, where he thought there might be a chance of finding him.

He was unsuccessful for more than two hours; and at length, quite wearied, he went into a questionable kind of hotel, which was, in fact, a gaming-house by night, and sat down to have some refreshments. He was well known by the waiter who attended upon him, and after partaking of what he required to recruit his exhausted energies, he said—

"William, I have been hunting all over the town for Captain Murdo. Do you happen to know where he is?"

"Hunting all over the town, sir! Well, I am very sorry indeed to hear that, Mr. Hoffenden; for if you had but come here first——"

"Oh, you could have told me?"

"Indeed, sir, I could; for the fact is—of course I would not mention it to anybody but yourself, sir—he is now in this house."

Hoffenden sprang to his feet, and the expression upon his countenance was such as to make William repent that he had been so communicative even to him.

"I hope, sir, nothing's amiss," he said. "Really, sir, I hope there's no quarrel; because you see, sir, if there is, I shall have all the consequences upon my head, and I shall lose my place. Pray, sir, don't go to him if anything is wrong, sir."

"Pho—pho!" said Hoffenden, controlling himself by a violent effort; "you have nothing to fear. In fact, I will reward you, William. It's only a wager, you see, that Mr. Murdo and I have to settle between us—that's all. Where does he sleep? Can you show me his room, William? I will make it worth your while."

"Oh, yes, sir, of course I can; but you see, sir, I have no business up stairs, and would rather not be seen going. You cannot miss finding his room, Mr. Hoffenden. It's number sixteen, and the second door to your right, when you get up two pair of stairs."

"Thank you. I need not trouble you," said Hoffenden; and in another moment he was bounding, at a most rapid rate, up the staircase.

CHAPTER XXVIII.

CRIMINATION AND RECRIMINATION.—THE DANGER OF MURDO.—THE AGREEMENT TO
FIGHT.

HENRY HOFFENDEN paused for a moment or two to take breath, when he reached the
landing-place, after ascending to the second floor of the hotel. He did not wish to go
into Murdo's room as if he were in a state of undue excitement. What he meant to do,
he meant to do as coolly and calmly as possible.

No. 16 was staring him in the face the moment he turned to the right, and he placed
his hand upon the handle of the door. He dreaded to find it locked, in which case his
voice, in demanding admission, might betray him; for a man, whose passions are in a
storm, has little chance in succeeding in anything that requires dissimulation and cunning
to conduct it to a successful issue.

The door was not locked: it yielded to a touch.

Hoffenden entered a partially darkened room, and closed the door behind him. The
window-curtains, which were of heavy, thick damask, were drawn nearly close, so that
it was only a sort of twilight that came into the apartment; and the first act of Hoffenden was to dash aside the window-curtains, so as to admit a flood of light into the room.

It was the rattle of the curtain-rings upon the iron rod on which they moved, which,
no doubt, awakened Murdo, who looked up with a confused aspect, saying—

"Oh, William, I forgot to tell you, if any one comes for me, by no means own that I
am here."

Hoffenden did not speak; but he looked from the window where he stood towards
Murdo, who, for a few moments, was so confused by the glare of light that came upon
his face, that he could not exactly see who it was. The silence, however, of the person
who had thus made way into his room, first made him think that something was amiss,
and he started up in bed.

Then he saw and knew Hoffenden.

For an instant, even the effrontery of Murdo appeared to have deserted him; for the
mere fact that the man whom he had so much injured should seek him in his bed-room,
showed that something of a very unusual character was about to take place.

Still Hoffenden was silent; and that silence perplexed Murdo more than enough, for
he would have been glad to have ascertained, from the voice of Hoffenden, what were his
thoughts and intentions. That continued and mysterious silence, however, forced Murdo
to speak, for it was much more painful to him than it was to Hoffenden.

"Is that you, Hoffenden?" he said, with affected hilarity; "why, you are an early
visitor."

"And you are a scoundrel," said Hoffenden.

This was quite conclusive, and Murdo saw in a moment that, probably, as serious a
quarrel as any he had ever been engaged in was at hand. Bitterly he regretted not having taken measures, which he might have done, to secure himself against interruption:
but it was too late now; the time had come for action, not regrets.

He sprung out of bed, and commenced quickly dressing himself, without offering a
word to Hoffenden in reply to what he had said.

"You heard me," said Hoffenden; "you are a villain—an assassin. What hinders me
from, at this moment, ridding the world of a man who has committed more iniquity in it
than human lips can tell? I say, what hinders me, Murdo?"

As he spoke he drew from his pocket a pistol, and presented its shining barrel to the
man who had, fiend-like, played for a time the part of a friend, but to become, with the
greater certainty of hitting his mark, the most deadly foe.

Murdo was not a coward. He was constitutionally brave, and he felt, now that his first
surprise was over, that his safety wholly lay in the coolness and intrepidity of his own
behaviour. It required an effort so to do; but he made the requisite one, and turning
his full face to Hoffenden, he said in tones of deep solemnity—

"Beware—beware, I say, Henry Hoffenden, that you do that in your passion which
you will repent of at your leisure. There is always time enough for vengeance when you
are quite convinced it is called for, and that it is not now, I do not expect you to take

my simple word; but I do expect that even you will condemn no one unheard. It is contrary to my nature so to do. I know you, Mr. Hoffenden, better than you know yourself; you cannot take the life of an unarmed man."

"I have done so once, and at your instigation," said Hoffenden; but yet the pistol shook in his grasp as he spoke, and the old irresolution, which was part and parcel of his disposition, was coming over him. Murdo saw that he was comparatively safe, at all events, if not wholly so. It was his task now to seek to improve the advantage he had gained.

"Mr. Hoffenden," he said, "I will not at a time like this seek to flatter you——"

"Dissembling villain."

"Call me what you like; but, for your own sake, if you fancy I have done you wrong, for the sake of your own after reflections, meet me like a man. I pledge myself to give you a meeting with what weapons you like, and when you like; but do not act the part of an assassin."

"An assassin! It should not, and cannot be called assassination, to rid the world of a monster. If I hesitate, it is not that I view the deed with those feelings, but because I will not sacrifice myself needlessly even in the perpetration of an act of justice. I accept your offer."

"You are right, Hoffenden, you are right; but, since you are firm, perhaps you will tell me in what it is that I have offended you so grievously?"

"Can you ask such a question, and not fear to renew those sentiments with which I entered this chamber?"

"You may have heard much to my prejudice, that I will not deny; but, remember, Hoffenden, that there is no story which may not be told two ways."

"Enough, enough; I will hear no more."

"Nay, is this just?"

"Murdo, I am more than satisfied that you are a villain—let that suffice. There needs no words about any specific charge that I could bring against you. You are a villain, Murdo, and as such I brand you with the name. I will meet you as you propose but further argument with you I will not have."

"Be it so, then; you may possibly take the life of your best friend. I will be in a coach at the corner of Park-lane this evening, an hour before sunset, and will go where you please to direct."

"Agreed; I will think upon our route between this time and then. I will likewise provide myself with a second, do you do so likewise; and I pray that before night, one or both of us may sleep the long sleep of death; and, by the heavens above us, I care not if it be myself."

"It shall be, or I will know a most substantial reason why," muttered Murdo, and then he said aloud—"Well, well, I deeply regret it; but it cannot be said that I refused a meeting to any man yet, Hoffenden, and I am not going to do so now."

Hoffenden turned and left the apartment, feeling that his resolution as usual had failed, for, most certainly, when he first made his way into the bed-room of Murdo, his intention was to take his life, and then he would have made what exertions he could to provide for his own safety.

And did no thought of his wife and child cross his mind in that arrangement? Yes, it did. He did think of them, and he knew that they would have a good chance of being happier in the hands of perfect strangers, than while they were tied to him and his fortunes. What was he now, that his presence should be considered even as one of the destroyers of their peace? What a horrible conviction for any man to have regarding himself, who has those near and dear ties of wife and child!

But such actually were the feelings of Hoffenden. Oh! could he but have recalled the last few years of his existence—could he but awaken and find that all was but a dream, into what a Heaven of delight he would be then plunged. What joy—what extacy! But no; all was too real—too substantial. He lived, and he had made himself what he was.

Home, he did not now dare to go. What was home to him? How long was it since he could pronounce that word, and mentally append to it any of those endearing recollections and feelings which hallow the name to the poorest man, who can lay his hand upon his heart, saying,—

"God knows I am innocent of intentional evil."

Alas! how few in this wild, stormy world of dark and dreadful struggling, can say so much! Blessed is he who can, and he ought to welcome death, lest, by living on, he should fall from that high estate.

The circumstances of Hoffenden might now be considered to be in their most complex state, and it would be a mercy for him to fall even by the hand of such a man as Murdo; for by so falling, he would most unquestionably save an amount of misery, far more than equal to any he could encounter by the mere pain of dying; and yet he clung to life. That hope which

"Springs eternal in the human heart,"

did not quite desert him yet, and the proposition of Jane began, as the day advanced, to assume to his mind a much more feasible character, and he began to think that if he should kill Murdo in the encounter that was about to take place, he might do worse than lay his hands on what resources he could, and then make his way to some other land to seek for peace where he was not known.

At all events, it required consideration; and the thought did occur to him, that on the Continent there were plenty of gaming-houses; but he did not know that the cheating that goes on openly in a continental gaming-saloon, is about ten times what is done secretly and with dread of exposure in England.

But these were dreams which were never to be realised. Other events plunged Hoffenden still further into that vortex, from which there was no escaping.

CHAPTER XXIX.

THE MEETING AT ACTON.—THE RESULT OF THE DUEL.

IT became a matter now of moment to Hoffenden to get some one to accompany him to the meeting with the scoundrel Murdo, in the character of a friend, and he thought over the names of all he knew, with some anxiety, to discover one to whom he could apply.

Among them all, however, there was no one whom he thought he could trust, for he had a frightful dread of what Murdo might say in the event of anything going wrong with him in the encounter. And now, when he began to think of the really fearful secret which Murdo was in possession of, he more than once regretted that he had not at once, in the hotel, put an end to the villain's existence.

True, there would have been some chance of his, Hoffenden's, getting into some immediate trouble upon the subject; and yet, a pistol-shot from the very small weapon he had with him at the time, would have made but a slight noise in a closed room, but the bullet would have been quite sufficient to have produced death.

"Oh! fool that I was to hesitate about it," he thought, as he sat in a coffee-room of a French restaurateur's, in a street leading out of Leicester-square; I "might have rid myself for ever of this man; but now, alas! I know not what may happen prejudicial to me."

As he sat indulging in these gloomy reflections, a tall, sinister-looking, and most awfully ugly Frenchman came in, and seated himself at the table where Hoffenden was. He was frightfully scarred with the small-pox, and there was a frightful cicatrix of a wound across his forehead and one of his eyebrows, which gave him a most diabolical aspect, and appeared to have engendered a faint squint.

Hoffenden was not very much delighted at the close companionship of such a personage, nor was he a bit more prepossessed in his favour, when he ordered a repast of soup, which could not come to above fourpence; and when he had swallowed it, carefully pocketed the remainder of the bread, which was very imprudently supplied a discretion in that house, according to the fashion in Paris.

Hoffenden, in moving his foot under the table, slightly knocked the stranger, and, of course, apologised to him, the brief apology being received with perfect gentlemanly courtesy, so that a sort of acquaintance sprung up as the ice was thus broken between them.

Hoffenden found that the Frenchman spoke English but indifferently; and, as he announced that he had been in the army (what Frenchman has not?), a sudden thought struck Hoffenden that he might serve as well for a second to him in the duel with Murdo as any one else, and perhaps better.

"Sir," he said, "I cannot but think it a fortunate circumstance that brought me to this hotel to-day, since it has made me acquainted with so brave and so courteous a person as yourself."

"You is *very mush* better *den* too *goot*," said the Frenchman.

"Not at all, sir; and perhaps you will allow me to explain why I came here, and appeared to be in such deep thought when you came in, which, no doubt, you noticed."

"*Certainement.*"

"Well, sir, I have got embroiled in an affair of honour, which must come off this evening, and I am at a loss for a second. I was just counting over all my friends, and wondering to whom I could refer, as I have some objection or another to almost all of them, and I never like to involve married men in such affairs—you understand, sir."

"Certainly," said the Frenchman, with whose particularities of pronunciation we need not fatigue the reader; "you're quite right in that respect, sir; I am alone, and nearly a stranger in London, and I can only say that, if you choose to accept of my services, they are perfectly at your disposal."

"Sir, I scarcely know how to thank you sufficiently."

"Oh, do not thank me at all. The fact is, that during my military experience, I have seen so many little affairs of the sort, that I think nothing at all of this, and I consider it but just a piece of ordinary civility from one gentleman to another on such an occasion."

Hoffenden was very well pleased to have got over his difficulty so easy, and to have secured to himself a second, who, knowing nothing whatever of his previous history, could not be prepared for any uncomfortable revelation from the scoundrel Murdo; and if, indeed, any should be made, would probably have but a very insufficient understanding of it, from his rather limited knowledge of the language.

"If you have no other engagement," he said, "perhaps you will, as the day is getting on, join me in a bottle of wine here, before we go to the redezvous, and in that case we need not part."

"With pleasure, sir. But what weapons do you use?"

"Pistols, which I can borrow at a gunsmith's, as we go, without difficulty."

The Frenchman seemed to be quite at ease, and quaffed the wine, and talked upon the most indifferent subjects, fully proving the truth of what he had said, namely—that affairs of honour were so familiar to him that he thought nothing of them, only giving to them the attention of a passing moment, and only taking them as some of the most ordinary incidents of everyday existence. But as the time approached, Hoffenden, although he could not be said to feel fear, could not be entirely indifferent to the matter which might place him among the dead before two more hours elapsed.

But while the Frenchman, who told Hoffenden that his name was Grillet, seemed to be so utterly heedless of the passage of time, he was not so in reality; for ever and anon he kept his eyes upon a clock that was in the dining room, and when he saw that the hour had come when it would be necessary to start, he said—

"Sir, we have something to do before going to the place of meeting. Had we not better start?"

"Certainly," said Hoffenden, rising.

The bill of the hotel was paid, and they left it; first of all in search of a gunsmith's, where could be procured the pistols, which it was necessary Hoffenden and his second should take with them.

They found more difficulty in procuring such weapons, as a loan, than Hoffenden had imagined; and, after all, it was only by his leaving the full value of them, as a deposit, that he got a pair.

"I think," he said to the gunsmith, "as you know me, you are needlessly scrupulous."

"Not at all, sir," said the gunsmith. "But we never lend duelling pistols without their full value being left; not that we may at all doubt the honour of the gentleman to whom we lend them, but, you know, sir, there is a possibility that he may not have it in his power to return them."

"Exactly, exactly—I understand."

"I was sure you would, sir, and therefore not take amiss the little fact of our demanding a deposit."

Hoffenden said no more upon the subject, but handing the pistols in their case to the Frenchman, they left the shop together, and, quickly procuring a coach, directed the driver to take them to Hyde Park, by the Oxford-street entrance, to that favourite place of resort for nursery maids and blackguards.

Just at the iron-railings, near the corner of Park-lane, another coach was standing; and when the vehicle, which contained Hoffenden and his second came up, a gentlemanly-enough-looking man alighted from the former, and approaching, said—

"I suppose I have the honour of speaking to Mr. Hoffenden."

"Yes, sir," said Monsieur Grillet, "but you will please to observe that I am the friend of Monsieur Hoffenden, and you will do me the honour of speaking to me, and not to him."

"With pleasure, sir. If you will alight, we will in a few moments, I have no doubt, settle where the little affair is to come off."

The Frenchman alighted from the coach, and walked a short distance down Park-lane along with Murdo's second, who gave his card, which announced him as a Major Williams, although, upon close inspection of his general appearance, any one well acquainted with London life would have probably pronounced him as an assistant to a gaming-house, or a bonnet, as they are termed.

Monsieur Grillet, however, if he thought anything at all derogatory to the second of Hoffenden's opponent, kept such thoughts to himself; and it was agreed, at the suggestion of Major Williams, the party should go in the coaches, about three miles down the Uxbridge-road, and then, after discharging the vehicles, seek for some place where could be carried out, with the due and desirable degree of privacy, their intentions.

" There are plenty of fields and retired spots," said Major Williams, " where a duel may be fought comfortably, both to the right and left of this road."

" Monsieur is better, of course, acquainted with the country than I am," replied Grillet; " and I shall be happy to follow his directions."

This part of the business thus being settled so far satisfactorily, the requisite orders were given to the coachman, and, at as good a pace as hackney-coach horses could be expected to move, they went towards Bayswater.

The evening was now rapidly drawing in, so that it became a very doubtful matter indeed if there would be light enough for the duel to come off; and yet the twilight among the open fields lingers much longer in its reflected beauty, than it does in the streets of London; and as they got clear of the houses, and the smoke of the great city, the sky appeared to be getting lighter instead of darker.

" One could almost suppose," remarked Hoffenden, " that it was the dawn of morning instead of evening twilight."

" Yes, very true; but we have other things to think of. I believe you were the challenger."

" I was."

" Then your adversary, I fancy, will insist upon choosing the mode in which the duel is to come off."

" Oh, it will be the usual mode; I suppose about twelve paces."

" Very bad—very bad. A barrier duel is the best, when each man faces his opponent, first at thirty paces, and then is at liberty to advance ten paces, and fire when he thinks proper. Ah, there is some sport in such a duel as that, my friend."

" We don't like such a mode of doing things in England."

" No, I am aware of that; and as you have given the cartel to the combat, you must take your opponent's choice as to the mode of fighting. Are you a good shot?"

" Certainly not; but I am not quite a stranger to the use of the pistol."

" Well, my friend, you must aim at his knees, and then you will, if you keep in a good line, be sure to hit him. I fancy you will be placed back to back, and then made to turn and fire at once upon a given signal. In that case, do not shrink from his shot, but take it, and reserve your fire for half a moment, so that you shall have the chance of taking aim. You want to kill him?"

" He is a villain, and has been the bane of my life."

" Eh, bien! then you shall do your best to kill him, my friend. We shall see what we can do when we reach the ground, which, I suppose, will be soon. Ah, they stop; we shall get out here, I suppose."

This was so. Major Williams stopped the coach in which he and Murdo were travelling, and discharged it, upon which Hoffenden did the same by his vehicle. Then they all four proceeded some distance, until Major Williams paused at a stile on the right-hand side of the road, and said—

" This is a pathway across the fields to the little retired village of East Acton. It is nearly half a mile, and on the way there are some retired spots; suppose we go until we come to one of them, and there, as the light is fast fading, conclude the business. And if you please, Monsieur Grillet, I will speak with you as we proceed, so as to save time when we reach the ground."

This was politely agreed to by the Frenchman, and as he and Major Williams got some distance in advance, the latter, with an odd sort of laugh, said—

" Do you know the particulars of the quarrel?"

" No, not I."

" Well, it is a very trivial affair."

" Very likely; but one's honour feels a scratch as much as a deep incision."

" Very true; but here are really two valuable lives at stake. Now, sir, we have a way in England of satisfying the honour of both parties, and yet doing no harm to either. You know how many bloodless duels are fought here?"

"Oh, certainly, sir; but what way do you allude to?"

"Why, the fact is, we put no bullets in the pistols, but ram down rather hard a piece of wadding, which makes a great noise, and, of course, does no mischief at all; and I was thinking, as our two friends only quarrelled about a night-cap, we might save any serious consequences, by adopting such a course in this case."

"Agreed," said the Frenchman. "You load your man's pistol without a bullet, and I'll do the same to my man's."

"Very well; but what will be better still, perhaps, and thoroughly satisfy both parties, suppose you load for us, and we load for you, and then, of course, it will be all right."

"As you please, sir; as you please."

"Then we will stop here, if agreeable to you."

CHAPTER XXX.

THE ATTEMPTED TREACHERY.—THE FALL OF MURDO.

THE spot upon which Major Williams, as he called himself, now paused, was a very beautiful and sequestered one indeed. It lay in a little valley, to one side of which was a running stream, while on the other, thick clusters of trees prevented any one from seeing, from that direction, what was going on.

This valley was open to the west, so that all the light that still came from the clouds, that reflected the last rays of the setting sun, came with a soft and gentle radiance, streaming down it. Certainly, under the circumstances, there could not have been found a place better calculated for the scene that was about to be there enacted.

The Frenchman glanced around him, and then pronounced it to be as pretty a spot for a meeting, as could very well be found in England, he dare say; and then he and the major stepped aside to load the pistols, and to make other important arrangements. As for the two principals, they did not come within speaking distance of each other. We may fairly enough, from what we know of the character of Murdo, conclude that he was quite aware of the plan of operations which had been suggested by the major, and probably that fact might account for the great coolness with which he took the whole affair; for he certainly did not seem to be at all put out of the way by it.

As for Hoffenden, the deep sense of the wrongs he had suffered at the hands of Murdo, and his conviction of the fact that he had been but a mere tool in the hands of that bold, bad man, did not permit him to think of anything now that he was present, but of his probable revenge.

At all events he had no fear, and when the Frenchman advanced, and said—

"You will stand face to face, about twelve paces, holding your pistols' muzzles downwards, and at the word—fire—you will raise your hand and fire;" he merely inclined his head in token of agreement.

"Fire low," whispered the Frenchman. "Remember my instructions, and you must succeed. I am to give the signal; but, as it is to be by word of mouth, don't look at me, but at your opponent, and at the moment you hear me say—fire—you can blaze away."

"I understand."

"Hoffenden thought that he saw a covert smile upon the face of the second of Murdo; who, at that moment, made a pretence of suddenly startling, and exclaiming,—

"Hush! let us pause a moment; I thought I heard a noise as of footsteps and voices over yonder hedge; shall I go and see, or will you, Monsieur Grillet."

"As you please; I will keep the ground while you go."

Major Williams did go, carrying the pistol with him, which had been loaded by Grillet, and when he was out of immediate observation, he popped a bullet into it, wrapped up in a small piece of wash leather, and rammed it down.

Grillet had his back to the two principals, and Hoffenden fancied, by the slight movement of his elbows, that he was doing something to one of the pistols, but he had no idea what. It was no bad joke, after all, for the Frenchman, fully mistrusting the gallant major, was quietly putting a couple of slugs into the pistol intended for Hoffenden's use.

And thus was it that these two worthy seconds were playing each other the same trick, a course of proceeding that had the effect of neutralising both the tricks, and placing Murdo in a much more dangerous position than he thought himself in.

"Now, gentlemen," said Major Williams, as he came back; "I have ascertained that there is nothing there, and we may as well proceed to business at once. Monsieur Grillet has won the word, and, therefore, will give it. It is 'one, two, three, fire!'"

The principals were now placed opposite to each other, and the pistols handed to them. The seconds retired some distance, and then Grillet called out, in a loud, clear voice—

"One—two—three—fire!"

Bang went the two pistols, and the seconds rushed forward at once. Hoffenden was standing in his place, profoundly motionless, but Murdo was upon his knees, and his arms were held above his head in a very strange manner.

"Good God! How is this?" said Major Williams.

"Are you touched, Monsieur Hoffenden?" shouted the Frenchman.

"Yes," said Hoffenden, as he advanced, and showed that a bullet had grazed his arm.

At this moment, Murdo fell over upon his back with a groan of anguish, and began vomiting blood most awfully.

"Why, how is this?" said Major Williams, trembling like an aspen leaf. "How is this, Monsieur Grillet? you promised me you would put nothing in the pistol but powder and wadding. Good God! how has this happened?"

The Frenchman advanced close to him, and, fixing on him a glance of passion that made his eyes look like blazing coals, he said—

"Listen to me, monsieur. You made to me a dishonourable proposal. I knew you were a villain, and I affected to agree with it. I knew you meditated treachery; and, when you went across the bridge to see if any one was there, in consequence of the mock alarm that you raised, you put in a bullet to the pistol."

"And—and—and you——" faltered Major Williams.

"I put in a couple of slugs in mine, which has done for your friend; and now, sir, it is our turn."

As he spoke, Monsieur Grillet began busily loading the pistols again, and Major Williams, after casting a hasty glance round him, took to his heels at a rate which defied detection or pursuit. Grillet got the pistol loaded, and fired it after him, which seemed to add wings to his speed, and, in a few moments, he was out of sight.

All this passed very rapidly, and, when it was over, Hoffenden stepped up to Murdo and, folding his arms across his breast, stood regarding him with painful interest. The villain still lived, but he could not speak; for, when he attempted to do so, the blood came gushing from his throat in such floods as nearly to choke him.

"Come away," said Grillet. "I have seen enough of wounds to know that you can do nothing for this man. He is dying—nothing can save him; and it is time you looked to your own safety by flight. I was in hope to have got rid of Major Williams—but that he has prevented by his flight, so that you have no other resource now for yourself, as he will speak of the affair."

"It's horrible!" said Hoffenden.

"What is horrible, my good friend?"

"The sight before me. Look at him. Saw you ever such a ghastly sight?"

"Yes, many such; and am none the worse for any of them. Come away. He would have taken your life freely enough; but the chances of fortune have made you the victor. The slugs have gone into his lungs, and he will not be able to say another word in this world. Come away."

The wretched Murdo appeared to be conscious of what they were saying, and, as they were about to turn from him, he made an effort to speak, and produced a horrible, unearthly sort of sound. It was his last in this world. He bent his body like an arch, the head and heels alone touching the ground, for the space of about half a minute, and then with a sudden fall down, he went, and was dead.

Hoffenden turned away with a shudder. The sight was one not likely to be for ever forgotten by him, although in his memory he had another reminiscence to the full as horrible as that. When he looked around him he found that he was alone.

CHAPTER XXXI.

A CHANGE OF SITUATION.—THE NIGHT VIGIL.—THE CLOCK STRIKES ONE.

WITH frantic look, and scarcely knowing what he did, and why he did it, Hoffenden hurried to his house—that house which might have been so full of joy, if he had not profaned it by the fell passion of gaming, which had made him what he was.

In reply to his hurried knock, one of the servants opened the door, and then said, immediately—

"There is a gentleman, sir, who wishes to speak with you."

"I can see no one," said Hoffenden. "Say that I can see no one—I want to see no one. Tell him to go away, and come again. Anything he pleases, so that I am not pestered with his presence now. Do you hear me?"

"Yes, sir. But—but he won't go away."

"Kill him, then—kill him!"

"Hold, sir!" said a man, advancing through the half-open doorway of one of the rooms that opened to the hall. "You will not, I am sure, refuse me an audience."

Hoffenden at a glance knew who it was; it was Foxley, the officer, and there was really a something about his tone and look which seemed to say, "if you do refuse me an audience, be it at your peril; and you will soon repent the indiscretion."

Hoffenden made an effort to recover his composure; it was in vain, though. He could not stand out against the fixed, steady gaze of that man, who knew, at all events, sufficient of his criminality to be of the worst account for him, and who, for all he knew, might likewise know of the recent duel.

"You must see me," said Foxley, laying an emphasis upon the pronoun. "You will see me."

"Yes, yes; I did not know exactly that it was you, Mr.—a—a——"

"That will do; and, as my business is very urgent, if you will step into this room, Mr. Hoffenden, in which I have been waiting your coming for some time, I will tell you at once what brought me here."

Foxley spoke much more like the master of the house than Hoffenden did; and the servant looked astonished at the wonderful change in his master, who was evidently unable to hold his way with the stranger. Hoffenden at once followed Foxley into the room indicated, and the latter closed the door very carefully; and then, as if time was no object, pointed to a seat, saying—

"You may as well hear at your ease what I have to say, Mr. Hoffenden."

"What—what is it?"

"You are agitated. I wonder that such a trifle as shooting such a man as Murdo can have such an effect upon you—you, a man of courage!"

"I kill Murdo! Gracious Heavens! what do you mean by such an expression?"

"Pho! pho! Mr. Hoffenden, it is of no use keeping up any concealment with me; I have means of acquiring information which would surprise you."

"So—so it seems," stammered Hoffenden, as he sat down, looking as pale as death.

"You are alarmed," added Foxley, "and without reason, for I am one who always listens to reason. Let us talk this matter over confidentially now. You have committed crime enough to place you within the grasp of the law, as you well know; but in the death of Murdo you have done yourself a service, because you have got rid of one who knew too much, and you have only to pay one person for secrecy instead of two."

"I do not understand that allusion."

"Do you not? Then I will tell you how you may understand it. You paid Murdo, and dared not shake him off, because he knew of the murder of Andrew Ewart."

"Hush! Oh, hush!"

"Enough. And he paid me, because I likewise knew of it. Now, of course, as what money I had of him came from you, now that you have only me to settle with, you are better off by far."

Hoffenden groaned.

"How much may I expect," added the thief-taker, "for keeping this dangerous secret?"

"Name your own sum, and you shall have it."

"Good. I will have one half of your income, be it what it may, and I will call this night for an instalment; and beware of playing me false, for if you so much as cheat me, or attempt to cheat me, out of a farthing I shall assuredly discover it, and have signal vengeance. Now you know your precise position; you can make it worse if you please, but better you shall never make it. I will be here to-morrow by ten in the morning, and be sure you have your accounts accurately prepared to show me. Farewell for the present. I do not know now what you have to do but to be as happy as possible."

Hoffenden could only mumble out an almost unintelligible assent, and then Foxley left him, as if with the most perfect confidence in the helplessness of his victim.

It was this assumption of confidence in the impossibility of any one escaping him, or playing him a trick, combined, certainly, with a well arranged system of espionage, which made Foxley so universally successful in his villanies. People did not make an effort to escape him, from a hoplessness of its success; and he owed probably much more to the fears of those whom he chose to oppress, than he did to his real power over them.

Hoffenden sat for some time in a kind of stupor after Foxley had left him. That interview had disarranged all his ideas completely. He had come home to make preparations for flight; but, without intending any joke about so serious a piece of business, we may truly say that Foxley had put to flight his preparations.

"What will become of me?" he murmured at length. "Oh, wretched destiny, what will become of me? To what horrors may I yet be doomed?"

He shuddered, and was about to utter some other words indicative of the distraction of his spirits, when he heard the door open, and, upon looking up, he saw Jane enter the apartment.

She showed, by the sudden start she gave, how much she was surprised and shocked at his altered appearance, and then she burst into tears, and sank into a chair, for she was really unable to support herself. It was some minutes before a word was spoken on either side; but Hoffenden at length broke the dreadful silence by saying, in a voice of deep anxiety—

"Jane, Jane, there have been times when you have stood between me and evil; and if ever there was a time when I required my better angel at my side, it is now."

"Oh, Harry, Harry! to hear you talk to me thus gives me a hope that you are not entirely lost. Tell me—tell me what new misery is in store for us?"

"In a few words, Jane, I can tell you all. Murdo and I have fought a duel, and he is dead."

"May Heaven have mercy upon him!" said Jane, with a shudder. "Oh, Harry, what will come of this? Speak to me. Your looks are wild and disordered. Tell me what will come of this, Harry? What can I do to aid you?"

"There is danger—great danger. The law calls such an act murder, and I have enemies enough, too, so to construe it. What would you advise? I dare not face out the affair, which now, before many hours have passed away, will be well known, and my apprehension may follow. I dread the consequences."

"Then fly—fly. But—but, Harry——"

"What—what sudden thought comes over you to make you shudder and look so scared as if—as if your whole soul was intent upon the remembrance of something almost too dreadful for words?"

"It is so."

"Speak—I charge you, Jane, to speak. What horrible suspicion have you?"

"I must speak, if the words I utter produce an answer which shall blast me for ever. I must speak, Harry. Harry, do you know aught of Andrew Ewart? It was hinted by that dreadful man, Murdo, that there was a secret connected with his fate that would make me loathe you. Oh, tell me at once—tell me by one word that you are innocent of anything against him, and I will follow you to the end of the world with joy."

There was for a few moments a kind of spasmodic twitching of the features of the face about Hoffenden before he spoke, and then he said, in a strange, hollow voice,—

"I am innocent."

"Thank Heaven! But why—oh, why should innocence speak in such a tone, or betray such a word of agitation?"

"Jane, I am agitated about other things; and, moreover, is it not enough to still almost the beating of my heart to think that you should find it necessary to ask me such a question. Be content; I am innocent."

Jane Hoffenden was content upon the subject. She could not believe it possible that her husband could deceive her in so awful a matter. It was an immense load of care removed from her heart to find that it was capable of telling her he was innocent of the frightful crime which had been more than hinted at as having been committed by him, when the villain Murdo was endeavouring to shake her virtue.

"Yes, Harry, yes," she said, as the tears coursed each other down her cheeks, "I will forget all the past, and we will leave this place for ever."

"What say you, Jane, to some other country, where we can commence life as it were afresh?"

"Be it so, Harry. Your home shall be a home."

"Enough. We will go to the New World, Jane, and there be at least free from the cankering anxieties that would for ever beset us in this hemisphere. I will get what money together I can, and we will start to-night, Jane—yes, to-night. I have no doubt but that all will be well there. We can make our way to some seaport, and from thence take shipping for America."

Jane eagerly embraced the proposition. She fondly hoped that new scenes, and the activity of a new mode of life, would wean her husband for ever from the dreadful vice of gaming, which had produced all the evils they at that time groaned under. Indeed, with crude and indistinct notions of America, she thought that he might look in vain there for the opportunities of gambling, which, in a great city like London, were presented to him at every turn.

"And Harry," she said, as she flung herself into his arms, "a short time will make me again a mother, and our little one shall breathe the air of a purer sky than this. Oh! we may surely yet be very—very happy, Harry, if we will choose to be so. Let us go to-night by all means. Oh, let us go to-night."

"It shall be so," said Hoffenden; "make up such few articles as you wish to take with you into as small a parcel as possible, and we will go to-night.

CHAPTER XXXII.

THE FLIGHT FROM LONDON.—THE FISHING VILLAGE NEAR LIVERPOOL.

IT certainly is a very complimentary thing to the Jewish fraternity, for in addition to being God's chosen people, they are on every occasion, when any roguery is to be transacted, everybody else's chosen people likewise.

Hoffenden at once left his home, and went to one of the children of Israel, to whom he said,—

"I know that if I show you it is to your advantage to keep a secret, you will do so, and likewise assist me as far as you see that, by your so doing, you put money in your pocket."

"Whoever recommended you to me," replied the Jew, "was a discerning individual."

"Very good; I have fought a duel, and dangerously wounded my opponent, so that it is necessary that I should get out of the way, and wait on the continent until I know whether he is going to die or not. Being, however, a little pushed for ready money, I have come to you for assistance."

"Ah! very good, sir. But the security—the security."

"Certainly; I have a house with £2,000 worth of furniture and effects in it. Give me £500, within four hours after satisfying yourself that what I say is the truth, and you can take everything away to-morrow by virtue of whatever legal document you may think it necessary for me to sign, to give you such power."

"Agreed," said the Jew; "take me to your house, and shew me the goods."

This was done, and after Mr. Isaacs had satisfied himself of the value of the property, he conducted Hoffenden to a brother Israelite, who was an attorney, and who prepared a document, which was amply sufficient to enable Isaacs to take possession of the house and all its effects, in defiance of everybody but the landlord and the taxgatherer, the respective amounts due to such personages being duly deducted from the £500, which, together with the attorney's expenses, certainly considerably reduced the amount; so that by the time the transaction was concluded Hoffenden had only £410 left, with which, however, he was forced to make himself as contented as he could.

The child had fortunately been sent only on that very day to a preparatory boarding-school, in the vicinity of London, and so was no encumbrance to the flight. But Hoffenden fully intended to fetch him away by some secret means before absolutely leaving England, for which there would probably be ample time, as many days might pass before he could find a means of getting away.

It was nine o'clock in the evening, when Jane Hoffenden, by direction of her husband, left her home—that home she was never to look upon again, and waited for him at a neighbouring shop. She had contrived to slip out without any of the servants seeing her; but Hoffenden was not so fortunate, and a footman came forward very officiously to open the door for him.

"I shall be back in an hour," said Hoffenden.

"Yes, sir, if you please, sir," said the footman, as he closed the door, and then he added to himself—"An hour, indeed; I think I see it. You are a wonderfully altered customer if you are back again before breakfast time to-morrow, I'm thinking; but that's no business of mine, and you may stay out for a month, for all I care, old fellow. Now for a nice cool glass of sherry, and I will say that much for Hoffenden, he keeps decent wine, really."

Jane was waiting most nervously and anxiously for Hoffenden at the corner of the street, and when he got there, she placed her arm most eagerly in his, saying,—

"Come, oh, come quickly. Let us turn our backs on London as quickly as we can; I did not think I had so little courage until now. How do we proceed?"

"This way—this way, Jane. I have got a post-chaise in readiness a few streets off, and another hour or two will, I fully expect, place us sufficiently beyond any imminent danger. Then we shall be able to breathe freely."

He hurried her on until they came to a stable where the post-chaise was in readiness. The postillions cracked their whips, and in another minute they were whirling along at ten miles an hour towards Liverpool.

It was, in reality, Foxley whom Hoffenden was running away from, although he made Jane believe that it was from fear of being apprehended on account of the duel with Murdo; so that while he was hoping that in consequence of the suddenness of his departure, the officer would be puzzled to know in which direction he had gone, Jane was, with no small amount of thankfulness, congratulating herself that time had been given to Hoffenden to escape before the consequences of the duel should become known.

There was a feeling of curiosity in her mind which would have been gratified to know the precise particulars of the death of Murdo, but she dreaded so much the very pronunciation of his name, that she would not ask Harry a question upon the subject; and the first twenty miles of their journey were completed in nearly unbroken silence.

When the horses, however, were changed for the second time, some little degree of confidence, in consequence of the impunity from pursuit, came over them.

"We shall be safe," said Hoffenden, " I think."

"Oh, yes, yes, we shall, Harry; and this will be the commencement of unusual happiness for us."

"It may be. I do not place the death of Murdo much to my conscience. It was in fair fight, and for a fair quarrel, and he was equally armed against me as I was against him; so that I cannot blame myself."

"Think no more of him; the very name of that man is a horror to hear."

"It is—it is, Jane; I will mention him no more."

They travelled the whole of that night, and by the morning had, of course, got a considerable distance on their way. It was no part of Hoffenden's intention to go into Liverpool so openly as in a post-chaise, but he intended to dismiss it at the last stage, and then to find some village near the sea, where Jane could stay while the child was procured from the boarding-school, and he, Hoffenden, made preparations for their departure from the port of Liverpool.

This was certainly managing the affair as well as it could be managed; and, not having the fear of immediate pursuit, for they had left no available clue behind them, they stopped at the large inn which was the posting-house at the last stage before entering Liverpool.

Then, to the surprise of the post-boys, Hoffenden dismissed the chaise; but, as he paid very liberally, all remarks were stifled completely.

What he now wished to do was, at that point, to break the clue to his future movements in case Foxley should find out where he had gone; and when he came to consider that that ingenious individual had found out, in a manner quite unknown to him, Hoffenden, the fact of the duel and the death of Murdo immediately that those circumstances occurred, it certainly was not impossible that he might light upon a guess of what direction the Hoffendens had taken in their flight.

After staying, then, at the inn about an hour, and just as the evening shadows were beginning to show themselves, he sent for the landlord, and said to him,—

"I dare say we shall stay here about a week, if you can conveniently accommodate us. Are there any pretty walks about the neighbourhood?"

"Oh, yes, sir. There's the little village of Allowby, about three miles further on, close to the sea."

"Very good. We shall return in an hour."

He and Jane walked out, and when they got some distance from the inn, he said,—

"Now, Jane, do you think you can walk as far as the outskirts of Liverpool, which is a distance of about five miles from here? You should ride, but that would be just getting a witness to tell which direction we took. I propose getting into the suburbs, and then providing ourselves with some obscure home, preparatory to our starting on our expedition to the new world."

"Oh! yes, yes, Harry. Anything—anything you please. I can walk very well—quite well."

It took them two hours to reach the suburbs of Liverpool, and then they asked at the door of a cottage if there was any lodging to be had; and the reply was, that she, the woman, did not know of a lodging, but that there was a furnished cottage hard by, which, if they wanted it for a week or two, they could have by paying rent in advance for the use of it.

This Hoffenden at once thought was much more desirable than a lodging, in which they would be liable to a constant surveillance as regarded all their movements; and in half an hour he had paid a month's rent in advance, and was fairly in possession of a pretty enough, but scantily furnished cottage, with a long, straggling bit of garden, and a charming view, from some of its windows, of the sea.

"This is the very thing, Jane," said Hoffenden; "and, if needs be, we can wait here a considerable time before we ship ourselves for America. We shall be free from all remark, and not half so likely to be discovered in a place we have completely to ourselves, as in one which other people were likewise in."

In this Jane acquiesced. She was too happy in the apparently returning affection of her husband to make any objections, even if she had seen any to make.

A few common necessaries were bought of the villagers, and brought into the cottage; and, probably, that night's repose was the most profound that Hoffenden and his wife had enjoyed for many months. At all events, they had no apprehensions, and it would have been quite impossible to have enjoyed anything approaching to such a state of peaceful repose in London.

Alas! what would have been the state of mind of poor Jane, had she known that he who slumbered by her side had dyed his hands with the blood of Andrew Ewert. Surely it was a mercy that she knew it not, or the dreadful thought would have driven her to distraction.

The morning came, serene and beautiful; and the sea looked so bright and fair, that Jane's face wore most unusual smiles.

After breakfast, Hoffenden said, with quite an appearance of gaiety,—

"Now, Jane, you will keep house while I go to Liverpool, and inquire about the shipping likely soon to start from that port for America. We must not waste our resources longer here than we can help, you know."

"Certainly not," said Jane. "Only tell me when you will be back, that I may know when to expect you."

"By mid-day at the latest."

With these words he left, and pursued the road, which soon led him to Liverpool, that second London in extent, but certainly not second to any place in vice.

Liverpool has all the bad qualities of a large commercial town and a seaport combined, and there are not many natural beauties about it to compensate for such drawbacks. When Hoffenden reached it, he found the streets and quays thronged with people, and he was wandering listlessly along, when some one gave him suddenly a smart blow upon the back, and he turned round almost sick from apprehension that it was Foxley, or some of his myrmidons.

It was a vexation, but still it was a great relief to him, to find that it was an old gaming-table acquaintance from London, named Rochet.

CHAPTER XXXII.

THE TEMPTATION AND ITS RESULTS.—JANE'S DETENTION IN THE COTTAGE.

"Why, Hoffenden, what brings you to this part of the world?" said Rochet.

"Oh, nothing particular, nothing—only—for—a—a change, that's all; no other reason, I assure you. I—I am going back soon."

"Well, I'm glad I met with you. I suppose you know the houses here? I tell you candidly, I am keeping out of the way of John Doe and Richard Roe."

"Oh, that is it, is it? You were always famous for an acquaintance with those gentlemen."

"Yes, much too close an one, I can assure you. But I suppose you know the houses here, as I was saying?"

"What houses?"

"The houses of play, to be sure. There's one, they tell me, that goes by the name of Morris's, that is well worth going to, and where capital stakes are played for. Suppose we have a try; I should say that London hands, as we are, cannot come to much mischief."

Hoffenden shuddered as he replied, "No, no, I cannot, I cannot; I have not brought down funds for such purposes, I assure you. Do not ask me to go; besides, at this time of day, you know it is not the thing at all."

"Oh, you need not trouble yourself about that, for the house I name is a peculiar one. They light it up in the daytime just the same as at night, and, by shutting up all the windows, and drawing all the curtains, they give the appearance of night to it. Damn it, man, come and look at it; nobody is going to force you to play if you don't like; but as it's only in the next street, you may as well come and see the place, if it is only from curiosity, and to say you have seen it."

"Well, well, I suppose there is no harm in that."

Hoffenden, as usual, yielded, and allowed himself to be led away by his old comrade to the house he named, and which would have well enough repaid a visit from mere curiosity, but which was the destruction of hundreds who came to look on, but, alas, stayed to play. That did Hoffenden.

It is night, and Jane Hoffenden is alone in the cottage; she has not strength to move or to cry for help—she lies upon a couch, and she clasps in her arms a dead infant. He does not come—no help—no footstep to bring her hope! Oh, horror! horror! horror!

*   *   *   *   *   *   *

"Seven's the main!" cried Hoffenden, as the clock struck twelve. "By God, I've lost again! What a run of ill-luck! Give me more wine."

"Play again," said a man, with dark whiskers, and a profusion of mock jewellery, with whom he had been playing for five hours. "Play again; luck will be sure to change, and I should be glad to give you your revenge. You have lost nine times consecutively, and it would be folly to suppose that such a game as that could continue. Play on."

"I will," said Hoffenden, when he had tossed off some wine; "I will. I am not exactly one of the leaving sort, as those who know me in London can testify. Another twenty pound on red. Lost, by heaven!"

"Oh! never mind that. Try again."

Notwithstanding the large quantity of wine he had drank, and a large quantity, indeed, it was, a feeling of faintness all at once came over Hoffenden, and he thought of Jane—she, who had so freely and so readily forgiven all his past errors, and been to him such a guardian angel in his troubles. He knew that the midnight hour was now past, and that he had been absent the whole day.

And oh! soul-harrowing thought! he knew, too, that of all the money he had brought with him, there now remained but a few pounds. He was nearly destitute. Frightful thought!

He felt that to continue such reflections would drive him mad, and he at once resumed play, as the only means of alleviation he had at hand for his state of misery.

The kind friend who had seduced him into this den of iniquity stood now behind him, as, indeed, he had done for the most part of the time the play had lasted, and Hoffenden, as he turned his head rather suddenly to make some remark to him, saw, or fancied he saw, a slight smile upon his face. The idea that he had been betrayed and victimised at once came across his mind.

His last stake was upon the table, and he sprang to his feet.

"Villain!" he shouted; "at least I will have revenge upon you!"

As these words passed his lips, he grappled with his foe, and would have strangled his old acquaintance, but for the immediate and active interference of those who were near at hand. Hoffenden was torn away from the man, who, probably enough, had a share in the spoil, and, when he turned to look for the person he had been playing with, he, as well as the last few pounds the wretched Hoffenden had staked, were gone.

"Ruined—ruined!" he gasped. He tottered towards the door, and in another moment he was in the open air, with the stars of a cloudless sky shining down upon him.

"Oh! Jane—Jane!" he gasped. "How can I look upon your face again? What is to become of us—oh! what is to become of us now?"

With a countenance positively ghastly, for it was the reflex of the feelings of his soul, he tottered out of the town, and took his way to the village where he had left his wife.

*   *   *   *   *   *

It was about half an hour before Hoffenden reached the village, that a stranger, mounted on a powerful horse, but which appeared to be much exhausted, gallopped into the little hamlet, and alighted at the door of the only cottage in which he saw a light burning. That cottage belonged to the wife of a watchman, who went off duty at four o'clock in the morning, and she was waiting his return home, which accounted for why she had a light burning at such a late hour.

The stranger knocked at the door.

"Who's there?" cried the woman.

"A stranger. You do not know me. But I wish to ask you if a man and woman have passed this way within the last twenty-four hours? The woman young and—and beautiful."

"Is the man fair?"

"Yes—yes. Oh! yes; and looks about him suspiciously."

"Oh! they are staying in the village. You will find them at a cottage a little way to the left, opposite; you cannot miss it, for it is the only one that has a vine growing all over the front of it."

"Thank you—thank you."

The stranger hastened onwards as he was directed, and in a few moments he reached the door of the cottage, and was about to knock at it, when a voice behind him cried,—

"Hold! who are you?"

He turned, and Hoffenden, for it was he who had spoken, beheld Andrew Ewert, whom he thought he had murdered in London. The idea that it was a spectre possessed him on the moment, and with a shriek of dismay he fell insensible upon the threshold of that little abode, the horrors within which he little knew or dreamt of.

CHAPTER XXXIII.

THE CONCLUSION.—THE CLOCK STRIKES FOUR.

Let us look into the interior of that cottage. Let us, with tearful eyes and grieved hearts, look at the young mother, abandoned at a time when all the love, all the gentleness, and all the consolations of humanity ought to have been heaped upon her.

"Hush! oh, hush!" she said, as she fondled the new-born babe in her arms. It had not yet ceased to breathe. "Hush, darling, hush, your father will surely come. Oh, God! what keeps him? Help, help! Can no one hear me—will no pitying soul come to me? Oh! 'tis horrible to lie thus alone—alone. Hark! What is that? The distant sound of a clock. No—yes, it is. One—yes, the clock strikes one, and I alone still. Oh! my child, my child! let me again hear your wailing cry, that I may know you live. Husband, husband, where are you now?"

A feeling of faintness came over her, but she shook it off, and did not lapse into utter insensibility. If she had, Heaven only knows if she would ever have unclosed her eyes again.

"Still dark, all dark," she muttered. "No—the light brightens. It has not quite left me yet. But he comes not. Oh, God! he comes not. Hush, hush. It is—yes. Thank Heaven, it is his step. Oh, joy—welcome, welcome, Harry. Husband—welcome—welcome—wel——no, no, no. The footstep passes on. It is not he—it is not he."

She wrung her hands, and wept. The child was silent. The silence of death was in that little chamber, but the fond mother still held it to her heart, and called upon it frantically to cry, that she might know it lived. And still he came not! At that moment Hoffenden was in the gaming-house, playing deeply, and quaffing the wine that was eagerly given to those who came into that pandemonium.

The clock struck one!

" Another hour—another !" half shrieked Jane. " Yet, another hour into the night, and he comes not. Oh, save me, Heaven ! Harry, Harry, are you dead ? Ah ! that noise. Is it a step ? No, no ; and yet I thought I heard a voice say, ' Weep no more, for thy joy is at hand.' Oh, God ! am I wandering in my intellect—am I going mad, mad, mad ?"

*   *   *   *   *   *   *

The clock strikes two.

" My child ! my little one, cold, cold. Oh ! no, no. Dead—dead upon its mother's breast. It cannot, shall not be so, my little one, my darling. Oh ! let me kiss thy little hand to life again. Cold, cold—all cold. Oh ! God—God !"

*   *   *   *   *   *   *

The clock struck three !

" Not yet ; he comes not yet to see the living and the dead, and I am not yet mad. What is life, reason, hope to me now ? Why am not I mad ? Oh, God ! why was I sent into this world to be the most unhappy wretch within it ? Husband !—help—help—help ! He comes ; I hear him now. He comes. Ho—ho—ho ! I am not yet mad ; and yet what strange lights are dancing in my eyes !"

She shrieked aloud, and then dropped insensible over the dead body of the child.

*   *   *   *   *   *   *

The clock struck four !

Andrew Ewert bounded over the insensible form of Hoffenden, and made his way into the cottage.

" Jane, Jane," he cried—"'tis I, Jane. Speak—oh, speak to me, if it be but a word. 'Tis I, Andrew Ewert."

All was still. The candle she had lit in the early darkness of the coming night had burnt down in the socket of the candlestick, and all was obscurity. Yet a dread that something horrible had happened was so strongly impressed upon the mind of Arthur, that he ran to the door of the cottage, and, in a voice that soon summoned up all the inhabitants of the village, he called,—

" Help—help ! Lights—oh, lights here ! Help—help—oh, help !"

In a very few moments several windows were opened, and then doors, and several of the villagers eagerly inquired what was the matter.

" I do not know," he replied ; " but, for God's sake, come, some of you, and bring lights, for I think that something horrible has happened here."

Curiosity, as well as compassion, urged them to be quick ; and, in a very few moments, a rush of persons, with lights, dashed over the prostrate form of Hoffenden into the cottage.

Oh, what a sight there presented itself ! On a couch lay the apparently dead body of Jane, and when they lifted her up, they saw the infant quite dead. A medical man, however, who was promptly on the spot, pronounced that she still lived, and had her conveyed to a warm bed : when, by the aid of such stimulants as he thought it safe to use, he soon restored her to a state of consciousness. He then gave her an opiate, which rendered her, in a very short time, unfit for conversation, and she slept for many hours, being in a happy state of oblivion during that time as to what had occurred.

When Jane was thus seen to, Andrew Ewert and some others lifted up from the threshold of the door the insensible form of the gambler—the man who had, from the consequences of that one dreadful vice, been the bane of himself and of all who were in any way dependent upon him, or connected with him by kindred or association.

Hoffenden was dead !

*   *   *   *   *   *   *

Our tale is over. Andrew Ewert, by the connivance of Maria, had escaped from a dungeon in which he had been confined by Foxley, who, finding him alive when he removed him from Hoffenden's house, had thought him a good hostage for money.

After a long and precarious illness, Jane recovered, and, in due time, became the wife of Andrew. They went, upon a small independent income, which had been left to him by a relative, to live in a romantic and beautiful part of Devonshire, where, in many years of happiness, no one could have recognised, in her blooming face and happy, sparkling eyes, any recollections of the Gambler's Wife.

THE END.